PUF

*The Mystery of Munroe Island
and Other Stories*

TO
DEAR PARTNER
WITH LOTS OF LOVE
&
BEST WISHES

The Mystery of Munroe Island and Other Stories

SATYAJIT RAY

Translated from the Bengali by Indrani Majumdar

Introduction by Victor Banerjee

PUFFIN BOOKS

An imprint of Penguin Random House

PUFFIN BOOKS

USA | Canada | UK | Ireland | Australia
New Zealand | India | South Africa | China

Puffin Books is part of the Penguin Random House group of companies
whose addresses can be found at global.penguinrandomhouse.com

Published by Penguin Random House India Pvt. Ltd
4th Floor, Capital Tower 1, MG Road,
Gurugram 122 002, Haryana, India

Penguin
Random House
India

First published in Puffin by Penguin Books India 2015

ISBN 9780143333289

Typeset in Minion Pro by Manipal Digital Systems, Manipal
Printed at Manipal Technologies Limited, India

www.penguin.co.in

MIX
Paper from
responsible sources
FSC® C043100

Contents

Contents

Introduction

I'd be lying if I told you I had read Shonku as a child. For starters, I went to a boarding school in the hills where my Bengali teacher was a waddly wobbly wheezer who spat through the gaps in his rotting teeth as he spoke and smothered us with vaporous clouds of halitosis that drove me to study the plebian language of rickshawallahs and phuchkawallahs instead, Hindi. In other words, it eventually stood me in good stead.

The truth, of course, is that Shonku landed from the Red Planet into our *Sandesh* when we were studying for our Senior Cambridge and solving algebraic puzzles and geometric theorems and staring like idiots at calculus, logarithm tables and dividers and protractors. All this was under the stern gaze of an enormous and powerful Irish Christian Brother called Cooney, who looked like a bulldog and dressed in an unwashed black habit all year long that smelled of the tobacco which spilled from his pipe into his pockets and everywhere he went. This monstrous Irishman would whimper 'meow' under his breath so his clouded pet alley cat could hear him and follow him around with its tail held erect and twitching.

Now let me put two and two together in arithmetic progression and tell you that it was on one rainy afternoon in Shillong that that smelly bundle of linguistics, our Bengali teacher (for he, like Shonku, spoke several languages that he probably picked up on his trek through Japanese battle lines in Burma into India, like our Bengali Chemistry professor had), terrified of Cooney and allergic to his cat, slunk into the shadows of our hallway with a snuff-smeared handkerchief stuffed up his nose, to let the monsters pass and whispered, 'Byata Irish Byomjatri aar Newton,'* and thus, quite fortuitously, introduced us to the crazy world of Professor Shonku—and sneezed.

Worlds in which sailing ships sailed through Southern seas, in waters traumatized by Black Hole Brandon the Pirate with a gouged-out hole for an eye, suddenly disappearing in the mysterious Bermuda waters with all hands on board, or flying to Tibet to hover over unicorns in Utopia, or where under the curse of an enraged fakir, Professor Shonku brings a dinosaur to life from its skeletal remains. Ray mesmerizes you with extraterrestrial beings and potions and magic

---
* That dratted space traveller and his cat

and inventions that are creations of a mind which dwelt in fantasies and romance that would one day produce *Goopy Gyne Bagha Byne*, arguably the most successful film in Bengal's fantastical box office history.

From the corridors and laboratories of Scottish Church College in Calcutta to the world of the Third Reich, Subhash Chandra Bose might have gone to Germany to meet Adolf the Führer, but his college's young physics Professor Shonku had gone there to teach Herr Goering a trick or two and slyly slip away from Nazi Germany before the world war began.

Indrani Majumdar's charming volume of work isn't a translation at all. Indrani seems more like a mesmerized raconteur of Professor Shonku's adventures and Satyajit Ray's magical mischief in prose. How else can you interpret 'holding a freshly-delivered egg in your hand is strikingly similar to the experience of gazing at so fine a sky'?

While I sit back on my rocking chair, by a log fire in the mountains where the air is thin, having popped a tablet of 'Cerebrilliant' and snorted a line of 'oximore' that jumpstarts an addled brain, I watch my Persian cat lick the saucer clean of 'Marjarin' that has the power to immortalize the purring Newtons of this world and contemplate strafing the globe with 'Hypnojen' from sleek black stealth bombers and UFOs, so we can forever forget the atrocities we perpetrate on fellow men and destroy Shonku's 'Remembrain' so we would never remember them again. Shonku's worlds are an enthralling escape, a consummation, in a sea of troubles, devoutly to be wished.

This is a thrilling volume for all ages of man. Gripping, analytical, suspenseful and amusing. I loved it—cover to cover.

Victor Banerjee
June 2015

Dr Schering's Memory

2 January

What a splendid morning! The clear blue sky dotted with fluffy white clouds, as well as the bright sunshine, can almost give you the mistaken feel of autumn. The pleasure you get holding a freshly-delivered egg in your hand is strikingly similar to the experience of gazing at so fine a sky.

Of course there's another reason for my happiness. I'm actually resting after a very long time. This morning I finished working on my latest gadget. After returning from my garden to the laboratory, I sat down to take a long look at my new invention; this act of introspection gives me a feeling of great satisfaction. The device doesn't look much when viewed from the outside. At the most, it gives you an impression of a fashionable helmet or hat. The inside of this helmet contains 72,000 wires interwoven intricately into a dense electric circuit. It's the result of three years of untiring hard work. Let me give you an easy example to demonstrate how the invention works.

Just now, as I was resting on my chair, my man Friday, Prahlad, brought me a cup of coffee. I asked him, 'What fish did you buy on the 7th of last month?' After scratching his head a couple of times, he said, 'I don't remember this, Babu!' Then I asked him to sit on a chair, placed the helmet on his head and pressed a button. Prahlad's entire body shook for a while and then suddenly became still. In addition, his face bore a completely vacant look. I repeated my question.

'Prahlad, on the 7th of last month, what fish did you purchase?'

Upon hearing the question this time, there was no change in his expression and his lips parted only to utter the word, 'Tyangra.'

When I removed the helmet from his head, Prahlad stared blankly at me for a moment. He then suddenly jumped up from the chair and, with a beaming smile said, 'I now remember, Babu—it was Tyangra!'

Prahlad is only an example. This contraption can refresh anyone's memory at any given point of time. Apparently every human being's head has a collection of 1,000,000,000,000,000—i.e. one hundred trillion—memories, some clear and some hazy. These include scenes, incidents, names, faces, tastes, smells, songs, stories and countless other details. On an average, a person loses his or her memory of the first two years of life quite easily. My own memory is far superior compared to others. I still remember a few things from when I was eleven months old. But then, too, a few of my childhood memories have also faded a little. For instance, when I was a year and three months old, I remember the local magistrate Blackwell, cane in hand, taking a walk with his dog by the banks of the Usri. The dog was white in colour but I couldn't remember its exact breed. But when I put the helmet on and recollected the scene, I immediately identified the dog as a bull terrier.

I've named this invention Remembrain, that is, a machine that helps your brain to remember old memories. Yesterday I sent an article about this in the English journal, *Nature*. Let's see what follows.

23 February

My article has appeared in *Nature* and ever since I've been receiving countless letters in response. People from Europe, America, Russia and Japan have all showed their eagerness to study this machine. On the 7th of May, there will be a science summit in Brussels where I have been requested to demonstrate this apparatus. In the world of scientists, none seem willing to believe that such a machine could be conceived, though they all are well aware of my calibre. The fact remains that the enigma of memory is still well beyond the realm of science and neurology. My own understanding is that when a fact enters your head it takes the form of a memory. I think each memory is equivalent to a chemical substance and each memory is marked by a different molecular structure. As years go by, memory fades away as no element can remain constant forever. My machine creates an electric current in the head to recharge the structure of the memory, which in turn helps to refresh one's memory.

I know many will question me on how I managed to work on such a machine despite not unravelling the basic mystery of memory. Even one-fourth of the knowledge that we now have about electric power wasn't available a century ago. Yet, despite such lack of knowledge on this subject, amazing inventions were carried out in the world of electrical gadgets. Similarly, I too discovered my own equipment, Remembrain. In short, this would be my reply.

I was very amused by a letter I received in response to my article in *Nature*. An American millionaire industrialist, Hiram Horenstein, has mentioned that while writing his memoirs he could not clearly remember the incidents which had taken place before the age of twenty-seven. He plans to use this machine in order to revive his memory and to do so he is ready to recompense me adequately. In my reply, I mentioned very gently that my machine had not been invented to fulfil the desires of whimsical millionaires.

4 March

My morning began with reading the news of a horrible accident in Switzerland. Within half an hour I received a long telegram about this very accident. What a clear case of telepathy! The news which the paper reported was basically this: two noted scientists, Auto Lubin from Switzerland and Dr Heironimus Schering from Austria, were travelling in a car from the city of Landeck in Austria to Walenstadt in Switzerland. In the recent past, these two luminaries had been working on some scientific research, the subject of which was hitherto kept a secret. Both Lubin and Schering had been sitting at the back of the car. While driving down a hillside, the car fell into a deep gorge. A cowherd from a nearby village spotted the ruined car dangling precariously from a height of one thousand feet. Lubin's crushed body was located lying close to the car. Dr Schering had a miraculous escape. His body was caught in a bunch of bushes thirty feet below the road.

The moment this news reached Walenstadt, Norbert Busch, the Swiss biochemist, arrived on the scene. Lubin and Schering were both on their way to visit Busch in order to take a break. Busch put the unconscious body of Dr Schering into his spacious Mercedes Benz and brought him home. The newspaper had reported this much. The rest of the news I received via the telegram which Busch sent me. I must mention that I have known Busch for over ten years. We first met each other during a conference held in Florence. Busch has written—

'Though Schering's body bears no mark of injury, the wound in his head has erased his memory completely. And the additional news is, the driver is absconding and so are the research papers. The doctors, psychiatrists, hypnotists and others have all failed to revive Schering's memory.'

Busch has asked me to join him in Walenstadt immediately. Busch will bear the expense for this trip himself. He states at the end of the telegram, 'Dr Schering is an outstanding individual. The science fraternity will eternally remain grateful to you if you bring him back to his normal self. Please let me know about your decision soon.'

I'll never find a more opportune moment to test the true potential of my machine. I need to organize my trip to Walenstadt right away. My machine is cent per cent portable. It weighs only eight kilos. There's no question of paying the airlines for extra baggage.

8 March

After landing in Zurich, I enjoyed the sylvan surroundings of the mountains as I was driven to the tiny town of Walenstadt, sixty kilometres away from Zurich, in Busch's car. I reached around 8.45 a.m. Soon I'll be called for breakfast. Meanwhile, sitting in my room I made a quick entry in my diary. Surrounded by trees and flowers, biochemist Norbert Busch's house is built upon an area of 14 acres against a picturesque landscape. The house has wooden floors, a wooden staircase and wood-panelled walls. My room is west facing, on the second floor. When I open the window, I can see the Walen Lake surrounded by hills. Packed in a plastic bag, my machine is resting on a table next to the bed. I don't think there'll be any flaw in my hosts' hospitality. Just now Busch's three-year-old son, Willie, offered me a packet of chocolates. The child is very friendly and lovable. He freely roams around the house, reciting nursery rhymes and humming songs and jingles. Within minutes after my alighting from the car and greeting everyone, Willie came towards me and holding out a black cigar case said, 'Will you have a cigar?' I'm a non-smoker but trying not to disappoint the child I thanked him and took out a cigar from the case. If one needs to smoke at all it has to be a cigar; a high quality Dutch cigar like this one.

Six people are at present living in this house. Busch and his wife, Clara, Master Willie, Busch's friend—who is also Willie's teacher—the charming and quiet Hans Ulrich, and Dr Schering and his nurse, whose name probably is Maria. In addition, two policemen are constantly on vigil outside the house.

7

Schering's room faces the east. In between our rooms, there's a landing and a staircase leading to the ground floor.

Soon after reaching the house I went to meet Schering. He is of an average height, aged around fifty with blond hair showing a bald patch at the back. The shape of the face is somewhere between square and round. When I entered his room, he was sitting on a chair next to a window, playing with a wooden doll. When he saw me enter, he turned his head in my direction but didn't get up from the chair. I realized he has forgotten the very basic manner of greeting a man by standing up. When I saw his face, I was stuck by a certain doubt. I asked him, 'Do you wear glasses?'

On reflex, Schering's left hand had reached near his eyes and then he put his hand down. Busch replied, 'His glasses have broken. A new pair has been ordered.'

After meeting Schering, we went to the drawing room. Following an exchange of pleasantries, Busch sheepishly confessed, 'To be very frank, I wasn't that enthusiastic about your new machine. In fact, I sent you that telegram partly at my wife's request.'

'Is your wife a scientist, too?' I asked, looking in Clara's direction.

Clara smiled. 'No, not at all. I work as my husband's secretary. I was very keen that you come. I have deep respect for India. I've read a lot of books on India and happen to know quite a bit about your country.'

If Busch has some reservations about my machine, he is sure to change his mind today. This evening, I'll try to unlock Schering's blocked memory.

At this point I couldn't help but enquire about the missing driver. Busch said, 'The cops are still investigating. He could be hiding in one place out of the two. He could either be westbound from the place of the accident, towards Remus, about four-and-a-half kilometres away, or eastbound—about three-and-a-half kilometres away, towards Schleins. The investigations are under way at both these locations. In addition, one team is also combing the forest areas adjacent the hills.'

'How far is the site of accident from here?'

'Eighty-five kilometres. The absconding driver has to take shelter somewhere as it snows at night in that region. My fear is that he could have passed on all the documents to an accomplice.'

8 March, 10.30 p.m.
There is a bright fire in the fireplace. A strong and cold wind is blowing outside. Despite the tightly-shut windows, one can clearly hear the howling of the wind.

Busch is amazed to realize my true potential as a scientist. Now, it'll be difficult to gauge who's a bigger fan of mine—he or his wife.

Today at six in the evening, we all assembled in Schering's room along with my device. He was still sitting in his chair like a zombie. He gave us a glazed look when we entered. After greeting him, Busch said in a jovial tone, 'We'll put a cap on your head today. Is that all right? It won't hurt you at all. You can continue to sit in the same chair.'

'A cap? What sort of a cap?' Schering asked in his deep yet mellow voice, sounding a bit uncomfortable.

'Just take a look.'

I took the gadget out of my bag. Busch handed it over to Schering. Just like when he was playing with the toy in the morning, he felt it and gave it back to me.

'Will this give me pain? The injection did hurt me that day.'

After receiving our assurances it wouldn't hurt, he relaxed and leaned back in the chair, letting his arms fall loosely by each side of the chair. Other than the mark of a sticking plaster on the wound near his neck, I didn't notice any overt sign of injury.

I faced no difficulty in putting the helmet on Schering's head. Then I pressed the red button and the battery of the helmet began to function. With a jerk, Schering's body turned stiff and wooden, and he stared at the fireplace blankly.

The room was deathly silent. I can still visualize the whole scene. With the exception of Schering himself, I could hear everyone breathing. Clara was standing in front of the door. The nurse was standing at the back of the bed, looking at Schering in fascination. Busch and Ulrich were standing on either side of the chair, bending forward in sheer tension.

I whispered to Busch, 'Would you like to ask him questions? Or should I? It'll work equally well if you do.'

'You might as well start.'

I pulled out a stool from the corner of the room and sitting down in front of Schering began my interrogation.

'What's your name?'

Schering's lips parted. In a low yet clear voice, he answered.

'Hieronymus Heinrich Schering.'

'It's for the first time . . .' Busch said in a choked voice, 'for the first time he is telling his own name!'

I put forth my second question.

'What's your profession?'

'I am a professor of physics.'

'Where were you born?'

'Austria.'

'In which city?'

'Innsbruck.'

Inquiringly, I looked at Busch. Busch nodded to say that it was all falling into pattern. I turned my attention back to Schering.

'What's your father's name?'

'Karl Dietrich Schering.'

'Do you have any siblings?'

'I've a younger sister. My elder brother is dead.'

'When did he die?'

'During the First World War. On the 1st of October 1917.'

In between my questioning, I was glancing at an astonished Busch. His repeated nodding confirmed Schering's answers.

'Did you go to Landeck?'

'Yes.'

'For what purpose?

'I'd some work with Lubin.'

'What work?'

'Research.'

'On what subject?'

'BX 377.'

Busch whispered to say this is the code for their research. I returned to my questioning.

'Did you finish your research?'

'Yes.'

'Was it a success?'

'Yes.'

'What was the subject of your research?'

'We had invented a new formula for an atomic weapon.'

'Were you returning to Walenstadt after finishing your work?'

'Yes.'

'Were you carrying the papers of this research?'

'Yes.'

'The formula as well?'

'Yes.'

'Was there an accident on the way?'

'Yes.'

'What happened?'

Busch placed his hand on my shoulder. I know why. I'd been noticing a state of restlessness in Schering. He now licked his lips, and blinked his eyelids once. The veins were swollen at his temples.

'I . . . I . . .'

Schering stopped speaking. He was now breathing heavily. I'm convinced that he has grown anxious as he had let out the secrets of his invention.

I pressed the green button to stop the battery. There was no point in further questioning him under the present circumstances. We could wind up the rest tomorrow.

The moment I removed the helmet from Schering's head he leaned against the chair. He then took a deep breath, shut his eyes then opened them at once, looked around and said, 'A cigar . . . a cigar . . .'

I wiped the sweat from Schering's forehead. Busch looked a bit embarrassed. He cleared his throat and said, 'But there are no cigars. No one smokes a cigar in this house. Would you like a cigarette?'

Ulrich took out a packet of cigarettes from his pocket and offered him one. Schering didn't take any.

I asked, 'Did you have a box of cigars of your own?'

'Yes, I did,' Schering replied. He looked tired and restless.

'Was it a black case?'

'Yes, yes.'

'In that case, it's with Willie. Will you please look for it, Clara?'

Clara immediately left the room in search of her son.

The nurse took Schering's hand and helped him lie on the bed. Busch went near the bed and with a smile said, 'Do you remember it now?'

In response, Schering stared at Busch looking very surprised. In a calm voice he asked, 'Remember what?'

This question from Schering didn't please me at all. Busch, too, looked puzzled. He gathered his wits and calmly said, 'But you've answered all our questions correctly.'

'What questions? What have you asked me?'

Now I briefly described our question-answer session held a few minutes ago. Schering remained quiet for a while. He gently put his hand on his head and looking at me asked, 'What did you put on my head?'

'Why do you ask this?'

'I'm in pain. I feel as if hundreds of pins are pricking inside my head.'

'You've already had a head injury. When you fell down the hill you injured your head and lost your memory.'

'I anyway had a head injury. Why should I fall down the hill?'

All three of us stared at each other.

Clara returned. She was carrying the cigar case I'd already seen. She gave it back to Schering and apologized, 'I don't know when my son took this to his room. Please don't mind.'

Busch once again cleared his throat and said, 'I hope you now remember that you smoke cigars.'

Schering took the box in his hands and closed his eyes. He genuinely looked tired. We realized it was time to leave this room.

After putting back the Remembrain into my bag, we returned to the drawing room. I was going through a mixed feeling of elation as well as anguish. If you regain your memory after wearing the helmet, why must you lose your memory all over again? Does that mean Schering's head injury is rather grave?

The other three did not look that dejected.

Ulrich was, of course, ecstatic about my machine. He said, 'There's no doubt that your invention is a real milestone. This is no mean feat: to bring out the right answers to all the questions you put to him, knowing he had a complete loss of memory!'

Busch said, 'Actually the door to the memory is so tightly shut that it's not completely opening up yet. All we can do is to wait till tomorrow. Once more we need to put the helmet on him. Our part would only be to extract answers from him. We have to find out what transpired in the car before the accident. The rest will be handled by the police.'

Around 8 p.m. Busch called up the police to get the latest report. There's still no news about the driver, Heinz Neumann. Does that mean Neumann, along with the formula BX377, has been buried under the snow forever?

9 March
When I didn't get any sleep till 2 a.m., I finally took Somnonil, a pill of my own invention, and fell into a deep sleep for three-and-a-half hours. In the morning, when I was just thinking of checking my machine to see if it was functioning fine, I heard a knock on my door. I opened the door and saw Schering's nurse. She looked agitated.

'Dr Schering is calling for you. There's an urgent need.'
'How's he now?'
'Very well. He slept soundly last night. The headache is no longer there. He is a completely changed man now.'

Still in my nightgown, I went to Schering's room. He greeted me with a bright smile and wished me good morning. I asked him, 'How are you?'

'I've completely recovered. And my memory is all back. Your machine is indeed a marvellous one. But just one request. Whatever I have disclosed about our research in response to your question, please keep to yourself.'

'There's no need to mention this. You can completely rely on our discretion.'

'One more thing. I want to find out about Lubin. I want to know where he is. Is he, too, lying in bed, injured?'

'No. Lubin is dead.'

Schering's eyes widened. 'He is dead?'

I said, 'It's by the sheer grace of God that you've survived.'

'And the papers?' Schering sounded desperate.

'Nothing has been recovered. What's really worrying is that the papers along with the driver have disappeared. Do you think you can enlighten us about this?'

Schering slowly nodded his head and said, 'Yes, indeed I can.'

I drew up a chair and sat next to his bed. The people in this house were yet to wake up. Never mind. Since such an opportune moment was right here, I'd continue with the conversation. I asked, 'Why don't you tell me what had happened exactly?'

Schering said, 'After leaving Landeck and crossing the border of Finstermuntz, we were in Switzerland. Travelling further for a few kilometres we reached the small city of Schlientz. The car halted there for fifteen minutes. After having beer in a shop we resumed our journey, but within ten minutes the car appeared to have developed some trouble and the driver, Neumann, stopped the car to locate the problem. He seemed to check under the bonnet and then called for Lubin. The moment Lubin went towards him, Neumann struck him with a wrench on his head, rendering him unconscious. Naturally, I stepped out of the car. But Neumann was a very strong man. I lost out in the scuffle and he struck me on the head with that same wrench, knocking me unconscious too. After this, I remember nothing.'

I said, 'It's easy to predict the rest. Neumann put both of you in the car, pushed the car into the gorge and then fled with the research papers.'

I'd heard the phone ring a while ago. Now I heard the stomping of feet on the wooden floor. Busch ran into Schering's room. His eyes were gleaming.

'They have found some papers in the gorge near the accident site. The writing on them has more or less disappeared but it's not difficult to guess what papers these are.'

'Which means the formula hasn't been lost!' Schering exclaimed.

Busch looked quite perplexed when he heard these words from Schering. I explained to him what had occurred this morning. Busch said, 'I hope you can now gather what happened—perhaps Neumann never took the formula. He may have fled carrying the cash and a few valuables with him.'

'How can you say that,' said Schering, sounding very worried. 'Apart from important documents we also had some not so important papers. The papers which have been recovered from the gorge may not have any connection with the research papers.'

Schering is right. It can't be ascertained from a few faded papers that Neumann hasn't taken the formula with him. Anyway, Busch and I decided that after having breakfast, we both would visit the accident spot, leaving Schering with Ulrich. We're hoping against hope that we may recover a few more papers which may contain the formula. The accident site between Remus and Schlientz is twenty-five kilometres away. At the most it'll take us a quarter of an hour to reach there. I feel it's much more important to look for the papers rather than for the driver. It doesn't matter if they are all washed out. I have the expertise to decipher such texts.

Now it's 8.30 a.m. We'll leave in ten minutes. Though I've no clear idea why, somehow I feel a bit bothered. There seems something wrong in this whole affair. But I can't exactly pinpoint what it is.

But I'm certain about one thing, though. There's absolutely nothing wrong with my machine.

10 March, 11 p.m.
I've come out of an unending and terrifying nightmare. I'm yet to recover from this ordeal. I know I'll finally come out of this only when I get back to Giridih and its normal

environs. I could never believe that such a horrifying incident could take place against the backdrop of such a charming city. I could hardly believe that a horrifying incident like this could take place . . .

When Busch, Hans Berger of the Swiss police and I left for the accident site yesterday morning, I looked at my watch. It was quarter-to-nine. One could see ice everywhere—on the roads, on the hills and on the peaks. Even though the windows of our car were rolled down, judging by the restless trees one could gauge the speed of the wind. Busch was driving; I sat next to him and Berger was sitting at the back.

It took us one hour and ten minutes to reach our destination. We had halted for three minutes in Remus where we met a man from the police department. I was told that they still had no news of Neumann. Investigations were on in full swing and they had even announced a reward of 5000 francs for finding Neumann.

The natural surroundings of the accident site are beautiful. The gorge alongside the road is three-and-a-half thousand feet deep. When you look down you can spot a narrow river. I thought to myself that if the documents had gone floating in the river then the chances of recovering them were rather bleak. The road here is so wide that unless someone deliberately pushes a car or the driver loses his mind there's no chance of the car falling straight down the ravine. I could see some cops near the hill, and on the road across I spotted some jeeps and cars. Clearly they were keeping no stone unturned in this investigation. Busch and I began to climb down the hill . . .

There's a footway and the slope is not that dangerous either. From afar I could hear the ringing of bells. Perhaps some cows were grazing. Swiss cows wear big bells. And the sweet sounds add to the charm of the surroundings.

We first needed to see the site where the car had crashed as well as the spot where Lubin's body was found. A thick carpet of ice surrounded us and occasional blobs of snow fell off the branches of tamarisk, beech and ash trees.

However, even after hunting for forty-five minutes, we couldn't locate a single piece of paper. After climbing down from the spot of the crash for about 500 feet, what I discovered was simply unexpected.

This discovery was mine alone. Everyone was looking for pieces of paper. But my own scrutiny didn't escape the branches and the leaves of trees. I stood under an oak tree, thickly covered with leaves, and when I looked up what I observed was neither scraps of paper nor snow. My sense of observation is ten times more powerful than that of a policeman. I immediately realized that the object was a piece of cloth. I gestured at Berger and pointed my finger towards the tree. The moment he saw that, he swiftly climbed up a branch. Within minutes I heard his agitated voice. He screamed in his mother tongue, German—

'Da ist eine leiche! I can see a dead body!'

The body was brought down within five minutes. Because of the snow, even after so many days the body had remained intact. It was no trouble to figure out that the body was that of the driver, Heinz Neumann. The pocket of his coat contained his driving licence and some personal identity cards. Neumann's body showed signs of broken bones, and there were marks of injury on his face and hands. There's no doubt that he, too, had fallen out of the car on to the oak tree.

Does that mean that Neumann, after rendering both Schering and Lubin unconscious and while pushing the car with the bodies in it, himself slipped and fell down the ravine? Or could someone else have done him in? Whatever the case, the police department need not work any further to look for Neumann.

I must also mention that no research related papers were located in the pockets of Neumann's clothes. If these are located within the gorge, well and good, otherwise this was the end of the BX377 affair . . .

We left for Walenstadt at 11 a.m. We were both in a state of complete exhaustion. This was partly due to the exertion of climbing up and down the hills as well as the discovery of the body. Coupled with this, like the previous night, today, too, there was something that made me very uneasy. Occasionally, I react to a chain of thought—trying to connect to something—but that thought process swiftly snaps and goes into oblivion. Remembrain was still with me. I didn't feel like staying away from it. Once I thought of asking Busch to question Schering, but I soon realized I've no idea about the kind of queries to frame in order to restore his memory. I decided to drop the idea.

It was getting a bit cloudy and the moment our car stopped at the gate it began to drizzle.

Schering was as baffled as us when we told him about the discovery of Neumann's body. He said, 'The death of two people along with an absolute waste of seven years of sheer hard work.' He took a deep breath and then remarked, 'It's good in a way.'

We looked at Schering in surprise. He seemed dejected and said, 'I anyway had no wish to work on any weapon of mass destruction. The offer first came from Lubin. Though I'd initially protested, I inadvertently got involved as Lubin was a very close friend of mine since college days.'

With a smile, Schering looked in my direction. 'Do you know what inspired us to work on this invention? I'm particularly telling you since you're an Indian. Lubin knew Sanskrit. He happened to have read an amazing scripture written in Sanskrit kept in the Berlin Museum. The name of this scripture was *Samarangan Sutram* (Techniques of Warfare). It mentioned countless descriptions of combat mechanisms. After reading the books, Lubin conceived the very idea of this invention. Never mind . . . perhaps what has transpired will prove to be good in the end and actually be a blessing in disguise.'

I've heard of *Samarangan Sutram* but never had the fortune to read it. But the fact that Indians had devoted very special thoughts to warfare mechanisms long, long ago becomes quite apparent when you read the Mahabharata.

There was no point in detaining Schering any more. When we had been away he'd called up a friend in Altdorf asking him to come and fetch him. Altdorf is seventy-five kilometres away from here. Schering's friend said he'd come in the evening to pick him up.

*

All afternoon the four of us whiled away the hours in conversation. Around 3.30, a brand-new, fashionable red car appeared in front of our house. A well-built man more than six feet in height and aged around forty, wearing a leather jerkin and corduroy trousers, alighted from the car. Judging from his tanned face I could gather (and was later told what I thought was right) that his actual passion is climbing and that he has climbed the highest mountain, Monte Rosa, in Switzerland, five times. Otherwise he is a lawyer by profession. Needless to mention though, he is Schering's friend, Peter Frick. Schering bade farewell to everyone. Once more, he highly praised my appliance and then left for Altdorf.

After ten minutes of his leaving, when Clara was about to serve us lemon tea and cake on the table, like a flash everything became clear about what had been bothering me for so long. And right then, alarming everyone in the room, I jumped up from the sofa, looked in Busch's direction and said, 'Let's go. We need to reach Altdorf right away.'

'What does that mean?' Ulrich and Busch spoke in unison.

'Never mind the meaning. We can't afford to lose any time.'

Noticing my eagerness to get going at once, even at my age, both Busch and Ulrich got up immediately. Running up three steps at a time I asked Busch, 'Have you got a gun? I haven't brought mine.'

'I've a Luger automatic.'

'Bring it with you. And if the police officer is still here, ask him to come with us. Also, ask them to be ready with the police force at Altdorf.'

After picking up the machine from my room, the four of us got into Busch's car and raced towards Altdorf. Busch was an expert driver. Within a minute he had picked up speed of 120 kilometres per minute. In this country, the person who sits in the front has to tie the seat belt like you do in a plane. The car is designed in such a way that unless you tie the belt the engine won't start. Not only that, in case there's need to suddenly brake, two soft pillow-like cushions appear from the dashboard, stopping you from falling forward and injuring your face.

We faced no sudden brakes.

On the way none of us spoke. Perhaps judging by the look on my face the others didn't dare ask me any question. Except for me, the group was clueless about this expedition.

Within a few seconds of crossing the thirty-kilometre signage, we spotted Schering's red car. I called out, 'Overtake the car and stop!'

Blowing the horn, Busch overtook the red car and from a distance waved his hand. He stopped his own car at an angle so that Schering's car couldn't help but stop.

We got out of the car. Taken by surprise, both Schering and his friend came towards us.

'What is it?' questioned Schering.

I stepped forward. Even though Schering tried to look normal, his lips had gone dry and pale. His friend, Peter Frick, stood three steps behind him. I calmly said, 'I feel like having a cheroot. Having smoked one last night, I've become addicted to your Dutch cheroot. I hope you still have the cigar case with you?'

These plain words, spoken softly, was like fire striking dynamite. In a flash, Schering's friend pulled out a revolver from his pocket and fired at us. I felt the bullet graze my right hand and embed itself into a corner of the roof of Busch's Mercedes Benz. Then I heard the sound of another shot; Busch had shot Frick with his gun and the revolver slipped out of Frick's hand and skidded on the ice on to the side of the road. With his knees folded, Frick sat down on the road; his face was contorted with pain as he held his injured left hand.

And Schering? Letting out a wild cry, he began to run in the opposite direction but both Busch and Ulrich pounced on him with tiger-like fireceness and grabbed him. And I— the noted international scientist Trilokeshwar Shonku—took out my unique invention, the Remembrain, and putting it on Schering's head, switched on the battery.

Sandwiched between his two captors, Schering stood motionless. With the machine on, his face had become vacant, as if he was meditating, looking at the far-off snow-capped mountaintop.

Now my show began.

I shot forward a barrage of questions aimed at Schering.

'How did Dr Lubin die?'

'By suffocation.'

'Did you kill him?'

'Yes.'

'How?'

'By strangling.'

'Was the car on the move at that point?'

'Yes.'

'How did the driver Neumann die?'

'Neumann observed the scene of Lubin's murder in the rear view mirror. At that point his steering went out of control. The car fell into the gorge.'

'And you fell along with it?'

'Yes.'

'Did you think you would kill both Lubin and Neumann and throw them into the gorge?'

'Yes.'

'And then abscond with the formula?'

'Yes.'

'What would you have done with it?'

'I would have sold it.'

'To whom?'

'To whoever bid the highest.'

'Do you possess the formula papers?'

'No.'

'Then what do you have?'

'The tape.'

'The formula is recorded in it?'

'Yes.'

'Where's that tape?'

'In the cigar case.'

'Is that a tape recorder in reality?'

'Yes.'

I took the helmet off his head. The police, with striding steps, walked up the wet road towards Schering.

*

I was thinking what an amazing thing our brain is and what strange games our memory plays. Yesterday, Schering asked for a cigar; Clara offered him the case yet he didn't light up one to smoke. At that point, I should have made the connection but I didn't. Even this morning, in his room, I neither saw any sign of a cheroot nor could I smell one. In the normal course, the cigar case should have been on the side table but it wasn't there. This afternoon we had sat in the drawing room for quite long but even then he hadn't smoked a single cigar.

The cigar case is now lying on my table. It's made of gunmetal and intricately devised. You can find a cigar when you open the case but below the layer of cigars is an almost invisible button that when pressed opens a hidden compartment which accommodates a tiny tape recorder along with a microphone. Running the tape, I could hear the entire formula of BX377 recorded in Schering's own voice. If one can record something else over this recording, Schering's dangerous formula will get deleted for eternity.

Isn't that Willie's voice? He is again humming a ditty.

I take out the microphone and switch on the recorder.

Hypnojen

7 May

During the last sixty-six years of my life, I've received many invitations, on many occasions, from various sources across the world, yet this one stands out. A telegram arrived from a remote and unknown village in Norway; a telegram whose words count went well beyond a letter. When I counted, there were 133 words in the telegram. The name of the person who sent it had been hitherto unknown to me. I had neither come across this name in any biographical dictionary nor read it in any encyclopedia. I did find the name mentioned in a twenty-five-year-old German *Who's Who*, where it stated that a gentleman by the name of Alexander Craig was the owner of a diamond mine based in Brazil; he apparently died in 1913. Obviously, this Alexander Craig is a different individual. But whoever he is, the question remains, why is he so desperate to meet me?

The telegram informs me that a first-class plane ticket is on its way and the moment it reaches me I must leave immediately for Norway. A car will be waiting for me at Oslo airport. The name of the driver and the number of the car have also been mentioned in the telegram. This same car will take me to the residence of this mysterious Mr Craig. It states that it'll take three-and-a-half hours to reach his house. Further, it also mentions that I'll stand to gain in this visit as I'll be introduced to a celebrated and world-renowned scientist by Mr Craig. Who is this amazing and eccentric gentleman? Why would he spend so much money in sending me this telegram?

Whatever the case, Norway is now going through the phase of the midnight sun. At the place which I'll be visiting, at this point of time i.e., in May, there'll be no dark nights. I have never experienced this before. As a result, I'm now mulling over the definite possibility of accepting his offer and will soon let him know about my consent. I need not invest any money to do so as he has already sent me a prepaid telegram, though, even if I try, I won't be able to put in more than a dozen words.

May 9
While I was leafing through the pages of an art book, I came across a painting by the famous sixteenth-century Italian artist, Tintoretto, and noticed a line written right below the

painting in very small letters: 'From the personal collection of Alexander Craig.' Certainly, there's no doubt left that a person who has a Tintoretto in his personal collection must be a very wealthy man, indeed.

I'm leaving the day after. I have let Craig know my plan. I'm mighty excited about this trip. I can sense that my journey to Norway will not come to naught.

11 May

It's been half-an-hour since we left Oslo airport, travelling in a Daimler driven by a chauffeur in uniform. I said 'we' as two more persons other than me are present in the car. One of them is an English physicist, John Somerville, an old friend of mine. The other person is someone I am meeting for the first time. He is Hector Papadopoulos, a biochemist from Greece. Of the three of us, he is the youngest and doesn't look more than forty. His head full of thick, curly hair is matched by bushy eyebrows and a thick pair of moustaches. All three of us have been invited in a similar way i.e. by a lengthy telegram delineating the arrangements. I discovered this only upon my arrival at the Oslo airport. We're all in the same boat at present. Somerville, too, had not heard of Craig. Papadopoulos said he may have heard of him, but cannot clearly recall. The length of the telegram, the first class ticket, and now this expensive Daimler and the fancy uniform of the chauffeur all drive home the fact that there's no dearth of money in Alexander Craig's life.

At this moment we have all halted for a coffee break. It's now 3.30 p.m. It's not as cold as I'd expected. But then, any student of geography will be well aware of the unpredictable nature of Norway's weather. In this country, it is colder in the southern hemisphere as occasional warm winds from the Atlantic often blow over the northern region. As a result, despite the location at greater heights and the proximity to the polar axis, it is warmer here. We're having our coffee at a roadside restaurant. The atmosphere is wonderfully quiet and pleasant. In Norway, there's practically no presence of any plain and flat surface. The place is mostly all valley surrounded by snow-capped mountains. The driver, Pietro Norwell, tells us that Craig's residence is 330 kilometres from Oslo. It'll take us two-and-a-half hours to get there.

12 May, 9.30 p.m.

I say it's 9.30 at night simply by looking at my watch, though I know that if I look at the bright sky I wouldn't believe it. I must say, we've come to an amazing place. But one ought to talk about the people first rather than the place. Because this residence—one can call it a palace—was built by only one individual. It resembles a medieval castle. It appears to be 700-800 years old but in reality it was built

34

only in the twentieth century. I was quite keen to find out about the total expense made in its construction but when I saw the condition the owner was in, I realized it would be absurd to ask such an irrelevant question. Alexander Aloysius Craig was on his deathbed. He had called upon us with a predicament on his mind. Now I must recount the remarkable story of why he asked for the three of us.

At exactly 6.05 p.m. our car drove through an imposing gate and onwards for another five minutes down a picturesque meandering road under the shadows of poplar, aspen and tamarisk trees till we finally reached the main doorway to the castle. A uniformed middle-aged man came forward, and welcomed us into the castle.

The room we entered was a so-called waiting room but we were rendered speechless at the opulence of the interior. The presence of furniture, marble statues, a crystal chandelier, huge gilt-framed oil paintings, an elaborate Persian carpet, armour hanging against the walls, and iron suits put up against pedestals—in effect it took us back to the days of barons who looted millions and millions and led a life of luxury, lavishness and jollity. Though a scientist, I realized Papadopoulos had vast knowledge about various other areas, too. Glancing around, he remarked that the paintings alone would amount to a few million rupees. Personally, I could identify one Rembrandt and a Fragonard. God knows what else is scattered around the rest of the fortress.

After we had waited for ten minutes, the man returned to tell us that Mr Craig was now ready to meet us. As we followed him, we passed through two more enormous rooms filled with countless priceless objects and finally entered a somewhat smaller and semi-dark room. I could spot a solitary lamp whose light was focused on a peculiarly massive, crafted bed. The figure lying on it was nearly as old as the antiques in the house. The man who was reclining against the pillow looked very ill, but his eyes gazed at us with a sharp expression. It was, of course, none other than the owner and master of this castle, Alexander Craig. He was covered with a satin quilt, his emaciated hands resting on his chest. He released the right hand from his left one and stretched it out in our direction. All three of us shook hands with Craig.

Craig nodded his head in the direction of three leather chairs positioned right next to his bed. We took our seats. He then gently pulled at a silk cord hanging next to his right hand. We heard the faint sound of bells and a creature appeared noiselessly from the dark corner of the room and stood next to Craig. I'm using the word 'creature', because 'man' wouldn't be correct. I've never seen such a man in my entire life. He was seven-and-a-half feet tall, with bluish-black skin the colour and smoothness of well-polished steel. He wore a knee-length dark red gown made of velvet, joined at the waist by a sliver band. The features of his face coupled with his perfectly sculpted bald head gave the impression of a mythological god.

This stranger now bent over Craig and pressed the sides of his temple with his right hand. He continued to press for about ten seconds and then loosened his grip. Immediately, one could observe a tangible change in Craig; it was as if his body had gained a new lease of life. Resting his hands on the bed, he pulled himself up into a sitting position. Taking a deep breath, he said in clear English, 'I've brought up Odin with my own hands and he is a trustworthy servant. Among his many other abilities, he has this capacity to revitalize an ailing person for a brief period so that the person is able to normally converse with his friends.'

Mr Craig stopped talking. When I heard Odin's name I realized my assumption had not been all wrong. Craig himself regarded his nurse as a divine being. In Norwegian mythology, the figure of Odin ranks very high amongst the other celestial figures. Odin's figure now quietly receded into the darkness.

Both Somerville and I were rendered speechless as well as alarmed. As Papadopoulos was a lot younger, he was quite restless—he had cleared his throat twice and was constantly squeezing his hands.

'Odin and Thor,' Craig said. 'They both do most of my work. You'll get to know Thor in due course.'

Thor is the name of yet another powerful Norwegian god.

Papadopoulos could no longer restrain himself.

'You'd written about a scientist.'

A smile appeared at the corners of Craig's lips. His eyes sparkled.

'That scientist is on his deathbed right now,' Craig said. 'He himself had invited you to come over. His name is Alexander . . .'

Papadopoulos looked quite disappointed. I hadn't expected this reply either. We all looked at each other. Craig resumed talking.

'It may not be that easy to believe this, but very soon you'll get some proof. Out of the forty rooms in this castle, one is a laboratory. Over the past ninety-two years I've been conducting numerous experiments.'

Craig paused for a moment. The reason was obvious. He could very well guess that when we heard his age as ninety-two this would obviously pose a few questions in our minds. He himself offered us the answer before we could question him.

'Due to my own scientific capacity, I was able to add to my longevity three times. But this time it's proving impossible.'

Every time he paused, I could feel an extraordinary stillness in the atmosphere. Not a single sound could be heard in the entire castle.

'Napoleon and I both share the same birthday. It's 5th May 1821.'

'You're a hundred-and-fifty years old?' Papadopoulos sounded flabbergasted as he asked the question in a loud voice.

Smiling gently, Craig remarked, 'If you're so taken in by this fact alone then I wonder how would you react about what is to follow next?'

Papadopoulos fell silent. Craig continued to talk.

'I was a student of science in the university. I was a favourite student of Prof. Rasmussen. He would tell me: "You should be teaching, researching . . . you have an assured future." But there was another side to my personality. I was addicted to adventure. I left home at the age of twenty-seven. From Europe, I landed up in South America. My mind diverted to gambling. And my luck turned out to be extraordinarily good. I acquired more than a hundred thousand reals in just one night alone, playing roulette in Rio de Janeiro. I invested that money in diamond prospecting; Africa was yet to discover diamonds. As a result, I decided to stay back in Brazil. All my possessions—this grand assemblage—what lies behind it are diamonds. Do you know how much this diamond costs?'

He held up his right hand. On his middle finger was a ring with a huge sparkling diamond. He didn't wait for our answer.

'I returned to my own country after staying in Brazil for twenty years. By then I was a multimillionaire. That's when the idea of building a castle struck me. I was obsessed with the idea of collecting precious objects. And I needed an appropriate place to house them. I built a castle. I began to live in it alongside these items. Many people do not like to stay alone. But I quite enjoyed it. It was only me and my objects of desire. After that I never left home. Whatever I have collected since has been acquired strictly through correspondence. The post office delivers whatever I order. Then one day, when I'd crossed the age of sixty, out of the blue, my one and only companion, my dog, died. The thought then dawned on me—one day I too will die, I'll have to leave behind this entire treasure. I began to wonder if through an artificial process, with the help of science, one can increase one's longevity. The laboratory was created. After forty-five years, the words of Prof. Rasmussen finally rang true. I could still undertake hard work. I started my research. You can see the result of that work. But . . .'

The three of us were listening to him spellbound. Papadopoulos had stopped squeezing his hands. Craig had now started breathing heavily. I noticed he looked exhausted.

'But . . . my invention cannot keep anyone alive for an indefinite period. I was aware of this and hence I had to invest heavily both on finance as well as on time, working on another experiment.'

'Mr Craig,' this time Somerville opened his mouth. 'Do you mean to say that despite having lived for 150 years you still long to live? Getting on with years, one gradually loses interest in all attachments, isn't it?'

With wide eyes Craig looked straight at Somerville. 'But I haven't got over my attachments, John Somerville.'

Ignoring his own condition, once more in a loud voice, he stated, 'My ultimate mission is yet to be accomplished . . . My final adventure!'

While uttering these words, Craig's head had risen from his pillow; the moment he finished speaking the head slackened. His devoted servant, Odin, had again appeared from the darkness and stood next to him, probably waiting for his orders.

Craig composed himself and when he spoke again, his tone was quite normal. 'We cannot make a human live indefinitely. His death is inevitable. But . . .'

For some unknown reason, Craig looked straight at me and completed my sentence, 'But a dead man can be revived at least once.'

The room went still. From a distant room we could hear the beautiful tunes from three clocks ringing in 7 p.m. When Craig spoke again, his voice sounded rather feeble. He was running out of energy.

'I'm not saying this without the support of my research. There's one person in this house who continues to do my work after being revived from his own death. I will not survive beyond tonight. Even Odin will not be in a position

41

to pump in fresh energy into me. Odin will help you tomorrow morning. He will carry my dead body to a special room. Please follow him to this room. Everything will be ready there. A chart will bear all the instructions. Other than scientists, no one else will be able to follow this chart. You all will be able to understand the instructions. Odin will lay me down on a particular place. Then the rest of the work will be yours. Your work will begin twelve hours after my death. After three hours, you'll begin to notice signs of life in me. At this point, your work ends. As I can't depend on one person, I've asked for all three of you together. I know you won't disappoint me. Nor will you betray me.'

Craig shut his eyes. It was getting very difficult to follow him now. Papadopoulos' voice broke the silence.

'After accomplishing this task, we're free to leave, isn't it?'

Craig's eyelids parted for a while. Possibly the two corners of his lips produced a faint smile. And at that very moment, he became unconscious.

Now Odin stirred. With his right hand he pressed the button of a black box which was on the table next to the bed. In an instant we heard Craig's voice again. 'I'm grateful to all of you for accepting my invitation. My servant Nils will show you around the fort. You can ask him any questions. Whenever you require any food or drinks he'll arrange for you. Goodbye for now.'

The servant named Nils was standing outside the room. The moment the recording stopped, he escorted us out of the room and we began our tour of the castle. While passing through a corridor, Papadopoulos asked Nils, 'Do you know any Greek?' Nils shook his head and said, 'Only English and Norwegian.'

'How old are you?'

I know why Papadopoulos asked this question: Nils definitely looked very old for this present job.

'Eighty-three,' Nils answered.

'How long have you worked here?'

'Fifty-five years.' He paused and then added, 'Last year on the 7th of December, I died. My master brought me back to life.'

Is everyone here out of their minds or are they all lying? Or has Craig tutored them to give such precise answers to our questions?

'You must be feeling quite fit now?'

Papadopoulos had questioned him with a touch of banter, Nils's answer was, however, absolutely matter of fact.

'I've never felt fitter.'

We toured the castle for a couple of hours. Each room could be described as an art gallery or a museum. We were shown all the rooms except for one, which was secured with a heavy padlock from the outside. When asked why that particular room was locked, Nils remained silent.

Undoubtedly, this must be Craig's laboratory as no other room we saw bore any evidence of scientific research.

My bedroom is marked by ultimate opulence. My entire house in Giridih would easily fit into it. The entire fort is centrally heated; each room bears a thermometer. The mercury points at 75 degrees Fahrenheit. The moment I sat down on a velvet sofa and was about to take out the diary from my pocket, I heard a knock on my door. Somerville and Papadopoulos entered. Typically, the former was composed; even if he was agitated you could never tell. On the other hand, the minute the excitable Greek gentleman stepped in, he chose a strong Greek word to articulate his present state of mind that roughly translates into English as 'What the hell!'

Somerville sat next to me and asked, 'Is it worthy of people of our calibre to participate in this farce? After all, we are not any Tom, Dick and Harry—we have a certain position and reputation to live up to in society.'

'But, look, John,' I said, 'since we are here thanks to Craig's money and have accepted his hospitality, we can't afford to get angry so easily. Tomorrow he will die. Then let's see what happens. At that point we can find out if he is a charlatan. Even if he doesn't die, then there isn't much we can do in any case. He can't surely keep us captured till he dies.'

Papadopoulos hit his right fist into the palm of his left hand. 'Luring us to meet other scientists, look how he has bluffed us all. Tch, tch.'

One thing was bothering me. I couldn't help but comment on it.

'I, too, could have agreed with you both but one thing is holding me back.'

'What's that?' They both echoed together.

'Odin.'

The moment I uttered his name Papadopoulos strongly protested.

'Odin? This pompous brute, who was presented before us with make-up on, a clean shaven head, and with that dramatic dress on—what's there to doubt? Don't you think pressing at one's temples to reactivate one's energy is a sheer act of quackery? The entire operation of Craig's is a hoax. He claims to be 150 years old! Out of his entire big talk only one thing is convincing—making money through gambling. I strongly feel this collection of his fancy art which adorns all the rooms are either stolen goods or forged stuff. Don't know what sort of a goon we're in the clutches of . . .'

I interrupted him. 'Odin wasn't batting his eyelids.'

Both Somerville and Papadopoulos looked unbelievingly at me. 'Are you sure?' Somerville asked.

'I looked straight at his eyes for five minutes at a stretch. It's not possible for anyone to look at you in such a state for that long. I feel he is a mechanical being i.e. a robot. I've had a similar experience with a robot once before.'

Somerville said, 'Even then, does it prove that Craig himself is a scientist and has created this robot?'

'No, that can't be. We'll get to know his real potential only if he can revive a dead person—'

I couldn't finish what I was saying. The lights of the room suddenly grew dim, almost plunging us into darkness. As the curtains of the windows were closed, no light could enter the room.

'What happened?' Papadopoulos asked, sounding frightened. 'How could this . . .?'

Drowning Papadopoulos' question, an eerie grave voice boomed across the room.

'The master is dead!'

Complete silence followed. Papadopoulos's face turned pale. Somerville stood up from the sofa. Then we heard the very same voice again.

'The master will live again!'

Moments after these words were uttered, the lights came back to the room.

'A speaker must be concealed somewhere in this room,' Papadopoulos remarked.

'That is obvious,' Somerville said. 'But whether this news is true or this prophecy will prove to be valid is the main question.'

Papadopoulos got up and started pacing up and down. 'This gentleman's theatrics are crossing the limits.'

That thought had crossed my mind, too, ever since we got here. It had grown more intense during our tour of each room. The mere idea of building such a castle in the twentieth century itself was so dramatic. And that room bearing a huge lock in front of the door was no less theatrical. According to Papadopoulos, the room contains smuggled goods; but I'm not totally convinced. If Craig had stolen some of these items from any noted museums, the thefts would surely have been reported in some paper, and come to our notice. Either Craig is being unnecessarily secretive or indeed some mysterious stuff has been hidden there.

At exactly 8 p.m., Nils emerged to tell us that dinner was ready. What a royal feast! The fellow who was serving us also looked very ancient; but none of us dared find out the length of time he had been serving Craig. I could not have digested the food, even if it was such gourmet fare, had I known it was being served by a dead man, resurrected.

Around 8:30 p.m. we all said goodnight to each other and retired to our respective rooms.

When I pulled away the curtain to see if there was still any sunlight outside, I realized the room was actually situated within the walls of the fort. Instead of the sky, what could be seen was a dark corridor. I could spot a wall which was perhaps within ten yards of the window. A suit of armour stood against the wall.

I sat on the bed. God knows what our future holds. I'm repeatedly thinking of one thing: a comment by Craig—'My ultimate mission is yet to be accomplished . . . My final adventure . . . !'

What work is Alexander Aloysius Craig referring to?

Do we have a role to play in this adventure?

When can we get freedom from this state of captivity?

13 May, 6 a.m.
As we'll be called downstairs soon, I'll write about last night's episode in my diary now.

In the middle of the night—looking at the watch later, I realized it had been 2:30 a.m. I got up when I heard a knock on my door. I'm a very light sleeper in any case, but the added discomfort I was feeling about a few things in this place ensured that I wasn't sleeping too well. I opened the door and saw our Greek friend, Hector Papadopoulos—his eyes wide open and his forehead dotted with drops of sweat despite the cold weather.

The fellow rushed into my room, breathing heavily, and could utter only a few words–'I've opened the lock!'

Good lord! What was this renowned scientist up to in the middle of the night?

'What lock?' I asked with great trepidation. In reply I heard a few more words—

'The forbidden room.'

The gist of what Papadopoulos told me was this:

When we noticed the locked door and not having received the right response from Nils, Papadopoulos was determined to enter the room anyhow. With this plan in mind he stayed up till twelve and then left his room. Despite the darkness in the corridor, he finally reached the room with the padlocked door. He then opened the lock. When asked how this was done he took out a small vial from his pocket. He told me it was some kind of acid; if a few drops of it are poured into the keyhole of the lock, all the contraptions of the lock automatically melt away and the lock opens up. This happens to be his own invention. When asked why he was carrying this stuff along he said this was just one of many such small inventions he had brought here to show to the 'world's most remarkable scientist'.

I was curious. 'What did you see in the room?' I asked. To this he said he didn't have the courage to enter the room alone because as he opened the door he detected a smell similar to the smell of a zoo.

We decided to take Somerville with us and visit the room. Ideally, I should have prevented Papadopoulos from doing so, but the moment I heard about the animal odour, even my own curiosity aroused. Somerville is obviously a light sleeper; we didn't have to knock at his door more than once. Taking great precautions to avoid using the torch, we made our way slowly by the faint light that came in from the windows and skylight overhead along the corridor. We finally arrived in front of the unbolted door. Opening the door ajar I, too, got a whiff of the animal smell but it wasn't as strong as Papadopoulos had described. Papadopoulos obviously has a very sharp sense of smell. We all marched into the forbidden room.

It was a huge room with no window. The impenetrable darkness of the room was slightly broken thanks to the light coming in from three skylights in the ceiling. This room was entirely different from the rooms in the rest of the castle. There were no valuable paintings or precious artefacts here; what was present were only work related items. If you can imagine an enormous room which included a scientist's study, laboratory and workshop—this room was one such. One side of the wall was marked by a bookshelf containing numerous books, the majority of which were scientific books. In the middle stood three long tables, all bearing chemicals and other equipment. In front were two rows of steel cabinets and in between the cabinets was a wide mahogany table. There's no doubt that Craig sat behind this table to do his work. Behind that table, on the wall hung an enormous world map. And certain areas of this map were marked by small coloured flags stuck with pins. Focusing the torch on the map, I realized the pins were fixed on all the capitals of each country.

'Hypnojen.' It was Somerville. He had started going through Craig's papers. He muttered this word while leafing through the first page of a fat leather-bound notebook. I had never heard this word before.

I moved towards Somerville. He had sat down on a chair with the notebook opened in front of him on the table. The words 'Hypnojen Related Notes' were written in red ink on the first page of the book. Below that was written 'A.A. Craig' and right below that were dates mentioned, going back over four years. We both began to leaf through the notebook. After reading a few pages, no doubt remained regarding Craig's scientific knowledge. There was nothing phony in the calculations and chemical formulas mentioned in the book. But what was this Hypnojen? If you go back to its Latin origin, it amounts to some hypnosis related sleep inducing medicine. Was it connected to some cerebral reactions in one's mind?

The first few pages of the notebook discussed a proposal that chilled the blood in our veins. With rising disbelief and terror we finally finished reading it. Alexander Aloysius Craig had outlined his 'ultimate mission' or 'last adventure'. The mission was essentially this—to establish himself as the singular ruler of this world. The rest of the world would live under his thumb. All the treasures of each and every museum, library and art gallery of this entire planet would belong to him alone. And this would be made possible with the help of this 'Hypnojen'.

Craig's Hypnojen is a vaporous component. Craig has described two easy methods by which this vaporous element or gas could be released over a city; one was through pipes or tubes and the other was by throwing a bomb from a plane. The bomb would be made of plastic and would automatically release the gas in all directions, seconds before hitting the ground. One got a fair idea about the outcome of this act from Craig's notebook. When a particle or a molecule from the gas enters a person's body through his breath, that person comes under a spell of hypnosis for the next twenty-four hours. One bomb would be enough to hypnotize the total population of a city like London or New York for an entire year. And the advantage is that the bomb will not otherwise destroy the city in any way. If one gets to control the mind of the people then where's the trouble in ruling over them?

While we were coming to terms with this incredible plan by Craig—was this all real or just a bunch of loony thoughts—a faint scream turned our attention to the other direction of the room. We saw Hector Papadopoulos standing in front of a door a little farther down from us in a state of sheer panic.

We ran to him. When Papadopoulos stepped back we came in front of the door. The feral stench was much stronger now. And the reason was quite obvious. In the room—a smaller one in comparison—a few yards from the door, we noticed a pair of green, glowing eyes staring at us. This antechamber was even darker as there was only one skylight overhead, and when we focused the torch in the direction of these eyes, a terrifying scenario appeared before us. A black panther stood in the middle of the room, looking straight in our direction. The vicious nature of this particular animal of the tiger family is well known. With a peculiar groan, Papadopoulos fell to the ground with a thud in a faint. However, I noticed something unnatural in this animal's manner. Somerville put a hand on my shoulder to stop me but I paid no heed and walked into the room.

I went towards the panther and knelt down in front of him. It was beyond my imagination that a ferocious animal of this nature could look so blank. I focused my torch right into his eyes. It would be wrong to describe them as harmless. Perhaps a foolish expression would be closer to the truth. This animal had become witless, as if he was waiting to obey someone's orders; he was no longer in possession of his own power or his own mind.

I noticed something else. There was a tag hanging from the panther's neck. A date of six months ago was written on it. Craig had obviously experimented on this animal on that day.

In the meantime, Somerville had focused his torch on the other side of the room. We were fascinated to see a series of glass boxes spread across the room. Each box contained a deadly creature—the majority of these were either insects or reptiles in nature.

We proceeded towards the first box. The top showed a label with a date. Inside the entire glass case was a black krait, all coiled up. When the snake saw me he raised his head but didn't expand his hood. I opened the lid of the box, put my hand in and partly took out the snake. He was harmless. I put him back into the box.

I looked at my watch and noticed it was almost 3:15 a.m. I wondered what state our Greek friend was in now. When we walked out of the antechamber, we saw that he had got up from the carpet and was now sitting on a chair. I said, 'It's time we return to our rooms. We have work to do tomorrow; we'll be sent for at eight in the morning.' Papadopoulos looked at me with fear in his eyes. 'What if Craig really comes back to life?'

I said, 'Well! Then we have to admit that there's no other scientist to match him in this world.'

'But what if he uses this gas on us?'

'If we see such signs we need to work out a strategy to disarm him. Won't we be able to arrive at a solution if we all apply our minds together? '

'Shonku—'

Somerville tapped on my shoulder. His eyes were focused on a particular steel cabinet. Selecting one among them, his torchlight now moved on to a specific drawer. It was labelled—'H. Minus.'

'Can you figure out something?' asked Somerville. I said, 'Perhaps I can. This is possibly the antidote to drive away the spell of Hypnojen.'

Somerville moved forward and opened the drawer. I stood next to him.

Inside the drawer, on a bed of cotton lay a carefully placed solitary bottle—slightly bigger than the size of a homeopathic bottle. 'Crystal,' said Somerville. He was right. The bottle contained white powder. When he opened the bottle, a whiff of a sweet, pungent smell entered our nostrils. Somerville instantly closed the bottle.

I thought I would experiment this on one of the hypnotized creatures in the next room but that was not to be. A fourth figure had appeared in the room. It happened so quietly that none of us realized till the light from Somerville's torch fell on him. Odin. He stood tall in the doorway. The voice that had announced Craig's death was the same voice that now bellowed across the enormous room.

'You've committed an offence. My master will resent it. Now return to your rooms.'

It was indeed very wrong of us—though the person to be really blamed is our Greek friend.

Left with no choice, we all headed towards the door. As we passed him, Odin stretched out his hand to Somerville. Like an obedient child, Somerville placed the bottle in his hand. Odin then put it inside the side pocket of his gown and turned towards the door. The three of us followed him through the corridor, climbed the stairs and walked back to our rooms. Odin escorted each of us to our rooms and then vanished into the dark passageway, as quietly as he had appeared.

I checked the time in my watch. It was 3:45 a.m. I went back to bed. I knew there was no way I could get any sleep under these terrifying circumstances yet I knew even if I just lay down with my eyes shut, it would help me to gather my wits. With what we had observed and heard in the last few hours there was plenty to reflect on.

14 May

Craig had spoken of his last adventure; the way things were shaping up, it was becoming quite apparent that this would turn out to be the last adventure of our lives too. That it did not turn out that way was for one and only one reason . . . no, I shall narrate everything in due course. I must maintain the sequence of each event.

At 7 a.m. Nils served us breakfast in our rooms. A little later, I heard the same voice echo through a hidden speaker in my room.

'The master is waiting for you. Kindly come to his room.'

The three of us met on the landing of the staircase and, having greeted each other good morning, proceeded to go down. None of us said a word. Papadopoulos appeared restless as well as nervous. I noticed he hadn't even shaved properly. I doubt if he had had a proper breakfast. In any case, I won't perturb him with queries.

The curtains of Craig's room had been drawn, letting in the sun. Now there was no darkness in any nook or corner of the room. The sunlight had fallen on Craig's bed; even on Craig's face. It was clear that the face was one of a dead man.

Odin was standing next to the bed. With ease he picked up his master's body in his arms, turned his head in our direction and said, 'Follow me.'

Once again in single file, we walked behind him. After crossing three long corridors and reaching the other end of the fort, we came to an open door that led to a spiral staircase going down. It meant that this special room of Craig's was down in a cellar!

Following Odin, we climbed down thirty steps and when we reached I saw the kind of room that one reads about only in novels. There were no windows in this dungeon-like room and no possibility of any natural light. Instead, the room was glowing with a bluish electric light. There was an operating table in the middle of the room with a light hanging from a shade above it. A number of glass tubes, electrodes, indicators, various switches and buttons to be turned on or off and a helmet with wires sticking out of it all surrounded the table. Near one of the legs of the operating table stood a teapoy which held numerous medicinal bottles—each of a different colour. None of this was unfamiliar to me; but the end result which would be obtained when all these items applied to a dead body was not clear to me.

After laying down Craig's body on the table, Odin left the room. A chart hanging next to the table explained in clear and minute details about our course of action. The chart had divided the body into three parts—the head; the upper torso and finally the lower torso, that is, from the waist to the tip of the toes.

'Five minutes to go!'

We were startled by this new voice.

'Read the instructions carefully and proceed!'

Our attention shifted to one corner of the room. Another humongous monster was standing there. His outfit, too, was like that of Odin's gown except that his was blue in colour. He was marked by another difference—he was carrying an immense hammer.

'Thor!' Somerville and I almost chorused together. Among the Norwegian mythical gods the position of Thor comes right after Odin. And everyone of course knows of Thor's famous weapon, the hammer. I soon comprehended that this Thor was made in charge of the special laboratory. And that he was to ensure the operation was carried out smoothly. Without wasting any more time, we worked out our duties. Notwithstanding numerous fears, one was also very curious to face results of such an unbelievable venture.

I told Somerville, 'I'm handling the head, you take care of the middle portion and Papadopoulos will look after the area towards the feet.'

I observed a strange change in Papadopoulos when he heard me. Sounding desperate, he said, 'I beg you. Please leave me out. I'm not capable of accomplishing such a task.'

We both were completely taken aback by his reaction. What was he trying to say?

'What do you mean, you're not capable?' I said fervidly, showing great annoyance. 'Being a scientist yourself, won't you be able to follow such clearly written straightforward instructions?'

Papadopoulos hung his head. 'I'm not a scientist. My brother Hector is the scientist. I am his twin. My twin . . . he is not well. He is now admitted to a hospital in Athens. After receiving Craig's invitation I came in place of Hector out of sheer greed.'

'Greed for what?'

'Greed for valuable items. I knew of Craig's precious collection. I thought if on such an occasion . . .'

Somerville interrupted him. 'Are you the same Nikolas Papadopoulos who, ten years ago tried to steal a painting by Pieter de Hooch from Holland's Rijksmuseum and was arrested?'

Our Greek friend's head bowed down even more.

'Two minutes to go!' announced Thor in his thunderous voice.

Papadopoulos dropped himself into a chair by the staircase. After spilling out the truth he looked much relieved.

Somerville and I got into action. The work was not too difficult and could be handled by two people. Within a couple of minutes we got everything readied, following the chart's instructions. It was now 9 a.m. We were ready.

The body was on the table, its emaciated hand bearing thin nerves and veins, and its bloodless and ashen face marked by endless wrinkles. It was not difficult to believe this man was almost 150 years old. Craig lay on the table— senseless and lifeless. His head was now covered by the helmet, which had seventeen electrodes protruding from it in different directions. The entire body was wrapped in a white sheet. Only the head, two hands and the feet remained uncovered. Many more tubes were visible from two sides of the temple, neck and from his hands and legs. Within the exposed part of the body, twelve areas of the skin were penetrated by pins in the manner of Chinese acupuncture.

We received fresh instructions, once again in Thor's voice:

'Now press the switch.'

We pressed the white button next to a glowing red bulb on the right side of the table. Instantly we heard a sharp vibrating noise like that of a flute which was joined by a deep sound resembling a Tibetan chant which ricocheted off the walls and rumbled through the underground laboratory. I just couldn't work out from where the second layer of this sound emerged.

We knew nothing would happen before 12 noon. I still had my doubts if at all anything would emerge as the apparatus and instruments used here showed no signs of anything unusual or original. Except for the fact that I've no knowledge of what liquid was exactly being passed into his body drop by drop, through a tube inserted into his nose. To be very frank, I would not have believed anything at all— but judging by the effect of Hypnojen on these ferocious animals which we encountered this morning—we were left with no doubt about Craig's ingenious scientific mind.

Being preoccupied, I had not noticed that Papadopoulos was missing. Could he have escaped? Somerville, too, looked surprised at his absence. 'For all you know, he may very well be removing paintings from the wall and putting them into his bag.' Since the very beginning I'd had my doubts regarding this Papadopoulos and now I feel somewhat relieved that my conjecture, after all, turned out to be true.

At 11 a.m., I concentrated fully on the dead body. A green shadow had appeared on Craig's entire face. Somerville was standing close to me. He placed his own hand in mine.

The hand was cold. Even someone of Somerville's stature emerged weak and frightened right now. I gently pressed my hand on his hand to give him some courage. When I looked at Thor I saw he was standing in the same position. Like Odin, he, too, is devoid of any eyelids.

When it was five minutes to twelve, I noted my heart was beating rapidly. Chiefly because Thor had left his earlier position and, taking four giant steps forward, was now standing right behind us. Upon hearing a mechanical sound we saw his hand slowly rise up to a certain level, along with the hammer, and then pause. That meant, if we commit any error at this last moment, the hammer would strike our heads.

With only a minute to go, Thor in his own voice began to chant peculiarly. He was requesting his master to return— 'Master, come back! . . . Master come back! . . . Master come back!'

In the meantime, all other sounds had stopped. This included the vibrating flute-like noise, the Tibetan hymn, and the beating of drums that had started an hour ago. Eventually, everything had died out except for the sound of Thor's voice.

And now Somerville and I looked at Craig's dead body in sheer amazement. The green colour on his face was gradually fading away and instead a layer of red was appearing on his face.

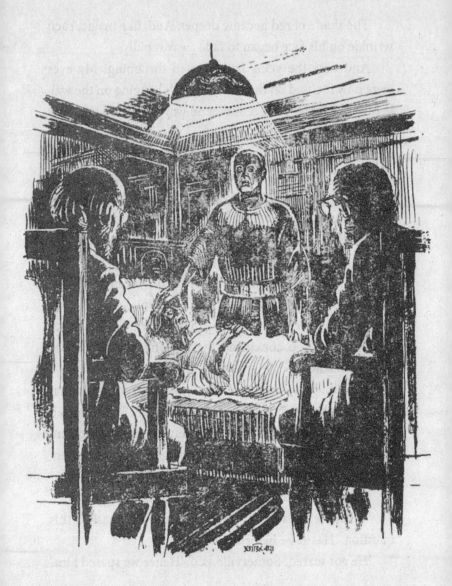

The shade of red became deeper. And, like magic, each wrinkle on his face began to fade away rapidly.

And now the veins have started throbbing! My eyes were now focused on the electric watch hanging on the wall behind the table. The second hand was slowly ticking away towards 12 o'clock. Four . . . three . . . two . . . one . . .

'Master!'

Thor's jubilation was followed by a horrible ghoulish shriek and we both lost our balance in sheer fright and fell to the ground. Even in that state we saw Alexander Aloysius Craig releasing his two worn out hands with great zest and raising them. And then Craig sat up.

'Are you convinced now? Are you convinced now?'

Due to Craig's brandishing movements, all the glass items of the operating room began to clatter.

'Now are you convinced that I alone am the world's greatest scientist?'

We both remained silent. And I could strongly feel that Craig was thoroughly enjoying our silence when I noticed his face parting with a grisly grin. But at that very instant the smile disappeared. He looked straight in our direction. 'Where is Papadopoulos? Why can't I see him?'

Craig had finally detected the absence.

'Where is Papadopoulos?' Craig once again asked this question. 'Hasn't he helped you?'

'He got scared,' Somerville said. 'Hence we spared him.'

Craig's face turned grim. 'A coward deserves only one reprimand. He has offended science. He has acted like a fool by trying to escape. This castle has only a doorway to enter but not an exit to flee.'

Now Craig's attention turned towards us. His anger was replaced by a strange sense of curiosity.

He climbed down from the table and stood before us. His brazen attitude showed that along with his new life he had also regained his vigour. His voice bore no sign of old age.

'I do not need Thor or Odin any more,' Craig said in a grave voice. 'You both will now replace them. There's a limit to intelligence in a mechanical being. You both have the intelligence. You'll follow my orders. You will become attendants to the man who is going to rule over the people of this entire world.' Still talking, Craig moved to one side and opened the door of a cabinet to take out something. It was a thin rubber mask. He put it over his head and his right hand proceeded towards a switch. I knew that the moment he pressed that switch a lethal gas from an invisible source would be released and then eternally we both would . . .

'Master!'

Craig's hand stopped. Nils was panting near the staircase, looking dazed.

'Professor Papadopoulos has fled.'

'Fled?'

Craig was astounded.

'Yes, Master. The professor went to the locked room. As the lock is broken, Henrique was guarding the door. Henrique had a revolver. The professor fled when he spotted him. Henrique followed him. The professor jumped out from the large window on to the cornice of the west facing wall of the fort. The professor was very quick, very—'

Nils could not complete his sentence. One could now hear a new sound. This sound was so utterly unexpected that even Craig, seeming baffled, removed his hand from the switch.

The sound was now much closer to us. Nils's face had turned as white as a sheet. He immediately ran off. And in that instant, letting out a huge roar, an animal entered the laboratory. The blue light was reflected on his smooth, black, hairy body. The tag with the date was still hanging from his neck.

A strange groan came out of Craig's mouth. With great difficulty he uttered two names, 'Odin! Thor!'

But Thor had almost turned into a statue—he was standing motionless and still. Craig took the hammer from Thor's hand. Strongly securing it into his hands he retreated two steps. I knew the hammer wouldn't be of much help to defend us if the animal attacked; but I also knew the animal was not targeting us. He proceeded step by step to the man who had turned him into a witless fool.

I've often observed that at the height of any crisis my mind always remains clear. When I saw Craig's hand was moving towards the switch to release the gas and disarm us as well as the tiger, I ran to him and pulled the mask off his face. And in that instant the panther leaped on him. I now ran towards the steps even as I heard Craig's piercing scream. Then I heard a familiar voice calling out our names.

'Shonku! Somerville!'

We had reached the corridor on the top but couldn't fathom from where exactly Papadopoulos was calling us. In this maze it's often very difficult to trace the source of the sound.

There was a right turn ahead of us. We came up to the forbidden room after taking this turn. This was now open. In front of it is lay the blood-smeared body of a man. Henrique had become the panther's first victim.

At the head of the corridor we could now spot Papadopoulos; he was holding a revolver, no doubt taken from poor Henrique. After taking a few steps he suddenly halted and waved to us and called, 'Come on. The road's clear!'

The three of us crossed three rooms and after passing through the waiting room door, we arrived at the entrance to the castle. Thanks to that lone revolver, we crossed all hurdles in order to escape. Using the same revolver, we were able to commandeer the Daimler and the driver, Pietro Norwell, to take us to the airport. Given that we all had our return tickets and passports with us, we faced no more difficulties.

We felt safe only when we reached the main road. I turned to Papadopoulos, 'What happened? You jumped over the window and landed on the cornice, and what followed then?'

Not removing the weapon pointed in the direction of the driver, Papadopoulos said, 'Well, that was easy. After landing on the cornice I headed straight towards the room located outside the zoo. And does it take too long to notch up a few grooves of the stones using your hands and feet to reach the skylight?'

'And then?' Both Somerville and I asked together.

'Not much was left to be done really. I had the bottle with me. After opening the bottle, I put my hand inside the skylight and spread the powder from there.

We both were utterly amazed. I asked, 'How come you had the bottle with you? Odin had put it in his pocket.'

Papadopoulos revealed two layers of teeth below his bushy moustache in a smile.

'In my youth, in a year, I've picked the pockets of at least a thousand people on the main avenue of Athens. And now I can't pick a pocket of a robot in a dark corridor?'

He then opened his left hand which was gripping something. In awe we saw that his hand was holding a big diamond ring, glittering with all the colours of the rainbow. 'Of course, nothing is easier than pulling a ring off a dead man's finger,' quipped Nikolo Papadopoulos.

The Black Night of Professor Shonku

7 June

Numerous people from various countries have often asked me if I believe in astrology. Each time my reply has been the same—I'm yet to come across an astrologer whose words of wisdom or whose actions have moved me enough to firmly believe in him. However, three months ago when Avinash Babu brought along an astrologer to my house, the events following it have changed my mind; I can vouch that all of his predictions turned out to be absolutely true in every sense.

Although I must admit I would have been far happier if his forecast hadn't turned out to be so accurate. He had said, 'Three months from now a very grave situation will come your way. You'll face the curse of Saturn. The situation will be so dangerous that even your own death will prove to be a better option.' When I asked if I would be able to free myself from such a situation, he said, 'You'll attain freedom only if you can destroy your ultimate enemy.' Naturally I asked him who this adversary is. He gave a cryptic smile and answered, 'You, yourself.' This prediction still remains a mystery but there's no doubt that even my own death would certainly be an infinitely better option than the crisis I am facing now. The crisis was brought about through a letter which I received today.

Two months ago, I had received an invitation from Madrid to attend a scientific conference. The organizer of the conference, the renowned zoologist, D'Sants, had written, 'We are particularly keen for you to participate. Without your presence our conference will not attain the same level of success. I hope you won't disappoint us.'

Three days after receiving this letter, my dear friend Somerville wrote from London putting in a special request for me to join a conference at Madrid. I had no desire to disappoint D'Sants. I always try to travel abroad at least once a year in order to revive my contacts; as well as engage in discussions with scientists from different countries and from all age groups simply to renew my own thoughts and views. This has now formed into a regular habit. With the result that, despite my advancing years, my mind, soul and body forever remain rejuvenated.

I'd already received the reply within two weeks of accepting and acknowledging the Madrid invite. On June 15, eight days from now, I'm to leave for the conference.

And out of the blue I received this letter today. The letter contained only three lines. In a gist—the organizers of the Madrid meeting have withdrawn their invitation. They didn't mince their words. They no longer want me to participate in this seminar. I was puzzled. The letter offered no explanation.

What was I to follow from this? Whatever could have happened that they had to consider debarring me? I had no answer, no idea if I would ever attain any answer either. I can no longer write. My mind and body are both exhausted.

10 June
I received a letter from Somerville today.

> *Dear Shonku*
> *I don't know if you've returned to your country. I couldn't sleep for two nights after reading the reports in the newspapers about your lecture in Innsbruck last month. Undoubtedly you must be suffering from some acute mental ailment; otherwise I cannot believe you could voice those words. After reading this news I called up Prof. Steiner in Innsbruck. He said he has had no news of you since your lecture. I fear you might still be in Europe and have fallen sick. If this is not the case and if this letter reaches you please send me a telegram immediately informing me about your well-being.*

Also please explain through a letter about the reason for your unbelievable behaviour.

Yours truly,

John Somerville

P.S.—*Here's the newspaper cutting just to let you know how this was reported in the* Times.

First and foremost let me state, I'd never been to Innsbruck in my entire life.

And now let me tell you about the *Times'* report. In sum this was the account. 'On May 11 in the Austrian city of Innsbruck, the world-famous Indian scientist Prof. T. Shonku delivered a lecture on the progress and development of science. The gathering was marked by the presence of many local as well as internationally noted scientists. Prof. Shonku directly attacked each of these scientists in offensive language. This incident created utmost commotion and furore amongst the audience, many of whom charged towards the dais to attack the speaker. An unidentified listener from the audience picked up a chair and threw it in the direction of Prof. Shonku. Hereafter, an Innsbruck resident, the chemist, Dr Carl Gropius, stepped forward to save the speaker from the assault.'

Just as Somerville had requested, after receiving his letter I immediately wrote out a reply and personally put it in the post. But what can I expect in return? Will

Somerville believe me? Will anyone in a sound state of mind be convinced that instead of me some clone of mine had gone to Innsbruck to deliver this lecture in order to destroy me? I've been friends with Somerville for the past thirty-three years. If he doesn't believe me then who will? The report states that Dr Gropius saved 'me', that is, this mysterious second Shonku. I know Gropius. I had met him seven years ago in Baghdad at an international seminar on inventions. I had found him to be a quiet and amiable person. I also wrote him a letter along with the one I sent Somerville.

I'd never found myself to be so utterly helpless. I fear I've to live in Giridih like a hard-core criminal the rest of my life carrying the horrible burden of this inexplicable scandal.

21 June

I received a letter from Gropius—and a very significant one. I've to arrange to leave for Innsbruck today itself.

The fact that the *Times* report wasn't an exaggerated one was confirmed when I read Gropius's letter. The microbiologist from Romania, George Popescu, had aimed a chair at me when I'd apparently ridiculed and dismissed his noteworthy research on enzymes. Naturally, he had become very agitated. Gropius was sitting right next to me on the dais. He instantly pulled me by hand and pushed me aside to save my life. That chair put one microphone out of order and crashed two glasses of water.

Gropius wrote:

'I took your hand and got you straight out of the Liebnitsch Hall. It became impossible to control you as you were in such a severe state of agitation. My car was waiting outside. Somehow I managed to shove you in and we drove off. When I touched your hand, I realized you were running a very high temperature. I wanted to take you to a hospital but after a kilometre, when the car stopped at a red-light crossing, you suddenly opened the door and jumped out. Even after a thorough search I could not locate you. After receiving your letter I realized you'd returned to your country. I've no idea how you can get rid of this tarnished image you've acquired in the international scientific world but if you can bring yourself to Innsbruck I can find you a good doctor. After an examination, if they identify any problem with your brain or any neurological disorder then one can easily understand your behaviour of that day. And this will stand to your advantage. If you're indeed unwell there'll be no dearth of treatment in Innsbruck.'

Gropius had also sent me an image of that day's incident from an Innsbruck newspaper. In a flurry Gropius had put a hand on 'me' to push 'me' aside. I could not spot any difference between me and the 'me' in the photograph. Except for a slight anomaly with my spectacles—which I could see were almost falling off. The lenses looked opaque instead of clear. Amongst the people sitting on 'my' right and left, I could recognize two. One was the Russian scientist, Dr Borodin, and the other was a resident of Innsbruck itself—a young archaeologist, Prof. Finkelstein. Finkelstein had raised his hands towards me. Perhaps he, too, was about to strike me!

After giving it much thought, I realized I have to visit Innsbruck. I remembered that astrologer. He had said unless I get rid of this staunch rival there'll be no reprieve for me. I strongly felt that this person is still in Innsbruck, in hiding. My sole aim would be to look for him.

I've written to Somerville about my plans. Now let's see how things unfold.

23 June

Yet again, I'm stricken by a fresh bout of panic.

I was going through the entries I had made in my diary over the last three months. I noticed there was no entry from the 3rd to the 22nd of May. That's not unusual since I do not write every day unless there's anything worth mentioning. But I am feeling a bit uneasy as the incident had taken place in Innsbruck during that same period. Suppose it so happened that I had received that invite, gone to Innsbruck, delivered that very lecture and then returned from Innsbruck—yet this whole episode has now been wiped out of my memory? Is it possible to suffer from such a lapse of memory due to some mental imbalance? I could have checked on this very easily. But alas, none of the two individuals whom I meet on an everyday basis were in Giridih at that time. My retainer, Prahlad, had taken two months leave to go to his village. I asked the person who had replaced him, Chhedilal, 'Do you remember if I'd left Giridih during the last two months?' He rolled his eyes and said, 'If you don't remember this, then how can I?' Clearly, it was my mistake. You can't cross-check this with anyone. I could have verified this with one person though. My friend Avinash Babu. But he, too, had left for Chaibasha last Friday for his niece's wedding.

I couldn't locate any letter from Innsbruck in my file. I hope it's a case of a false alarm.

I'm leaving for Innsbruck on the 6th of July. God knows what's in store for me.

7 July Innsbruck. 4.00 p.m.

After boarding a train from Vienna, I reached Innsbruck at ten in the morning. The minute I stepped into this city, I felt the repercussions of the report of my lecture along with my photo in the newspapers. Three hotels in succession denied me a room. After coming out of the third hotel, when I was getting into a taxi, the driver firmly shook his head and said no. Finally, carrying my bag, I walked for forty-five minutes till I found a room in a small inn located inside an alley. Noticing the thick lenses of the owner's spectacles I assumed he couldn't see too well and hence there was no dearth of hospitality from his side. But my work would definitely suffer if I had to live in this state of being incognito.

Somerville was arriving tonight. I had written to him from Giridih informing him of my visit to Innsbruck. And I called him after my arrival here. He had some prior commitments, yet he has promised to visit me.

I had also called Gropius. I've an appointment with him at five this evening. He lives ten kilometres from here. He said he would send his car.

In the meantime, I'd also made another call to Prof. Finkelstein. It wouldn't be correct to hear the only one version of the report so I decided to speak with Finkelstein as well. He wasn't at home. The servant picked up the phone. I gave him my number and asked for him to call me back when he returned.

Surrounded by mountains, Innsbruck is a beautiful city. A lot of it had been destroyed during the war. Some of it has been newly built. But of course, I was in no state to enjoy the beauty of this place. My sole aim would now be to depend on the astrologer's judgment and to look for a way to attain my freedom.

7 July, 10:30 p.m.

I'm trying to write about my meeting with Gropius in a coherent manner. A little before five, a young lad working at this Alpine inn informed me that Herr Doctor Gropius had sent a car for Herr Professor Shonku. I was a bit surprised to see his car. At some point—at least thirty years ago—this must have been a very fancy car, but now it looked much run-down. Is Gropius hard up or just a miser?

By 5 p.m. I reached Grunewaldstraße. Gropius's house was located on this street. After passing through an old church and cemetery, the car took a left turn and entered a gate. The house matched the car. On my way to the house, the variety and profusion of flowers in gardens of the other houses had given such pleasure to my eyes but the path on two sides of the road from the gate to the main door of Gropius's house was marked by a wildly-grown garden.

Gropius himself looked in a worse shape since the time I'd met him in Baghdad. He should not have greyed so much within seven years. Maybe he had faced some tragedy in the family. I professed no curiosity in this regard as he looked much more concerned about my own health rather than his own.

When we sat face to face in the drawing room, Gropius observed me for two minutes. Finally I was compelled to ask him lightly, 'Are you trying to gauge if indeed I'm that Shonku?'

Gropius did not give me a direct answer. Instead what he said doubled my worry.

'Dr Webber is on his way. He will examine you. That day I was taking you to Webber's clinic but you gave me no chance. I hope you won't raise any objection this time. It's only I who firmly believed that you could speak of such things simply because you were unwell. But others around me didn't share my opinion. Given a choice, if they get to meet you, they'd love to tear you to bits. But if Webber's examination proves you're suffering from a mental disorder then perhaps they'll pardon you. And not just this, with the help of treatment you'll get better and perhaps you'll earn back your reputation.'

Left with no choice, I was forced to say that in the last forty years not once had I been indisposed. I faced no problem either with my physical or mental health.

Gropius said, 'Do you mean to say that all these noted scientists—Shimanovsky, Ritter, Popesku, Altman, Streicher, in fact myself included—are unworthy . . . Do you hold such low opinion of all of them?'

Trying my best to control myself, I spoke in a composed voice. I said, 'Gropius, I firmly believe that there's another individual who looks just like me and he, at someone's instigation, is doing such things only to upset me.'

'In that case, where's he now? After getting off my car did he simply vanish from this city? At least you possessed

79

your own passport, tickets and straightaway boarded the plane and returned to your own country. But it's not that easy for an imposter to flee from a city.'

I said, 'I strongly feel this person is still present in this city. It could be that he is not so famous a scientist, but had seen me in many places, and had heard my speeches. It's obvious he resembled me to an extent and the rest was covered by make-up.'

Gropius's retainer served me hot chocolate. Along with him a dog also entered the room. It was a Doberman Pinscher. Noticing me, the dog came near, wagged his tail, and began to sniff at my trousers. But when he looked at my face he growled. It was only when Gropius shouted at him saying, 'Frica! Frica!' did he move away from me and settle down on a carpet nearby.

'Does anyone else know of your visit here?' asked Gropius.

I said, 'In Innsbruck there's only one person who I think knows me. I'd called him after arriving here, but he wasn't home. I've left my number with his servant.'

'Who is he?'

With a slight smile, I said, 'He, too, was present during Professor Shonku's lecture. I spotted him in the newspaper cutting that you'd sent me.'

Gropius frowned.

'Whom are you talking about?'

'Professor Finkelstein.'

'I see.'

Gropius didn't look too happy when he heard this. After remaining silent for about half a minute he looked straight at me and asked, 'Do you remember what you said that day about Finkelstein's research?'

I had to shake my head and say 'No.'

'If you'd remembered, you wouldn't have called him. You'd said, even a three-year-old child has more intelligence than him.'

My heart trembled. I jolly well know that I'm not to be blamed for this outrageous speech but if people here actually think that this imposter is the real Shonku, then there'll be no end to my trouble. In that case can't I trust anyone else other than Gropius?

We heard a car pull up outside.

'Oh, Webber must have arrived', said Gropius.

I didn't like the doctor. Austrians are very polite, when compared to Germans, and so this doctor seemed fake. The fixed smile on his face also looked put on. His politeness was extremely laboured. It made me feel rather uncomfortable.

For half an hour Webber questioned me and physically examined me. I quietly suffered him. Before leaving he said, 'Gropius will send you his car. Come to my clinic in Godfistrasse tomorrow as I've all my apparatus there. It'll be a challenge to cure you.'

I thought to myself—I'm ten times healthier than you are. You haven't clipped your nails for at least two months, the cigarette paper is still stuck to your lips, due to your faulty speech you swallow up your own words—and you'll treat me for my mental disorder?

Gropius left the room to see Webber to his car. Bored, I wandered around the room. Noticing a photo album on a shelf, I leafed through a few pages and spotted myself in one photo. I don't have this photo with me but I clearly remember it being clicked. It had been taken in front of the Hotel Splendid in Baghdad. Gropius, the Russian scientist Kaminsky and I were standing next to each other.

'What baggage do you have with you?' Gropius asked me after returning to the room.

'Why do you want to know?'

'I feel you should come over to my place here. I'm suggesting this for your own safety. I've a big guest room; you've lived in this room earlier too—though you may fail to remember this. When you were here in May you had accepted my hospitality.'

Although I knew this was impossible, my head reeled. I asked him, 'Was it you who had invited me?'

In response, Gropius brought in a file from the next room. In the file among other correspondence, I saw two letters from me. This was exactly my kind of paper, my signature and the fonts of my Olivetti typewriter. In the first letter I wrote, as I was anyway going to Europe in May, there would be no problem in visiting Innsbruck. In the second letter, I mentioned the date on which I was to arrive.

The mystery now deepened and so did my state of crisis. As it is, no one had allowed me accommodation in any of the hotels; in addition to this, I can jolly well predict the attitudes of the people I'd openly abused in my lecture.

But I had to let Gropius know that it was not possible for me to move into his house.

'Tonight, my friend Somerville is arriving from London. Will it be fine if the two of us put up at your house tomorrow?' 'Who's Somerville?' Gropius asked me suspiciously. I gave a brief description of Somerville, adding, 'He is a special friend of mine; he is particularly concerned about me after he heard about this episode.'

'Do you think his worries will go away when he meets you here?'

Without replying I stared at Gropius. I knew what he would say and sure enough he said so.

'There'll be no doubt that your friend, too, like me, will be very anxious about your treatment.'

I returned to my hotel at seven in the evening. There had been no phone calls from Finkelstein. I had sat down on the chair to reflect on today's strange activities when the phone rang. It was Somerville. He was calling from the station. I asked, 'What happened? Aren't you coming?'

'Of course I'm coming, but was a bit fretful—hence I called you.'

'Fretful? Regarding what?'

'I needed to know if you're in one piece.'

'Well, I am in one piece and perfectly well.'

'Very good. I'll come within half an hour. Have lots to tell.'

From this call I could make out how deeply concerned was Somerville about me. But what news was he bringing?

Though my room had two beds, the size of the room being rather small I decided to reserve the next room for Somerville. When I'd returned to my hotel that room had still been available. But when I came out of my room to discuss this with the hotel owner, I noticed the light on inside the room and got a strong smell of a cigar coming out from the slightly ajar door. On inquiring whether any other room would be available I found out there wasn't. Hence Somerville would have to be accommodated in my small room.

Within half an hour Somerville arrived. I didn't know it had begun to rain; I only realized that when I saw Somerville take off his raincoat. He said, 'First order for some coffee and then we shall talk.'

After saying so, Somerville, too, gazed at me for a few minutes just like Gropius had. I'm now getting used to this response yet Somerville's reaction seemed rather different.

'I notice no change in your expressions, Shonku. I feel you're absolutely normal.'

I could finally heave a sigh of relief.

After the coffee arrived, I narrated the events of the entire day to Somerville. After hearing all, he said, 'Since the last few days, after going through some old German scientific journals I discovered a few articles by Gropius. He had written some articles previously but over the last ten years he hadn't written anything.'

'Written about what?'

'About his failure.'

'What failure?'

In reply to this, what Somerville told me left me not just surprised, but provided me with a clarity that I could see the entire episode in a completely new light.

'Your discovery of the Omniscope, your heavenly medicine, the Miracurol, your Linguagraph, your Airconditioning pill—each of these products was first discovered by Gropius. Unfortunately, every time it so happened that you'd already patented these before he could. In other words, in this race of talent, he lost out to you only by a narrow margin. Ten years ago, in his last article, with deep regret he mentioned that the idea of attaining fame due to an invention is often a matter of pure chance. He had also cited a few examples after going through a few ancient texts and scriptures. For instance, recognition for the laws of motion was attained by Newton, yet much before him, thirty years ago, a scientist from Italy, Fratelli, had already written about this same law of motion.'

I said, 'Just as the credit for discovery of radio by our Jagadish Bose had been snatched up by Marconi.'

'Exactly,' agreed Somerville. 'Therefore don't be surprised if Gropius has reservations against you.'

'Yes, I can understand this. But how will this resolve the mystery of the second Shonku?'

Somerville looked serious when I asked this question. He said, 'You'd last met Gropius in Baghdad seven years ago. Since then he has not attended any science conference. In May this year, for the first time, he participated in this meeting which had been initiated and organized by him. And–'

I interrupted Somerville and said, 'But I never received any letter for this meet.'

'Of course you would not have got one. But Gropius must have said he had invited you. In fact, he must have filed away a letter with your signature on it.'

I had to mention that I'd seen this letter with my own eyes.

'Have you corresponded with him earlier?' Somerville asked.

I said, 'After meeting him in Baghdad I'd written to him a couple of times and for five years in succession I'd sent him New Year cards.'

Somerville gravely nodded his head. He said, 'Gropius must have found a man who resembled you—the rest was concealed with make-up—and coached him beforehand about the subject of the lecture. Lured by cash, many will agree to take up such a job. This second Shonku had to shoulder no responsibilities; he had nothing to lose. He accomplished his mission, received his payment and left. But the real harm was done to the real Shonku and at the same time Gropius took his revenge. That reminds me, would Gropius have any recordings of your speech?'

The moment I heard this question I remembered Gropius carrying a small tape recorder with him in Baghdad. I replied, 'That's quite possible. And not just that, he also possessed a good coloured photograph of mine. In fact, I saw it today.'

With a note of regret in his voice Somerville said, 'The problem is, the possibility to locate this fake Shonku is very remote. Yet to prove Gropius's crime we need to produce this second Shonku.'

There was no telephone in this hotel room. There was only one in the passage for the use of three occupants on this floor. If the phone rang once it was meant for the person in room number one; for the person in the second room there'd be double ring and for the third person it would ring thrice. As the phone was producing a double ring I knew it was for me.

I opened the door and went out to receive the call.

'Hello!'

'Am I speaking with Prof. Shonku?'

'Yes.'

'My name is Finkelstein.'

Not wasting much time on formality I straight away referred to the real matter.

'Last May I think you were present during a science summit in this city. I saw your photograph in the paper.'

'Have you lost your glasses?'

While I was thinking about how to reply to his unexpected query, Finkelstein put forward yet another question.

'The glasses of your spectacles are clear or opaque?'

I said, 'Clear. And these glasses are with me. I have never lost them.'

'I thought so too. However, in that science meet, the Shonku who delivered that speech had dropped his glasses on the floor while leaving the hall. I picked them up. It was not just the glasses. There was something sticking on to the glasses. That is also with me.'

'What's that object?'

'I'll show it to you when you come here. Had I not found it, I too would have believed that the person giving that speech was the real Shonku and not a fake one.'

When I heard this I began to palpitate. I asked, 'When do I get to meet you?'

Finkelstein said, 'Now it's quite late and the day is also not very pleasant. Come to my house tomorrow at 8.30 a.m. Will it be very early for you?'

'No, no. I'll reach exactly at 8.30 a.m. My English friend, John Somerville, will also come with me.

'Fine. Bring him along. We'll talk then. I've loads to tell.'

I put the receiver down. Somerville was standing next to me. We returned to our room. After shutting the door, Somerville asked me, 'Do you know the person staying in room number 3?'

'Why do you say that? He arrived this evening.'

'The gentleman seemed too curious. Getting a whiff of the cigar I turned back and saw him standing near the slightly-ajar door. Why was he so eager to listen to your telephone conversation?'

I had no answer to this. I've no knowledge of this person either. I hope a lot of this mystery will be cleared after we talk to Finkelstein.

It's 11 p.m. now. It continues to rain. Somerville has gone to sleep.

9 July

Yesterday I couldn't write my diary. I was in no state to write. The astrologer's prediction has finally come into effect. I've got to admit one thing: for an ordinary person it's extremely difficult to compete with a scientist's wickedness.

Nonetheless, let me now concentrate to be able to narrate the extraordinary events of yesterday.

We had an appointment with Finkelstein at 8.30 a.m. After finding his address in the telephone directory, Somerville said, 'We can walk it to his place. It's not very far—we'll reach in half an hour.' Somerville was familiar with Innsbruck. Also, he was well aware of the risks of putting me into a cab.

We set out at eight. The road ran through the old city. I realized that Somerville was familiar with the shortcuts running through the various lanes. After walking through a narrow lane, we came to the picturesque Seal River. We walked by the banks of the river and further down we crossed a park, and then turning to the left, we reached a quiet street. This was Rosenbaum Alley, the street where Finkelstein lives. We faced no difficulty in locating house number 11.

This small yet beautiful house seemed just like a picture postcard. In front was a garden dotted with flowers of many hues. On the right side of the main door stood an apple tree as if to guarding the house.

We went up and rang the bell. An elderly servant came out and opened the door. When he saw me, the smile he came up with seemed a bit unnatural.

'Please come inside. Have you left something behind?'

It was as if a hammer struck my heart.

'Is Prof. Finkelstein in?' Somerville also sounded apprehensive.

'The master is still in his room.'

'Where's the room?'

'On the right hand side of the first floor. But just a while ago this gentleman was . . .'

Climbing three steps at a time we reached the first floor. The door of the room on the right side was open. Somerville took two giant steps ahead and on reaching the door exclaimed, 'My god!'

This was Finkelstein's study. Finkelstein was sitting with his back to us in front of the mahogany table, his head peculiarly thrown back and his hands dangling from the sides of the chair. When I walked up to him my fears were confirmed. You couldn't bear to look at Finkelstein's face. He had been throttled. The marks of fingerprints on the two sides of the windpipe were still fresh. What Finkelstein's servant did next sent a shiver down my spine. He let out an indistinct scream, looked at me wildly and seized the telephone kept on the table. His mission was clear. He wanted to inform the police.

Somerville's immediate reaction showed his presence of mind. With one blow he knocked down the servant. The man was rendered senseless.

'You have been trapped, Shonku!' Somerville said breathlessly. 'We need to keep calm to work further.'

'But what's that?'

My eyes were now focused on a pad kept on the table. Only one word in red pencil was inscribed on it—'erste.' That is, first. That Finkelstein wanted to write some more became more apparent when one noticed the mark of the pencil after that word. The pencil now lay on the floor next to the table.

We needed to be real quick in our plan of action. What was Finkelstein trying to establish by writing the word, 'erste'? First-second-third—what could be there in the room which could be described in this manner? Could this be an explanation about the bookshelves? I didn't think so. I could actually make a guess about the object whose location Finkelstein was trying to indicate. My spectacles.

We located them when we opened the first drawer of the table. In the midst of papers, pens and pencils we came across a cardboard box on top of which was written in German—'Shonku's glasses and hair.' We fled the spot carrying the box with us. The servant was still unconscious.

While climbing down the steps, I noticed footprints; this had evaded my attention while we had been climbing up in a rush.

The same signs could be seen outside, too; these had come out of the door, trailed towards the gate and finally reached the road. You could see both set of marks—the ones which went in as well as the signs of returning. Clearly, last night's rain is responsible for this.

When we followed these marks after going further down on the road we noticed that they disappeared on reaching the grass. Despite this, we continued to walk ahead. When for ten minutes we looked in all direction and couldn't spot any trail of the second Shonku, we headed back to the hotel. The minute the owner saw me he said, 'There was a call for you from Dr Gropius. He has asked you to call him back immediately.'

When we arrived on the second floor I noticed that the room next door, once more, lay vacant.

11 July

I sat on the bed and took the box out of my pocket. After opening it, I saw it contained not just my spectacles but also a small envelope. The glasses were exactly like mine except that the glass was grey in colour. Inside the envelope was a slip of paper on which was written—'During the science conference in the Leibnitz Hall, a strand of nylon hair found attached to the fallen spectacles of the Indian scientist, Prof. Shonku.'

Nylon hair?

The strand of hair was inside the envelope. It indeed looked like a grey hair but there was no doubt that it was synthetic.

This is how Finkelstein figured out that the Shonku who had attended the conference wasn't the real Shonku.

But at this point of my crisis there's no way I can get any help from Finkelstein.

We both jumped when we heard a knock on the door. Who could have come at this hour?

It was Gropius.

I introduced Gropius to Somerville and asked him to sit down, but he refused. While standing at the door, he said, 'I told you I'll pick you up today but it doesn't suit Webber. And apart from that, we have had a tragedy in our family today. One of my servants died due to thrombosis last night. Today is his funeral. I need to be there.'

We both had nothing to say in reply to this. After pausing for a brief spell, Gropius himself spoke again. This time he asked a question.

'Do you know that Finkelstein is dead?'

I remembered that the fellow from next room had eavesdropped when I was talking to Finkelstein. If he happened to be Gropius's agent then he must have passed on the information of my appointment with Finkelstein at 8:30 a.m. to Gropius. Yet, putting up an act of surprise and ignorance I said, 'Really? When did this happen?'

'This morning. A while ago I received a call from the Academy of Science. His servant Anton had reported it to the police and then had called up Grossman, the President of the Academy.'

We both remained quiet. Gropius took a step forward.

'Anton had spoken of a fellow—his skin was dark, he was bald, bearded and wore glasses; he had gone to visit Finkelstein this morning. Anton had also mentioned the name of this fellow.'

'If the description matched me so could the name,' I spoke in a calm voice. 'And there's nothing to be surprised as I had indeed gone to meet Finkelstein this morning. With me was Somerville. When we reached there we found him dead. He had been strangled to death in a heinous fashion.'

'Prof. Shonku,' Gropius said in an ice-cold voice, 'it's one thing to defame scientists through the medium of a lecture but to directly attack one of them and murder him is something else. Since you have declared that there's nothing wrong with your head, then I'm sure you know what the verdict would be for such a crime?'

This time Somerville opened his mouth. His voice, too, was perfectly normal.

'Dr Gropius, when you were taking away Prof. Shonku from the platform his spectacles had slipped off and had fallen down. The glasses were dark; somewhat like sunglasses. Finkelstein picked up that pair. One strand of hair remained stuck on the arms of the spectacle. That hair was made of nylon. From what Finkelstein's servant said today, we could gather that a Shonku lookalike had gone to meet Finkelstein half an hour before we reached there. We spotted his footprints on the stairs and noticed them outside the house and on the street as well. The murder took place soon after he went in. The assailant didn't wear any gloves. Finkelstein's neck bore clear marks of his fingerprints. How can you put the blame on the real Shonku when a doppelgänger had actually committed the crime?'

All of a sudden Gropius burst into an outlandish and malicious guffaw.

'Very soon you'll see how I shift this blame! Yesterday, in my house, Shonku had used my cup to drink hot chocolate, had gone through the pages of my photo album—wouldn't these contain his fingerprints? It is possible these days to recreate fingerprints, Prof. Somerville! This is Hans Gropius's discovery! In the recent past, I've let out this device to three notorious criminals of Europe!'

I hadn't noticed till now but in front of the door a man stood behind Gropius with his hands tucked inside his pockets. I knew this man. This was the same individual who had eavesdropped from the next room.

'How unfortunate that this is what awaits you at the end of the day,' Gropius said, looking straight at me. 'If indeed you lose your head under these circumstances there's always Webber's clinic for you. That's where the work on brain transplant has started on the basis of my own invention. Perhaps this time you will not be able to outplay me! Good day, Shonku! Good day, Somerville!'

Noisily, Gropius and his accomplice stormed down the stairs. I dropped down on the bed. Somerville began to pace up and down the room. Twice I heard him say, 'What a devil! What a devil!

I could clearly feel that a net was slowly folding around to trap me. If my fingerprints matched up there no way I could come out of it. Unless—

Unless one found the imposter Shonku and handed him over to the police.

'Since we are trapped,' Somerville said, stopping his pacing, 'we have to see the end of it. Even if we have to die we'll give it a good fight. But not otherwise.'

I realized Somerville was not at all hesitant to shoulder the entire responsibility of my personal catastrophe.

He opened the suitcase with his key and taking a revolver, put it in his pocket. In the Venezuelan jungles he had proved time and again that his grasp over science was as good as his skills as a hunter.

I, too, took my Annihilin pistol with me. It measures only four inches. I had, however, always resisted using this amazing weapon.

After locking the door we both climbed down the stairs and stepped out of the hotel. Spotting a taxi, we waved our hands to stop it, but when we went closer the driver noticed me and instantly shook his head and said, 'nein, nein'—no, no. But that same 'nein' soon became 'ya, ya' when Somerville shoved a note of 100 groschen into his hands.

A few moments ago, I had heard the sound of a siren. As our taxi began to move, I saw a police car proceeding towards our hotel but it slowed down when they noticed our cab.

This time Somerville shoved a 200 groschen note into the driver's hand and said, 'Please speed up; we have to go to Grunewaldstraße.'

The morning had been sunny but I could now see black clouds coming from the west side, enveloping the entire sky. As a result, the temperature had also dropped to at least twenty degrees Fahrenheit. Our Mercedes taxi moved at a thunderous speed evading the traffic.

After ten minutes of our journey we once again heard the siren from a distance. Somerville gently tapped on the driver's back. The car picked up even greater speed. The needle of the speedometer almost touched 100 kilometres. The credit goes entirely to the driver for bringing us to Grunewaldstraße within twenty minutes, avoiding any mishap on the way.

There was a procession on in front of us, forcing us to slow down. Around ten–twelve people carrying a coffin turned in to the cemetery on the left. I could identify two of them. One was the fellow who had served me the hot chocolate and the other was Gropius himself.

When our car crossed the cemetery gate and just before it was to reach Gropius's gate, Somerville shouted—

'Stop the car!—Turn your car back.'

The driver instantly stopped his car, and backed it all the way to the graveyard gate. As we got out, the sound of sirens pierced the silence of the cemetery. The police car, too, arrived and stopped next to our taxi.

A coffin had been placed right next to a freshly-dug pit in the cemetery. All the mourners present looked in our direction, including Gropius himself.

Along with one inspector and two more people, Finkelstein's servant Anton came out of the police car and immediately pointed his finger at me and said, 'He is that man.'

The police officer came towards me.

The padre had started the last rites.

'Prof. Shonku, my name is Inspector Dietrich. You have to come with us for—

Bang! Bang! Bang!

Somerville's revolver roared three times. And the roar was followed by the sound of splitting wood.

'Don't let him escape!' Somerville screamed—Gropius was trying to flee from the rear side of the graveyard. A policeman with a revolver in his hand chased him. Inspector Dietrich shouted, 'Whoever tries to run will be shot.'

Meanwhile, my eyes, wide open with amazement, were focused on the coffin. One of the three bullets had pierced one side of the coffin and entered it. The top lid had split into two and been dislodged from its original place, revealing the occupant of the coffin.

Lying in the coffin with a pair of unblinking large eyes made of stone was my own duplicate—the second Shonku.

Freezing the blood of the entire gathering, dislodging the revolver from Dietrich's hand, knocking Gropius senseless while he was being held captive by the police, the fake Shonku slowly sat up in the coffin. The bullet had pierced through his ribcage, exposing the machinery inside his body. Gropius had obviously created a robot in my image. And the blast must have damaged the machinery, because the machine started uttering the words of an old lecture: 'Dear honoured guests!—Today the words that I'm planning to talk about in this august gathering may not appeal to you all, but—'

I took out my Annihilin gun from my pocket. I'll attain my final freedom only when I can erase this gruesome twin of mine forever from the face of the earth.

*

Shonku's Golden Opportunity

24 June

I'm writing my diary sitting along the edge of the famous
Stonehenge, built 4,000 years ago on the Salisbury Plain of
England. Today is Midsummer Day i.e. the summer solstice.
When Stonehenge was under construction, the Stone Age was
just being taken over by the Bronze Age. After discovering the
use of metal, humanity began marching towards civilization
in leaps and bounds. The European civilization, of course,
appeared much later as compared to those of Egypt, India,
Mesopotamia, Persia and others, yet one would hesitate to
call those who built Stonehenge 4,000 years ago uncivilized.
These large standing stones brought in from far-off distances
have been placed erect on the ground. One stone is placed
horizontally on some of the upright stones. All have been
arranged to form a large circular enclosure.

Historically, it was believed this was a place of worship
for the Celts. But in the recent past, archaeologists have

concluded that it had actually been an observatory. This oldest observatory was one with a difference—because one has clearly noticed a correlation of the placements of these stones with that of the sun's positioning. But this becomes most obvious today, that is, the 24th of June when the sun is in the zenith on the Tropic of Cancer. It seems incredible now to think how in that age craftsmen managed to place those stones with such precision and design despite not having the expertise we have acquired today in the area of modern engineering.

My friend Crole has, however, espoused another theory. His hypothesis was that apparently people of that age had attained certain knowledge of chemistry whereby they were able to reduce the weight of these stones momentarily, making it much easier to build monuments like the pyramids and the Stonehenge. Wilhelm Crole has always firmly believed in the supernatural powers of the primitive people. He has thoroughly studied the subjects of ancient witchcraft, magic and spiritualism. He had accompanied me during our 'Unicorn' expedition. Right now he is sitting on the grass, leaning against a Stonehenge column, playing a very special flute which he had picked up from a cave in Tibet. The flute is made of human bone. Who knew that such an amazing German folk tune could be produced from this flute?

Other than Crole, sitting nearby, is another person who had accompanied us on the 'Tibet' expedition. He is pouring out coffee from a flask. He is my distinguished English friend, the noted spiritualist Jeremy Saunders. I've come to London on his invitation. Both Crole and I are guests at his house in Hampstead. We'll be staying there for another week or so. The summer this year in England is wonderfully pleasant. There is no rain. The sun, visible all day amidst white clouds in the bright blue sky, helps to keep both body and mind refreshed.

Now I must finish writing. Crole has stopped playing his flute. I have to go out with him to an auction house in London. Apparently a thirteenth-century Spanish manuscript on alchemy is to go under the hammer. Crole thinks he may acquire this quite cheaply as there's not much interest among people on the subject of alchemy nowadays. In this molecular age it's no longer impossible to create gold artificially.

24 June, 10.30 p.m.

A strange incident happened at the auction. By nature, the Bavarian Crole is a jovial and hearty person, and I've never seen him in such an agitated state before. The ancient manuscript on alchemy, which he hoped he could buy for about fifty pounds, could be his only after he ultimately shelled out 1500 pounds for it. That is, in our own currency it amounts to Rs 25,000. Only one individual was responsible for upping the price. In a state of desperation, he began competing with Crole and in no time raised the rate of this seven-hundred-year-old worn out bundle of paper from a nominal price to a sky-rocketing one. Judging by his dress and pronunciation he looked like an American. It became quite obvious that after facing this defeat by Crole, he hardly looked happy. I noticed a constant frown on his face throughout the time he was at the auction house.

Ever since our return, Crole has been poring over the manuscript, all agog. Even though the state of the papers is rather fragile, they aren't difficult to read as the handwriting is quite clear. Moreover, Crole is quite familiar with the Spanish language. I know that during the thirteenth century in Spain, there had been a great revolution on the subject of alchemy. This influence initially came from the Arabs and had spread to quite a few other areas of Europe as well. The king of all metals is gold. It's not just attractive to look at, it is imperishable. In epics, the sun is referred to as gold and the moon, silver. For thousands of years a certain section of people have laboured over the idea of creating artificial gold out of metals like copper, lead and such others. One refers to them as alchemists. As this method also included spells and magic charms not within the sanctity of pure science, hard-core scientists never took them too seriously. I'm in possession of a Sanskrit scripture called *Dhandaprakarantantrasar* which proved that our country had also practised alchemy. It describes many ways to generate gold. Here I quote one such means:

> 'Obtain oxidized ash of copper, lead and brass by burning them over slow fire. Thereafter dig a twelve-foot-deep pit in the ground. Fill it with copper ash, the ash of burnt wood apple tree and charcoal and set it on fire. Allow it to burn for a week, remove the ashes and further burn them in a fire made out of *biraju* wood. This process would help in obtaining liquid copper, and thereafter add half the amount of mercury equivalent to the amount of copper; further add extracts of *biraju* wood, *basak* plant and *sij* tree. The completed process will yield gold.'

As if this wasn't enough, it adds, 'Before the entire process commences you need to chant the *dhanda* mantra 10,000 times followed by another act of worship and end it by pouring oil on to fire to offer it as an act of oblation. Only this will ensure assured success.'

No wonder I had never thought of trying this out.

The reference to alchemists is to be found in all ages of history. Many kings of Europe employed alchemists in their courts and built them laboratories in the hope of replenishing the royal treasury if they ever ran out of gold. However, I've no knowledge if anyone has actually accomplished such a task.

All said and done, it's obvious that Crole firmly believes in such a theory. Otherwise why would he invest so much on a manuscript? According to Saunders, Crole has full faith that he can easily produce gold in his laboratory and then can make up for the expense of buying the manuscript. And if we do not laugh at his absurd idea we may get a share of his gold. After all, who knows!

25 June

After arriving in London, in keeping with my usual habit in Giridih, I got up at five in the morning to go for my morning walk. In summer there's mostly bright light at this time, but as Englishmen are not in the habit of waking up early, my favourite Hampstead and its streets were now devoid of people. I strolled alone in the dawn for an hour or so in these green fields which rolled like sea waves, thinking how this morning light and air helps me to refresh my mind. When I returned home, I found Saunders up and ready with coffee. Crole usually gets up by nine as he is in the habit of studying late into the night.

This morning, however, I was mighty surprised to find Crole, who had already helped himself to coffee and was anxiously pacing up and down the drawing room. Spotting me at the door he instantly halted and gazing fixedly at me asked a strange question:

'Your zodiac sign is Scorpio, isn't it?'

I nodded my head and answered, 'Yes.'

'Was the colour of your hair black before it greyed?'

I again answered in the positive.

'Are you in the habit of having garlic?'

'Well, I do once in a while.'

'Good. There's no way we can let you off. Because Saunders is a Leo and I'm a Taurus. The colour of Saunders's hair is tawny and mine is blonde. Neither of us consume garlic.'

'Why do you sound so cryptic?'

'There is no mystery, Shonku. Manuel Saavedra has mentioned in his manuscript that the process of creating artificial gold in the laboratory requires the presence of at least one person in possession of all these three virtues. Hence we need you.'

'Where am I needed? Will this operation take place in Hampstead itself? Will this drawing room of Saunders's house turn into an alchemist's laboratory?' I wasn't sure whether to take Crole seriously or not.

With all earnestness, Crole pointed out his finger at a map which hung from the drawing-room wall and remarked, '4 degree West by 37.2 degree North.'

Without glancing at the map I said, 'It sounds like Spain. Isn't this the location around Granada?'

'You're right,' said Crole. 'But I won't be able to figure out the exact name of the place without looking at the map.'

I walked towards the map. After calculating where my finger pointed to, I noticed only one name—Montefrio. Crole said, 'Montefrio was the birthplace of Manuel Saavedra, the writer of this manuscript.'

'Have you lost your mind?' I couldn't help saying. 'What makes you think that this seven-hundred-year-old house still stands? Apart from that, if the manuscript indeed mentions the means of making gold then this experiment can be done in any laboratory. Where's the need to go to Spain?'

Crole looked rather cross at my remark. He banged the coffee mug on the table and said, 'This doesn't fit into the slot of the kind of scientific experiments you're talking about, Shonku. If this were the case, then there would be no need to find out whether you ate garlic or if your hair had once been black. In this case, science needs to connect with zodiacal time, date, the geographic location of the laboratory, the examiner's state of mind, health and appearance—they all need to unite. This is not to be dismissed. Do not treat this as a joke. Moreover, why wouldn't a seven-hundred-year-old house still remain? Haven't you seen European medieval castles? They are still standing firm. Saavedra belonged to a wealthy family. The description which I got of the house can easily pass as a castle. So what if it's in a state of ruin. Can't we find a room there which we can turn into a laboratory? Of course, if we locate people still living in that house we need to strike a deal with them. I refuse to believe that offering them monetary compensation won't work. Alchemy is—?'

'What are you both arguing about so early in the morning?'

None of us had noticed when Saunders had entered the room. Crole was not ready to give up. He explained everything to Saunders. At the end he stated, 'We had journeyed to Tibet in search of an imaginary animal, yet when there's a strong possibility to create gold and we need to fly only two hours to Spain and do our work in one corner of a room, where's the problem?'

I noticed Saunders didn't react. Perhaps he withheld commenting because Crole was in such a state of excitement and also looked extremely obstinate. After a while Saunders said, 'I've no objection in travelling to Spain; probably Shonku, too, will have no problem. But in this experiment of yours, may I know what further elements you require other than Shonku's presence?'

'Crole replied, 'More than ingredients, the timing is important. Saavedra had instructed to start the work on any day either a week before or after the midsummer and exactly at 12 noon—because during the entire year only on those few days does the radiation of the sun remain most intense. The materials are all very easily available. The mention of mercury and lead are found in alchemy studies of all countries; here we have both. In addition to these we require water, salt, sulphur and a collection of branches, twigs and the roots of a few particular trees. In the case of implements, we cannot use anything other than soil and glassware—this is mentioned in all other books on alchemy as well—and we also need a furnace, a stove and a water tank in the middle of the floor—'

'Why do we need a water tank?' questioned Saunders.

'We need to save rainwater in it. I didn't find mention of this in any other book on alchemy.'

'Have they spoken of a touchstone?' I asked him. The tradition of touchstones has been acknowledged in all countries. Wherever I have read any descriptions of alchemy, the creation of a touchstone is the first step towards this experiment. Thereafter, when the other metals are put into contact with the touchstone, they turn into gold.

Crole replied, 'No. Saavedra has made no mention of a touchstone. These ingredients, as a result of a chemical reaction, form into a sticky matter. It's then followed by a phase of purifying this matter after mixing it with the rainwater. The liquid that forms then works as a catalyst. When any common metal comes in contact with this liquid, the metal transforms into gold.'

'Was this experiment a success in case of Saavedra?' Saunders asked.

Pausing for a while, Crole filled his pipe with tobacco and said, 'The manuscript is actually a diary. It wasn't meant to be used as a textbook. The more the experiment progressed towards success the more his language turned poetic. Of course, a banal statement like, "Today I created gold at this certain time", is not anywhere in the script but Saavedra has mentioned towards the end.' Here Crole picked up the manuscript from where it was kept on the top of the piano and read out from the last page: "Today I just don't feel like a scientist or a magician; I feel like I'm the greatest artist amongst all artists—the one who has attained a divine talent, whose pair of hands have acquired an infallible power to lend a touch of eternity to his creations." Now it's entirely up to you to interpret whatever you want from this account.'

Saunders and I exchanged a glance. The three of us remained quiet for a few moments. I can feel that Saunders, like me, has been infected by Crole's zest. As if to suppress his excitement, he asked a question.

'Doesn't this require any ceremony or incantations?'

Crole pulled at his pipe, released the smoke and said, 'There's one such thing required—when a spirit has to be be called upon—a day before the work starts.'

'Whose spirit?'

'The spirit of the world-famous Arabian alchemist, Jābir ibn Hayyān. You must have heard about this renowned person who lived in the tenth century. It's nothing much—

only to seek his blessings. That's all. This invocation won't be a problem with me around.'

I knew that Crole was a chairperson of a Planchette Committee based in Munich.

Crole turned to look towards the door. Following his gaze I noticed Saunders's Persian cat, Mustafa. 'We also need him.'

'What do you mean by "him"?' Saunders asked, raising his voice. Saunders is crazy about cats—almost like me. Three years ago during his visit to my house in Giridih, he had tied a red silk ribbon round the neck of my pet cat, Newton.

Crole said, 'Saavedra has given clear directions regarding the role of a cat. In the research room the presence of a cat will unfailingly help us to accomplish our task. Or else an owl can replace him. But I feel, as we already have a cat with us then he is better than an owl.'

Both Saunders and I had never directly promised Crole we would accompany him to Spain, though Crole repeatedly told us if we do not take the use of this opportune moment of the Tropic of Cancer, we would have to wait for another year.

After having our breakfast, the three of us went out to carnival at Hampstead. This is an annual ritual at this time of the year. After glancing at shops, a gambling den, the giant Ferris wheel and the merry-go-round, and walking through milling crowds of young and elderly people, we came across a well-decorated caravan on whose body was written—'Come and have your fortune told by Madame Renata.'

The lady herself was peering out from behind a curtained window. With a smile she wished us good morning. Gypsy fortune tellers are often seen in this country—particularly at such fairs. Crole immediately decided to have our fortunes read. Under his insistence the three of us got into the caravan.

Madam Renata's caravan was sparsely furnished. On top of a table stood a glass vase with a single rose and next to that was a glass ball—they refer to it as a crystal ball. By concentrating on this crystal for a long time the fortune tellers can apparently see clearly into the future of each of their clients.

Without any pretence, Crole said, 'Come on, Madam, please tell us if any significant incident is to appear in the lives of us three friends. We are about to venture together into a project.'

Renata placed her elbows on the table and concentrated on the crystal. We were sitting in three chairs around the table. We could hear the music of the giant wheel along with the cacophony created by the children out on the fairground. Crole had pushed forward his head towards the ball.

'I see the sun rising,' Renata whispered in an almost masculine voice. Crole suddenly stopped breathing. There's no doubt that he has assumed the sun to be gold.

'I see the sun rising for you,' once more Renata remarked. 'And—'

The lady remained quiet. This time my heart began to beat faster as well. In such affairs all elderly people tend to become childlike.

'And what?' Crole broke in. He was clearly running out of patience. But Madam Renata remained unperturbed. Her hands had covered the ball from both sides—perhaps to shield it from the outside light so that she could see the future scenario more clearly.

'And . . .' once more that rough, masculine voice said, 'And I see death. Yes, death.'

'Whose death?' Crole's voice quivered. He was again breathing heavily.

'The death of a radiant man.'

Madam Renata didn't reveal much beyond this. When asked what this radiant man looked like, she said, 'His face is a blur.'

Saunders got up from the chair. The lady had come out of her trance. With a smile she extended her hand. Saunders slipped suitable payment into that hand.

26 June

Not giving much thought about what could be arranged in Montefrio, we bought all the paraphernalia needed for our alchemic laboratory from London's Chor Bazaar or flea market in Portobello Street. After spending two and a half hours there, we had managed to procure clay pots, a glass flask, retorts, etc. One of Saunders's friends is a well-known film producer here. It appears that three years ago he had directed a film on the supernatural which was related to alchemy. For the scene of a laboratory, he had manufactured various ladles, cooking spuds, water pots, woks, and so on. Saunders had decided to hire some of these items.

Saunders's cat, Mustafa, is of course accompanying us. I personally feel that even if Crole hadn't mentioned him, Saunders would anyway have taken Mustafa with him as he cannot remain apart from his pet for too long.

I'm not very keen about the creation of gold, nor do I have any desire for it even if it's successfully produced. My interest is chiefly based on the ground that I've never been to this part of Spain before. Saunders doesn't have much work at present. Thus he, too, is moderately enthused about this outing. But the less one talks about Crole the better! Driven by intense excitement, he can hardly sit still for a moment. I have occasionally noticed him scribbling some geometric patterns in a notebook—the patterns reminded me of our tantric mandalas.

When I was packing my bag in the evening, I heard the sound of a doorbell.

Within minutes of the sound of opening the door, I heard a familiar voice. It was the voice of Crole's American adversary at the auction. Out of sheer curiosity I went down to see what was going on.

Saunders had shown the visitor into the drawing room. Crole must have heard the stranger's voice as he, too, came down within a couple of minutes.

The visitor right away took out three visiting cards from his pocket and handed one to each of us. The name on it was Rufus H. Blackmore.

'Rufus Blackmore,' said Crole, 'are you that person who wrote the book, *Black Art and White Magic*?'

'Yes, sir, the very same.' I looked at his face closely. It was oval in shape. His skin was extraordinarily pale. His black hair reached his shoulders and was tucked behind the ears. His cool and calm eyes were a surprise; we had seen the same pair of eyes glowering at us at the Collingwood Auction House.

*

He now took out three silver balls, the size of ping-pong balls, from the right hand pocket of his coat. Then before our dazzled eyes he went on to create at least twenty-five magical tricks out of these balls. The sparkling balls appeared and disappeared all at once. There's no way you can make out how they were made to move at such an amazing pace. So deft was Mr Blackmore's sleight of hand. At his last act, when he brought out these invisible balls from each of our pockets, we all involuntarily clapped.

'I can't help but praise you for your dexterity,' blurted Wilhelm Crole.

'What have you seen of my power?' Blackmore quipped with a dry smile. 'This was so basic. Do you know my real magic?'

And then Blackmore held one ball fixed between his index finger and the thumb, and said, 'This is made of silver and this silver has been created by me. You will not be able to find more genuine silver than this. Not even in any silver mine.'

We were quiet. Blackmore's calm eyes were now sparkling.

'Half the power of alchemy rests in my two hands,' continued Blackmore. 'But I could not succeed in creating gold despite trying over the last three years. I'm certain that Saavedra's diary describes the method. I heard about this diary from my guru. When I came to know that the diary was being auctioned, I flew in from San Francisco. I'd assumed I'd get it cheap but hadn't realized Mr Crole would be so obstinate. I could have overbid him that day but later I thought if we get to know each other personally, he himself would perhaps sell it back to me at the same price. I firmly believe that Mr Crole has bought this diary for his personal collection like any average collector. But I'm an alchemist myself. In all of America—possibly the entire world—I'm the most genuine alchemist. My guru is no longer alive. Now I'm the only person who can do full justice to this diary. I'm carrying the money with me. I want that diary.'

Rufus Blackmore now took out an attractive leather notecase from the pocket of his coat. Opening it he took out wads of ten pound notes and put them on the table in front of him.

'Please take it back, Mr Blackmore,' Crole said. 'I've no desire to let go of my Saavedra diary.'

'You're making a mistake, Mr Crole.'

'Maybe not. You may be a magician. But I've no proof of you being an alchemist. I'm not convinced that this silver ball is indeed your creation.'

For a brief moment Rufus Blackmore remained quiet. Then, looking daggers at us, he shoved the wad of notes back into his pocket and with a sudden jerk got up from his chair. He looked at Crole and said, 'Perhaps you know that 99 per cent of pure silver has been successfully created in a research lab through a chemical process. But we know of no instance of 100 per cent pure silver—except this silver, made by me.'

Saying this, Blackmore threw one out of the three balls towards Crole. The ball landed on Crole's lap.

'I know all three of you are scientists,' Blackmore continued. 'At least in order to find out whether my words are true or not, I'm requesting you to check out this silver. I'm giving you two days. I'm staying at the Waldorf Hotel, room 429. If you change your mind and decide to sell the Saavedra diary to me then please give me a call. If you do not sell it to me, the least I can say is: you're simply not capable of producing any gold.'

After this dramatic sermon, not waiting for a moment, Rufus Blackmore with strident steps walked towards the door. What he did next was inexplicable and unpardonable. Saunders's cat Mustafa was sitting on the threshold of the door. With the tip of this pointed patent leather shoes, Blackmore kicked the cat three yards away. Saunders exclaimed, 'What the hell!' and got up to attack him but Crole held him back. In any case by then Blackmore had reached the road. Crole said, 'He doesn't seem to be a decent sort. It's best not to provoke him.'

Mustafa was growling in anger and pain. After Saunders took him into his lap and petted him, he mellowed a bit. If this is the sample of an alchemist then it's best to keep alchemy at bay! But that is not to be. Day after tomorrow we are leaving for Granada. No idea what the future holds for us.

Montefrio, 29 June
It's raining. Judging by the sky I doubt if the clouds will disperse in a hurry. According to Crole, nothing could be more fortunate a sign, as one could now easily collect one of the main items required for the experiment. On the first floor of the Saavedra castle there's an open terrace where we are collecting rainwater in a plastic bucket. I think it'll fill up by the evening.

We're not staying in the castle; we've checked into a hotel. We need to stay in the hotel for another two days.

Not a soul lives in the Saavedra castle and no one knows for how long it has remained uninhabited. But everyone here knows of the Saavedra family. In fact, soon after we reached Montefrio, the very first person we met on the street readily gave us directions to the castle.

Since we had rested well in Granada, we were feeling quite refreshed and, deciding not to waste any time, followed that fellow's direction. Reaching the post office we took a left turn and began to proceed on a hilly road. It took us ten minutes to arrive at the second landmark. This part of Spain had been ruled by the Arabian Muslims or the Moors during the eighth century, and for the next seven centuries. The signs are evident everywhere. For instance, Granada's Alhambra fortress is, of course, world famous. We also spotted an ancient inn, belonging to the same era, in a state of ruins.

Near the abandoned inn, a boy was standing next to a tree. A mongoose with a rope round his neck was perched on the boy's shoulders. When he saw our taxi stop, he looked curious and came towards us. After we enquired about the Saavedra castle, it was he who informed us that no one lived in it. We explained our aim was not to meet anyone but only to see the castle. To which he said, if he is allowed to come with us in the car he can easily show us the way. Not just that—he also offered to help us as a guide. As none of us had any objection to this we took him in.

The boy is quite chatty. Without being asked, he gave us loads of news about himself. His name is Pablo and he has four brothers and seven sisters. He is the youngest. His father owns a liquor shop and two of his brothers help him run it. One of the other two brothers looks after a fruit shop and the other one plays music in a restaurant. All the sisters are married. Pablo is well versed in the history of Montefrio. The exact period in which each house had been built, who lived where, which king died in which war—he knows it all. He doesn't have a job as he is not well educated, though he occasionally earns a bit as a tourist guide. His real passion is to capture animals and tame them. He had caught this mongoose just three days ago yet the mongoose appears to have settled down rather well.

We decided to accept Pablo's offer to work for us during the period of our stay. He'll help us with various errands which will be recompensed. Of course, whether or not the work gets done will depend on our visit to the castle.

Inside the forest, after walking down a crooked path for about fifteen minutes Pablo ordered the car to stop at a certain point. We would have to walk the rest of the distance. 'How far?' asked Crole. 'Not much. A two-minute walk,' said Pablo confidently.

Even if it wasn't literally two minutes, after breaking through weeds and bushes for about five minutes, we arrived at the main entrance of the castle. It was not quite as large as a palace we had in our mind but big enough for hundred-odd people to be accommodated in it. This fortress has no protective ditch or moat around it. Straight from the road you could enter the main gate and walk through the curved path and then easily reach the main doorway.

Pablo could gather we wanted to go inside it and hence warned us. 'That castle now houses at least a few thousand bats. In addition to this, there are rats and snakes, too.'

Saunders said, 'How do you know so much about the interior of this house?'

Pablo answered, 'Once while chasing a salamander I entered this castle. This animal had been harassing me for a while. He made me chase him up to the terrace.'

Salamanders belong to the lizard family. I knew they were abundant in this region of Spain.

'What else did you see in this castle?' asked Crole.

Pablo replied, 'As regards furniture, there was nothing more than a few broken wooden chairs and tables. A few rusted arms were still hanging against the wall.' Apparently in some of the rooms the roof joists have come apart and are hanging loose, and one room is bolted from the outside so no one can enter it. But surprisingly the castle kitchen still retained a few old utensils. Pablo had picked up a clay pot from there to gift to his mother.

Hearing this, our curiosity heightened. 'Can you show us that kitchen?' asked Crole in a voice which tried to suppress his excitement.

'Why not?' said Pablo. 'Follow me.'

As we went inside, we realized our conjectures were not all wrong. Watching this room located on the southeast end of the Saavedra castle, not an iota of doubt remained that 700 years ago some alchemist had indeed used it as his research laboratory. A furnace, a water tank in the middle of the room, clay pots, glass jars, retorts—no item was missing though everything was covered in a thick layer of 700-year-old dust. There was also a furnace from that period which Crole studied carefully and remarked that it would work easily even now. It was interesting because we have seen pictures of a room with exactly such identical arrangements of items in many ancient books on alchemy—the only difference being the people who were working in it belonged to the twentieth century. But it's also true that along with Crole, my mind too has travelled to the middle age. The excitement that I sense in my nerves now must have also been felt by the alchemists of that era.

We inducted Pablo into our work schedule. We decided to pay him 1000 peseta per day. He will clean up the lab over the next two days so that we can start our work from the day after tomorrow. A couple of rooms need to be cleared up as well for the three of us will live inside the castle. Once we start our work on producing gold there's no way we can leave this castle. Pablo will arrange for our food. There's no problem in our sleeping arrangement as we all own sleeping bags. There would be no need for proper beds; the floor was good enough for us.

We returned to our hotel from Saavedra castle at 1.30 p.m. Within half an hour of our return it began to rain and immediately we sent Pablo back to the castle along with the plastic bucket to retain the rainwater. Now it's 8.30 p.m. This area is supposed to be quite dry; I guess it is only by sheer fluke that it rained.

*

Crole and Saunders called just now to say they are ready for dinner. I forgot to write down one thing—we have checked on the ball which Rufus Blackmore had given us and found that the silver used in it is completely pure. Hence we can no longer treat Blackmore as just a magician. We can no longer deny that he is also an accomplished alchemist. We now need to compete with him seriously in creating 100 per cent gold. In this regard all three of us are hell-bent on achieving our goal.

30 June, 10.30 p.m.

We have just returned to our hotel from the Saavedra castle. We spent the last two hours in our alchemic laboratory. Before we ventured into making gold, following the instructions marked out in Saavedra's diary, we completed one task. I'm now going to write about that. Let me mention in the beginning that the tenth-century world-renowned Arabian alchemist's spirit has already bestowed his blessings upon us. Tomorrow exactly at noon our furnace will begin to function. Work related items have all been gathered in our laboratory—all in sufficient quantity. We have installed a new strong padlock on the front door. From tomorrow we will live in the castle. Pablo will stay here, too. We have more or less explained to him about the work we are to embark on. The boy is so charmingly innocent that none of us hesitated in placing our faith in him.

In order to call for Jābir ibn Hayyān's spirit, Crole adopted an innovative method which involved the incantation of Latin and Tibetan mantras. The first one was rendered by Saunders, and the other by Crole. Following this, Crole, using his special flute made of human bone, played a medieval European devotional tune for about five minutes. I must mention that other than the three of us, there was also the presence of another being during the séance. And that was Saunders's cat, Mustafa, who had already caught three mice in this castle. Perhaps that is why he looks quite content.

After the chants and the flute rendition, like the usual practice of a séance, we sat around a table to meditate on Jābir ibn Hayyān. As both Crole and I were conversant with Arabic, we faced no problem in communicating with Jābir ibn Hayyān's spirit. Crole himself was the medium and therefore the spirit was to appear through him. His eyes were shut; both Saunders and I were looking at him with all our attention. The light in the room came from two candles. Their flames were swaying gently and with that our shadows on the wall quivered, too.

After gazing at Crole for fifteen minutes we noticed the sudden play of a shadow against the wall. Following the direction of the shadow we looked up at the wall and realized that a bat had taken shelter against a roof joist. Mustafa, sitting on Saunders' lap, was also gazing at the bat. There's nothing new about a bat swinging from a beam, but what made this one unique was that it was swinging like a pendulum, silently . . .

*

Crole was undergoing a change. The alteration could be observed not only in his appearance but also in his sitting posture. The body from waist to his head folded up and stooped forward, and with it the lower portion had risen from the chair and was rising even higher.

After a couple of minutes, Crole's body involuntarily took up a posture that resembled the position of a person reading his namaaz. Both Saunders and I clearly saw that his feet were no longer on the ground level. And the chair in which he was sitting was no more connected with any part of his body.

From somewhere we got the whiff of attar. The minute I sensed this, I also heard the soft sound of something being dropped. I noticed a pearl rosary on the table where Crole's head was resting—Muslims call it the 'Tasbih'.

Yet more wonder! In an instant the pearls loosened and spread all over the table and then rearranged themselves into a line of an Arabian script! It read, 'May you succeed.'

Soon, the pearls once again set themselves to form a new line. This time the words read, 'The value of gold.' I began to wonder what the spirit was trying to convey through these words. Just then these pearls joined together to create yet another sentence—'Value of life.' With this last message, all the pearls disappeared!

Crole's body now fell back into the chair with a loud noise. I explained the meaning of these words to Saunders. He said, 'Of course I could follow "to succeed", but what sort of messages are 'value of gold' and 'value of life'? What do they mean?'

Crole could not offer any satisfactory response to this. He said he had been in a deep trance. He had no knowledge of what he had done in that state.

I feel that we need not pay too much attention to the second and the third word formations. To succeed—that's all matters.

When we were coming out of the room after our séance, we glanced at the beam and noticed that the bat was still hanging there. Has he become a permanent resident of this lab?

1 July

Today we checked out of the hotel and arrived at the castle. Before leaving, however, an incident took place which perturbed us all. The person chiefly responsible for this is the hotel authorities and hence we gave a mouthful to the manager. Let me tell you all about it.

Even in a most ordinary hotel, the key of one room should not fit into another door. But upon our arrival on the first day we noticed that using Crole's key we could easily unlock Saunders's room. Despite that, as we loved the ambience as well as the quietness of the hotel, we had decided to stay on. Now Crole entered my room in a state of bluster. He reported that apparently in the middle of the night a thief had entered his room and ransacked it thoroughly. 'Have they taken anything?' I asked anxiously. 'No, they haven't.' said Crole, 'But they could easily have. Imagine . . . what if I had the Saavedra diary with me!'

I haven't mentioned that while we were still in London, Crole had copied the process of making gold from Saavedra's diary and written it in his own code before depositing the original diary in the bank. We have divided copies of this in three parts among us. Each one has been allotted three foolscap sheets. Now we feel we would have faced a lot of trouble if we hadn't worked it out like this. Saunders went straight to the manager's room and nearly struck him. The gentlemen was almost in tears and said that in the last twenty-six years—that is, since they had set up this hotel—not once had they had any case of robbery. The nightwatchman of the hotel, that Pedro fellow, is a little above sixty. Upon investigation, he said one tourist had arrived after 1 a.m. to look for a room. Pedro said no room was available. Then that fellow offered a cigarette to Pedro. Noticing it was a good quality French cigarette, he couldn't refuse. Right after taking the first drag his eyes instantly grew heavy with sleep. When he woke up it was 6.30 a.m.

'What did he look like?' asked Crole.

'The man was bearded and mustached and wore black glasses,' said Pedro. Pedro thinks that this man had not come in through the front door. It's not difficult to climb up the pipe on the southern wall of the hotel to reach the verandah of the second floor. And after reaching the verandah you can straight away reach the staircase using the corridor.

Now I was compelled to ask Crole how he had remained asleep with so much activity in his room. Crole said he had taken two sleeping pills so that before the work started he could rest well for one whole night. In any case, as none of Crole's money or any other stuff was missing and we are to check out from the hotel today, there's no point in lamenting now. The manager said as per custom he'll report this to police. In case any new tourist has arrived in any other hotel he would go and investigate.

*

After arriving at the castle, the three of us checked it carefully in the morning light. You cannot comprehend the complicated plan of this castle by studying it only once. To be frank, if we didn't have Pablo with us we would have lost our way on many occasions.

On the second floor of the eastern side of the castle we had heard about a locked room; today we finally came across it. A huge padlock hung from the door. Moving and stirring the lock didn't yield any result. It would be ridiculous to use the keys we have with us in trying to unlock the door. Crole said, 'We will be staying here in any case; one day we can take a hammer and use our strength to see if that works.'

Saunders looks a bit morose since last night. I think he is trying to relate the forewarning of the gypsy fortune teller to the words spoken by the spirit yesterday. He said, 'Madam Renata had predicted, "I see death", and the words the pearls revealed were. 'The price of gold is the price of life.' If I see my life in question due to the greed for gold, I'll be nowhere in the scene. And not just my own life, Mustafa's life is no less valuable than gold.'

Crole was turning out to be an incurable optimist. He said, 'There's no need to pay any heed to that gypsy's words. There can be no connection between gold and death. What the spirit of Jābir ibn Hayyān said only suggested that gold is an invaluable metal.'

In clockwork precision, exactly at 12 noon, we put fire to the furnace and began our work. There's no complication in our work's procedure—it's crystal clear—all we need are time and patience. We have devoted the whole of today just turning various herbs and roots of different trees into ash; and to measure out the ingredients—chiefly, mercury, sulphur and salt—weigh them in different quantities and put them in different containers. The rainwater has been retained in an oval-shaped water tank kept in the middle of the room.

Now it's 10 p.m. The three of us had taken turns to sleep since at least two of us have to be present during our experiment. Pablo, too, has slept for four hours and will keep a watch all night.

4 July

As nothing worthwhile happened yesterday I did not write anything in my diary. Today's work progressed in the right direction. But something took place this afternoon which I must record in my diary.

Around 12.30 p.m. when I heard the sound of an alarm from Saunders's clock in the next room, I realized he had to join back work and now it was my turn to rest. But I could strongly feel that I would not be able to sleep currently as my nerves were all alert. However, as I didn't want to upset our routine, the moment Saunders entered the laboratory I left. I decided to venture out a bit and explore this castle.

Intuitively my attention went towards the locked room on the first floor. Among all the twenty-six rooms in this entire fort, why one room must remain locked had become the subject of great curiosity as well as suspicion for me.

After reaching the first floor, I crossed the dark corridor and went towards the door. It was a humongous door—at least ten feet in height and certainly four-and-a-half feet in width. The body of the door had copper plated motifs on it. The iron lock had designs on it. I had a torch with me. While focusing the torchlight on the door from several directions, I noticed a small crack on the wooden surface. After removing my glasses I put my eyes right next to the crack. I had no hope of seeing anything at all. I assumed the inside of the room would be swathed in darkness.

But when I peeped through that quarter of an inch gap, as thin as a thread, I could see that the inside of the room wasn't pitch dark. Light was probably coming in through a skylight or a window and I could also clearly see that the colour of the light had a yellow tinge. Either the colour of the wall was yellow or perhaps the window glasses had a yellow shade.

133

It was not possible for me to investigate any further. Another person would, however, be capable of doing so. Without waiting any further, I came out of the castle to look out for him.

It didn't take too long to locate Pablo. In the garden of the castle, under an oak tree surrounded by weeds and shrubs, he was trying to lay a trap. He said he had spotted a hedgehog and planned to catch it. I said, 'The hedgehog can wait. First do me a favour.'

After showing the room to Pablo I said, 'Use the stairway to go on the second floor and check out if there's any terrace on top of this room. Also look out for any skylight through which some light can enter that room.'

Within ten minutes, Pablo returned puffing and panting. His eyes were sparkling. 'Professor, come along with me!'

Till we reached the second-floor terrace Pablo did not let go of my hand. In fact he almost dragged me throughout the way. On reaching the terrace he pointed with his finger,

'There's the skylight. Just glance through it once simply to see what amazing stuff is inside it!'

I was hardly satisfied with just that one peek. I managed to find a thick rope and after breaking the skylight glass, using the rope I let Pablo climb down the room. When he scaled up with the help of the rope, his hands carried an animal, a bird and a flower—all made of pure gold. The animal was a squirrel, the bird was an owl and the flower was a rose. After wiping these well with my handkerchief, the glitter which they produced dazed my eyes. There's no doubt that this metal is 100 per cent gold.

Also there's no doubt left that this gold had been produced by the Spanish alchemist, Manuel Saavedra, in the thirteenth century. Now I understand why this alchemist had called himself an artist. He was not only second to none in alchemy but an excellent goldsmith too. Even works by the noted sixteenth century Italian goldsmith Benvenuto Cellini's works come out as a pale shadow.

5 July

I decided that as of now I would not show these gold objects to Saunders and Crole. In the end, however, keeping Saunders in mind I showed these sculptures to them that very day. Within two days of starting our work Saunders had to an extent lost his high spirits—one reason obviously being it's very difficult for a scientist to take the course of alchemy seriously. I can understand this. But by virtue of being an Indian perhaps I can't pooh-pooh concepts like ghosts and spirits, hymns and chants. From the various kinds of experiences I've encountered in my life, I find it difficult to associate any scientific explanations behind them. But Saunders is a thorough-bred Englishman; he has no belief in mumbo jumbo or in spells.

Of course today Saunders has undergone a complete change and the only reason is the discovery of the Saavedra made gold. We have set out those items on display on a shelf in our lab. One can't describe how much the look of the room has changed. But then, with it, one needs to worry about burglars, as well. All three of us are carrying arms with us. Saunders is a great huntsman and Crole, too, knows how to use a pistol. My Annihilin gun is always there in my pocket. Hence there's no need to fear anyone.

Pablo is keeping a watch every night on a regular basis. The hedgehog has been captured in his trap. He is happily dealing with both the mongoose as well as the hedgehog.

I think we'll require two more days to finish our work. Today we produced that sticky matter. It's taken a very strange appearance. It turns different shades of colours seen from different directions, and due to the presence of mercury each colour reflects a silver tinge.

6 July

We have a real reason to worry. It seems that the thief is still after us. It was only after Pablo informed us this morning that we went out and noticed a new pair of footprints in the garden. We spotted these footprints in various places. And some of these had appeared near the window of our lab. Yet Pablo could not make out anything of this affair. But that's not unusual as other than the main entrance there are other ways to enter the garden. Many parts of this seven hundred-year-old wall have collapsed. Using the disintegrated areas any stranger from outside can easily come into the garden and move around without any problem. From now on Pablo needs to be much more alert.

It's 9 a.m. I've just finished my coffee and have started writing my diary. Right now, it's Crole's turn to sleep. But I doubt if any of us can afford to sleep today. Today we have to dissolve that sticky element into the rainwater and purify it continuously for the next seven hours. Then by God's grace we have to dip either a pot or a pan made out of some metal like tin, iron, copper, brass into that liquid using tongs to see if our experiment with alchemy will turn out to be a success. If not, then none of us knows about our next course of action. I suppose like obedient children we will return to our respective homes. If asked, I won't be able to explain why, yet I can intuit that our experiment is edging towards success.

7 July

The depths of dejection. The liquid was the result of great labour and diligence on our part, following accurately the alchemic procedures in the diary, but we could not make gold with it .

Whatever metallic items that I had with me I immersed into that liquid—yet noticed no change in any of them. However, I can strongly feel that this liquid has some distinct potential; it needs to be cold in temperature, but when I place my hands near the liquid, I feel as if countless invisible pins are pricking my hand. Of course, Saavedra has clearly warned in his diary that no one should come in contact with this liquid. Along with Mustafa, Saunders has gone out of this laboratory and is now sitting in the garden. Sitting on a stool, Crole is looking blankly at the oval water tank. The bat, from the top of his head, continues to hang. Ever since his entry on the first day he has never left the room. I soon realized that Crole was almost on the verge of insanity when I suddenly saw him charging at that bat. After he uttered a few abusive words in German, aiming the bat on top, he took out the revolver from his pocket and with one shot killed him. What an extraordinary bat—even after his death he continued to dangle just like before from the ceiling—except that drops of blood from his body began to drip onto the floor.

Hearing the sound of the shot, Saunders hastily entered the laboratory and comprehending the situation began to shout at Crole. Watching this precarious situation, I left the room. Finally, signs of fatigue set in me after facing the lack of success despite all our countess days of hard work as well as staying up at nights. In general, my adventures never meet with failure. But this time it's likely to turn into one.

7 July, 11 p.m.
This day turned out to be the most thrilling and memorable one of my life.

I had left the room after hearing the altercation between Saunders and Crole and within ten minutes a series of horrifying events took place. I am trying my best to coherently jot down how things happened.

After coming out of the lab, instead of going to my room I headed for the garden. A couple of minutes ago we'd had a bout of rain despite the sunshine. Standing outside, when I glanced at the east, I could see the peak of Spain's highest mountain, Mulhacén. Atop the peak, across the sky, reflected a beautiful pair of rainbows. As I stood gazing at the rainbow I heard a muffled scream.

I ran in the direction of the sound and found Pablo lying on the grass, unconscious. His jaw was bruised, one tooth was broken, and blood was oozing out of his mouth.

And soon after, suspicious noise started coming out of the laboratory. Rushing breathlessly inside, I reached the door and stood motionless. Rufus Blackmore, sporting a satanic grin on his face and holding a .38 colt revolver in his hand, stood facing both Crole and Saunders. Noticing me he said, 'The moment you cross the threshold you're sure to die!'

Saying this, he got his hands on the gold making formula kept on the table—to be precise he snapped up nine foolscap sheets. And then he began to proceed towards the shelf containing the gold objects on the right side of the wall.

What took place that next instant gives me goose bumps even now. I can vividly remember the state of terror as well as amazement we all were in.

Out of the blue, a mass of furry flesh flew across the air at great speed and jumping on Blackmore's chest fiercely scratched him in the face. Blackmore's revolver slipped out of his hand but the shot instead of hitting us struck one of the glass retorts.

Losing his balance, Blackmore stumbled into the water tank kept in the middle of the room. In the meantime, much gratified with his suitable revenge, Mustafa had returned to his master. The moment Blackmore's body touched the liquid, like a fish he made a heavy stroke to jump out but all at once the body became stiff and sank under the liquid. The three of us saw with amazement that the uncovered portion of his body—i.e. from his neck to his face and from his wrist to his hand—was in no time transformed into glittering gold!

Saunders in a near whisper muttered, 'The price of gold . . . the price of life . . .'

In other words, to follow Saavedra's formula of alchemy, he enjoined the use of a living being—like humans, flowers, animals and birds—for conversion to gold instead of metals.

Blackmore, the owl, the squirrel and the rose—had once been mortal natural live objects.

Now all of them are immortal.

The Mystery of Munroe Island

Munroe Island, 12 March

I have jotted down the events of the past three weeks in my diary, though at random. And whenever I get some free time, I try to arrange my erratic jottings in some kind of coherent order.

Needless to say, I have once again engaged myself in yet another expedition. This island may have had an original name 300 years ago when humans from the mainland stepped on to it, but its name never reached the ears of the civilized world. For now, we will refer to it as Munroe Island.

Our group consists of five people. One of them is my old friend, Jeremy Saunders, at whose instigation we have undertaken this journey. To discuss the initial phase of this mission I need to introduce Callenbach. He is part of our group. A resident of California, he is a professional photographer and a large, strongly-built man with a devil-may-care attitude. He is about forty-five years old, but judging by his conduct, he appears half his age, almost like an overgrown child. Callenbach has known Saunders for quite a few years. Last December, at the behest of the *National Geographic*, Callenbach had visited a few cities of north-west Africa to photograph their local festivals. There in the city of Agadir in Morocco, he had a strange experience. Agadir is a coastal city of Morocco, the majority of whose inhabitants are fishermen. Callenbach had visited a fishermen's colony to familiarize himself with its denizens and to depict their lifestyle in his photographs. When he entered the house of one particular fisherman his attention was drawn to a three-year-old boy. The boy was playing with a bottle which contained a rolled up piece of paper in it. Saunders's curiosity was aroused. He took the bottle from the boy and noticed that the bottle was stoppered with a sealed cork. He broke open the seal and pulled out the paper. It was a letter written in English. Judging by the style of handwriting it seemed to be quite ancient. After checking with the boy's grandfather, Callenbach was told that the bottle had belonged to their household since the time of his grandfather. As the fisher folk are Muslims who speak Arabic, there was no question of them reading the letter.

Callenbach had taken out the letter from the bottle and within a few days left for London after completing his work. He then showed this letter to Saunders. It was a letter consisting of a few words written in pencil.

> *Latitude 33°East—Longitude 33°North, 13*
>
> *December 1622*
>
> *In this unknown island we have found such an amazing plant whose immortal quality is bound to revolutionize human life. To disseminate this news, despite Brandon's severe warning, I've put this letter inside a bottle and will float it into the sea. Blackhole Brandon is now the all-in-all of this island. Therefore, after reading this letter if any people turn up here in search of this plant, they ought to be prepared to face a confrontation with Brandon. I'm about to become a victim at the hands of Brandon.*
>
> *Hector Munroe*

The first thing Saunders did upon receiving the letter was to visit London's marine department—where all ancient sea travel related documents are archived—to research the records of the years 1621–22, in case there had been any news of shipwrecks in the Atlantic Ocean. Among the three shipwrecks in the year 1622 the name of Hector Munroe was found in one list of passengers. His ship—the *Conquest*—was going from Gibraltar to the Virgin Islands in the Atlantic Ocean. It was shipwrecked near Bermuda. No reason was provided for the accident. The report by the marine departments states that no one survived. Yet the fact that Hector Munroe had indeed survived is proved by the letter in the bottle. As for the reference to Brandon in the Munroe letter, no one of that name was travelling in that ship. After further investigation, Saunders discovered that in the beginning of the seventeenth century there was a notorious pirate by the name of Greg Brandon. Apparently Brandon was devoid of one eye. All that remained in its place was a hole. And because of that he was named Blackhole Brandon. Driven by his greed for gold he had killed more than a thousand people. Jamaica at that time was the main haunt of English pirates. Perhaps the *Conquest* came under attack by Brandon's pirate ship and was destroyed. The reason for Munroe's survival could be that Brando himself had saved him. One needs to remember that Munroe was a doctor. In those days, a capable doctor was much valued, even in a pirate ship. At that time during sea travel if a ship was struck by diseases like scurvy, pellagra and beriberi, the chances of a sailor's survival were rather bleak. Hence the presence of a competent doctor—someone who could treat such cases as well as perform surgeries if necessary—became an indispensable part of any sea voyage. Hector Munroe certainly fitted into this scenario. However, how both Brandon and Munroe arrived at this unknown island remains a mystery.

Nevertheless, the upshot is that, after gathering all this information, Saunders was hell-bent on travelling to this island, despite the lapse of about three-hundred-and-fifty-odd years since the letter had been written. The moment I received a letter from him informing me about this venture, I immediately agreed to join him and I arrived in London within a week. Upon my arrival I realized that all arrangements for the journey were almost complete. Callenbach, of course, had told us that if this journey takes place he will definitely join us. After a chat with him, I realized he is dreaming of earning loads of money by taking pictures for television.

The fourth person in our group is a Japanese scientist, Hidechi Suma. Among his many inventions, one is a jet driven sea vessel called the Sumacraft. We realized its amazing potential by travelling 1500 miles on the sea. Even after facing many adverse situations, the Sumacraft did not once give us any trouble during the cruise. Suma had arrived in London to give a demonstration of this boat, and that's how he met Saunders. Suma is not just the inventor of this jet boat. He has brought along various other inventions which he thinks might be useful during our expedition. Suma is also a distinguished biochemist. And Suma's introduction won't be complete unless I also give him this credit: I'm yet to see such a disciplined and well-turned-out person like him. Whenever you see him, you feel as if he is still living in Osaka and is about to pick up his briefcase and leave for work.

Before I name the fifth person, let me tell you how he was inducted into the group.

As soon as he decided on undertaking the expedition, Saunders put in an advertisement in all London newspapers inviting people to join the venture. Five criteria were put in to confirm eligibility. 1—Previous experience of sea travel; 2—Prior experience of being part of at least two scientific expeditions; 3—A top degree in any branch of science; 4—Good health; and 5—Experience in the use of a firearm. Other than the first requirement, our fifth candidate did not qualify in any of the other obligations. He is a writer, not a scientist; he has never been on either any scientific or non-scientific expeditions; only once while in school, as part of a group he had climbed 1500 feet of the Ben Nevis Mountain in Scotland. This was no major achievement considering the actual height of Ben Nevis is 4500 feet. Then how has he managed to be included in our group?

The chief reason is that David Munroe is a direct descendant of Hector Munroe. After spotting Saunders's advertisement he straightaway landed up at Saunders's residence and requested to be included in the group. He said he had heard from his father and grandfather about Dr Munroe, who had been Shakespeare's contemporary. When the British navy defeated the Spanish Armada, the commander-in-chief of the British side was the Duke of Effingham, and Hector Munroe was his physician. In addition, David became determined to join the group when he got to know about the role of Blackhole Brandon. Since his childhood he had been reading tales of pirates; he has even heard a lot about adventures related to Blackhole. If we find any hidden treasure of Blackhole's on this island, this will turn out to be a memorable adventure for David. One must mention that David is only twenty-two.

Just a glance at the young David Munroe produces doubt regarding his health and ability to do physical tasks hard. It becomes clear when you notice his hands, which other than a pen would never have touched any weapon. His lost looks and soft voice; his shoulder-length unkempt golden hair—all these point to a limited physical capacity, however powerful his imagination may be. Yet Saunders decided to choose him as he could not ignore one of his credentials—David Munroe belongs to the same lineage as the writer of the letter which is in the bottle. Other than him we also have another companion. Its David's pet, a Great Dane called Rocket. There's no doubt left that if anybody is physically the fittest, it's the dog.

We have arrived here this morning. We covered 300 miles a day on the Sumacraft without any sign of land and we doubted if at all this portion of the Atlantic Ocean indeed has any such island. At sunrise, however, when Saunders looked through his binoculars and said he could spot a bit of land despite the thick fog, Callenbach instantly picked up his movie camera. I was a bit surprised, because, as a norm, much before a vessel approaches land one usually sees clusters of seagulls flying around and squawking to announce the proximity to land. Nothing like this happened this time.

After arriving here, I realized this was hardly surprising, as throughout the day, even after traversing for five kilometres, I could not locate many living beings except for a few insects and crabs near the beach. And not just that, we could not even locate any unknown species of plants. Other than the usual flora and fauna associated with this region, we did not discover anything new. But then again we have only walked around the western side of this island today.

We have camped near the seashore on the southern part of the island. There's not much vegetation in this part; only sand and rock. The island is small in size and more or less plain and flat, though the central part of the island, which is about five kilometres from our campsite, is comparatively higher in surface and dotted with large hillocks.

David is in full form. It's delightful to watch him play with Rocket. Within a couple of hours after our arrival we have noticed a complete change in the youth we had met in London.

It's Callenbach who seems to be having trouble. He sneezed thirty times non-stop soon after stepping on to the island. Thereafter, he began suffering from high fever accompanied by shivering. Needless to say, he could not come with us on our walk. Both Suma and he stayed back at the camp. Suma is arranging all his tools and implements to be used for our research. In addition, he has set up a small laboratory in order to chemically analyse any new species we may discover.

Despite being so ill, Callenbach says that within a couple of days we will leave this island. He thinks many such islands are present all over the Atlantic.

But I cannot put Hector Munroe's letter out of my mind. If the latitudes and longitudes match, then this is indeed the island mentioned in the letter. On this very island Munroe had discovered that amazing plant.

13 March, Noon

Callenbach's prophecy didn't work. There's simply no question of leaving this island within a few days. Let me recount everything.

Getting up this morning, we bathed in the sea and finished our breakfast. Just as we were planning to go out, David suddenly said he wished to venture out with Rocket on his own. The fact that he has gathered some confidence had become noticeable since yesterday. After all, he is a writer; it's quite a torture for him to hang around too long with elderly scientists for companions. We have come here to observe and analyse everything in minute detail and for that we need time and patience. David said he would like to search among the distant hillocks just to check out if there are any cave-like structures among them. He thinks one of these may hold Blackhole Brandon's treasures. 'I'll go, inspect and be back within half-an-hour,' he said.

I tried to reason with him and said that even if the island may not be inhabited by large animals there's a strong chance of it having poisonous snakes and scorpions. Hence there's no need for him to take this risk. David refused to relent. He said he would take Callenbach's pistol with him. Moreover, he had Rocket. Therefore there was no need for us to be so anxious.

As I was thinking of how to disarm this foolish chap's determination, I heard someone exclaim—'No—No, No, No, No!'

Suma had come out of his camp shaking his head.

'No—No, No, No, No!'

What was that? I was amused to see such strong words coming out from his normally smiling face. Suma was holding a small instrument which he placed on the sand in front of us and said, 'There is something big here. A living being. About 5.7 kilometres from here—on that side.'

Suma spread his hand in the direction of the hillocks. And then he showed us his amazing instrument, which he called a Telecardioscope. This machine could detect the heartbeats of an animal from as far as ten kilometres. Exactly how far and in which direction the creature is can be gauged from the machine's receiver by turning a knob. The moment the distance and the direction match, the instrument starts producing the sound of heartbeats along with the blinking of colourful lights. The distance of ten kilometres is indicated by the colour of deep purple. When the animal gets closer to you, like the sequence of a rainbow the colour changes from blue, green, orange, etc; finally when the animal is within a kilometre, the colour turns red. And with it the volume of the heartbeat increases, too. However, if the animal is within the radius of a kilometre, the machine stops responding.

'The animal is in the same spot,' said Suma. 'And I think it's quite big.'

'What do you mean by big? How big is it?' I asked.

'I feel it's bigger than a human being. Because the size of the animal and its heartbeat are inversely proportional. The general heartbeat of a human is seventy per minute. I find his to be a bit more than fifty.'

'Could it be a tortoise?' I asked. It's not unusual for them to live here. And any other animal bigger than a human, like deer or monkey, would have a heartbeat rate much faster than a human's.'

'The way he is lying low, fixed in one spot, it seems like a tortoise,' agreed Suma. 'But what a tortoise is doing so far away from the sea and in the middle of this island is a question indeed.'

Saunders, however, dismissed the theory of a tortoise. He feels it's a different animal and perhaps the only big one on this island. Therefore, there's no way one can allow David to venture out alone under these circumstances.

After we watched the machine produce sound and light for a while, Suma switched it off. I couldn't help but marvel at Suma's competence. A dog like a Great Dane can sense the presence of another being close to him much before a human can; but even Rocket would seem like a small fry next to this machine.

We were all ready to set out for the day but the only problem was Bill Callenbach. Consuming his own medicines has produced no result. After our return I'll give him my Miracurol pill. This invention of mine cures all ailments within a day except for the common cold. But right now this poor fellow is tossing and turning in his bed. Perhaps he has heard about the presence of an animal here which has sparked hope that his movie camera won't, after all, prove useless. Suma would stay on in the camp today, too. With another couple of hour's work his mini laboratory would be ready to function.

The three of us, along with Rocket, set off. If there's any sign of an animal nearby, Rocket would, of course, warn us. But as long as there's no animal approaching us there's no reason to fear.

Today, our mission was not towards the mounds in the middle of the island. I don't think that area contains much vegetation. Today we were to venture out to the eastern side of the island. Following the seashore we would enter the forest where the foliage is the thickest. All three of us were carrying arms. Saunders had his German Mannlicher rifle slung along his shoulder; David's pocket contained Callenbach's Beretta automatic pistol, and my vest pocket held my Annihilin. When Callenbach was told about my machine—which when used not just kills the object but also makes it vanish at that very instant—he had warned me that if any animal appears when he is around, I won't be allowed to use my weapon before he gets a chance to photograph it.

While we were walking it was decided that in case one wanted to wander away from the group then he had to shout out to inform the others about his whereabouts. Also, no one was allowed to stray too far from the group. Of course, this was decided only with David in mind. I can clearly see a marked change in David from his former aimless lazy self; he is now quite restless. Where we were walking right now, however, even if one of us deviated from the set direction, everyone remained visible as there were no large rocks or trees in our way.

One thought was crossing my mind time and again— Suma's instrument had suggested only one animal; could there be more than one? Perhaps not, since the total area of the island is in length as well as breadth certainly not more than ten kilometres. A week should be enough to examine the entire island.

After walking for about a mile along the seashore, the scenario began to change. Now we would be walking away from the sea and going into the interior of the island. Here on our left—that is, facing the sea—was a line of squat palm trees and the forest eventually grew thicker with banana, papaya, coconut and other large trees. There were no rocks visible any more and the ground below our feet was strewn with grass and weeds rather than sand.

We entered the forest. What really surprised me was the complete absence of any bird calls. I've never seen such an absolutely silent forest and especially in this part of the world you can see at least eight to ten specimens of the cockatoo alone. That apart, in this kind of forest you often hear the sound of reptiles moving through the grass; that sound was also absent here. It seemed like a haunted forest. Perhaps whatever trees that exist now may not survive in the near future, too.

After walking for ten minutes, the forest grew thinner and soon we arrived at an open space when suddenly all four of us were so shocked at what we saw that we came to a halt. David was ahead of us and stopped with a shout. What we saw when we caught up with David was this:

The clearing in the middle of the forest was scattered with animal bones, skulls and parts of rib-bones. Among these, with much difficulty, we could identify the remains of two deer, about four large-sized reptiles belonging to the chameleon family—probably iguana—and a few types of monkeys. On examination it was found that the bones were rather old.

This proves that the forest had at some point indeed been inhabited by animals. But we have absolutely no knowledge of how they became extinct.

David finally found his voice.

'It's the monster! The same monster ate up this entire lot of animals.'

The heartbeat which was heard on Suma's instrument a while ago has, in David's mind, turned into a monster! But it was too soon to infer that someone had eaten them; it could well be a case of natural death. But then why should animals of such diverse breed all come and die in one particular spot?

We began to proceed further.

Ahead of us was a forest consisting of mahogany and cedar trees. Bushes of jasmine, hibiscus and bougainvillea were also scattered all over. I've seen many mahogany trees previously, but here the trunk of each tree was marked by a luminous blue colour, a shade I'd never seen before.

After going closer I gathered the reason for this colouration. The colour came not directly from the tree but on its trunk were clusters, somewhat like a beehive, of tiny blue berries. I must also tell you about its scent. An indescribable fragrance had enveloped this part of the forest. The presence of this plant's amazing colour along with its aroma made all three of us stand transfixed for a few moments. When we came out of this spell, the childlike David jubilantly ran forward and was about to touch the fruits when both Saunders and I simultaneously shouted at him not to do so. And then when Saunders, after putting on rubber gloves, brushed his hands on the bunch, the berries easily came off the stem. We put about a hundred of these berries into a plastic bag and headed back to camp. Without any delay we must let Suma chemically analyse this fruit as none of us have seen such a thing before. I can intuit that the amazing plant mentioned in Munroe's letter has to be this one. It's obvious that this is a parasitical plant; it survives by drawing in enzymes from the mahogany tree.

Suma's miniature laboratory is ready; he has already begun his work on analysing the chemical process of these rare berries. We have come to know that the fruits won't harm our hands if we touch them directly. I've been to Callenbach's tent and shown him one of the fruits. He took one in his hand, felt it carefully and heaving a sigh put it back on his side table. It was easy to see his deep regret for not being able to capture this special moment of discovery on his camera. I have given him a Miracurol pill. We need to restore him to health. Callenbach has till now refused to have any medicine other than the ones from his own country. But left with not much choice he gave in this time.

13 March, 9 p.m.
Our conviction is getting stronger each day that our mission won't go to waste. It's very difficult to forecast its outcome but the way events are taking a turn, one feels we'll return home with some amazing experiences.

I offered only some chicken soup to Callenbach. His pulse was still very weak. It was quite worrying to see his emaciated appearance after such a brief spell of illness. Even under these trying circumstances he asked about that animal. Have we found him? Has he come nearer us or is his position still static?

For the moment the Telecardioscope machine is switched off. Suma is now single-mindedly analysing the chemical composition of the strange fruit. That his work is progressing in the right direction is proved by his occasional cheery shouts. Saunders and I are both intently watching his research. One can follow this procedure easily. The presence of each vitamin in it is now being processed. The term 'vitamin' had not yet been coined during Munroe's era. Science was still in its infancy and research on food products was to commence two and a half centuries later.

Around 3:30 p.m., while getting up from his chair, Suma uttered only two words. First he said, 'amazing' and then while tucking in a quarter inch of his handkerchief further into his coat pocket he added, 'and mysterious'.

Meanwhile, we couldn't figure out when Callenbach had got up from his bed and come to stand behind us. When our eyes met, he extended his hand and with force shook my hand and said, 'Great! Your medicine is matchless. I'm completely fit now.'

'What? Only within these couple of hours?'

With a smile, Bill Callenbach said, 'You can see that for yourself!'

That my medicine can cure anyone at such a rapid speed was unknown even to me.

'And please take this back. It was lying on my table.'

'What? But this is my pill!'

It took no time to solve this mystery. Under the delirium of fever, instead of my pill he'd consumed that blue fruit kept on the table and this had resulted in such a dramatic recovery. Moreover, the fruit had not just helped Callenbach to regain health but also brought radiance to his face.

Saunders told Suma, 'There's no need to do any more research; now let's return home after collecting as much of this fruit as possible. We'll cultivate this fruit and dismiss all pharmaceutical companies!'

Though Saunders said this teasingly, the tone of Suma's reply was rather serious. He said he needs to continue with his research. At least for one more day. Other than the presence of vitamins, the fruit also has many other elements which he is yet to identify.

At Callenbach's repeated requests, Suma stopped his work and switched on his Telecardioscope. We saw that the animal has remained on the same spot. 'But his heartbeat is slower,' said Suma.

This can be observed just by the sound of it. Yesterday it was fifty, and today it's below forty.

'Good lord!' exclaimed Callenbach. 'Is he going to die? With the presence of such a special creature on this island, why are you still wasting your time with that fruit?'

'We've anyway got the fruit with us, Bill,' said Saunders. 'Tomorrow we'll go and inspect the central part of the island. Please don't be so impatient.'

Grumbling, Callenbach returned to his tent.

14 March
Today we could not venture out. Thunderstorm, rain and lightning continued throughout the day. Callenbach, left with not much of a choice, took our pictures and interviewed each of us with the help of his tape recorder.

In the afternoon, after lunch, David regaled all of us with stories of pirates. Really, this fellow has such a rich stock of these accounts.

There's one piece of unfortunate news. According to Suma, other than the presence of vitamins in the berries, his little lab is not capable of identifying the other contents in it. He can do this only in a bigger laboratory back home. Of course, our initial mission of coming here has been accomplished well. So we can now plan to return home. At this point, Suma has expressly forbidden us from consuming this fruit. If just a single fruit can cure Callenbach within an hour, it's easy to decipher its full potential. To Suma it won't be a surprise if eating this fruit might prove to be harmful despite its benefits. I don't know if an extraordinary increase in one's appetite is a harmful sign because during lunch Callenbach alone emptied three tins of ham.

15 March, 7 a.m.
Bad news.
Callenbach, without informing anyone in the group, has ventured out alone.

It was David Munroe who gave us this news. He and Callenbach were sharing the same tent; out of the other two Saunders and I are using one, and Suma along with his machineries is occupying the other. When David got up at six in the morning he found Callenbach's bed empty and the camera related equipment kept on the table also missing. Immediately David stepped out of the tent and called out Callenbach's name a couple of times. But he received no response. Finally deciding to take his dog's help, he picked up the handkerchief lying next to Callenbach's pillow and made Rocket smell it. When he observed that Rocket was dashing off towards the small hills he called him back.

Having worked the entire night Suma had dozed off this morning. He was woken up to be given this news. He instantly switched on his Telecardioscope. A pulsing yellow light showed that Callenbach was three kilometres away from the camp and was proceeding towards the hillocks.

We will set off within five minutes. It's a lovely day today. All four of us will go out to explore. There's no end to Saunders's regret; he is constantly bemoaning, 'Why on earth did I bring this irresponsible man with us.'

15 March, 5:30 p.m.
The numerous extraordinary events, all taking place at once, have rendered my mind topsy-turvy.

We have travelled two kilometres to the east away from the rocky hillock in the central island and are now sitting on the sand by the seashore. Saunders is jotting down notes in his notebook. He has signed contracts with three dailies in London for his contribution on this expedition. This is the first time that he opened his notebook.

We haven't come across Callenbach yet; what we found were the case of his camera and the tape recorder. They are both in a dishevelled state. The movie camera is always strapped to his waist; if he has been captured by that unknown animal he would have been taken along with his camera.

David has taken Suma's Japanese Mikiki revolver and is doing target practice after having placed pebbles on a slab of stone fifty yards away. Judging by his performance, with only three day's practice, he is bound to become a skilled marksman.

Suma is taking a walk by the seashore. He is walking precisely forty steps at a time on each of his sides. Even after eight hours of travel, not a crease has appeared on his shirt, not a single hair is out of place.

The leather bag that is hanging from Suma's shoulder contains a remarkable weapon created by him, the Sumagun. It's about six inches in length; in place of a trigger there's a button which when pressed, produces, instead of a bullet, a needle-attached capsule which contains a deadly poison created by Suma himself. Death strikes within three seconds.

Now let me tell you all about our other remarkable discoveries. The fact that this island had once housed more people other than Brandon and Munroe has been proved by the presence of scattered skulls and bones inside a cave as well as some pieces of glasses, bottles, knives and earrings made of glass and metals. It seems that people belonging to Brandon's ship took refuge in this cave. We found about twenty-two cutlasses, the kind of curved sword used by the pirates. Unfortunately we could not locate any chest. But there are many such caves to be found in this area. I wonder what they may contain!

After coming out of the cave and wandering for about ten minutes, we heard Rocket bark. Following the sound we went forward and found Callenbach's camera box and the tape recorder lying there. Probably he tried to free himself of these objects and run away. But we have no idea if he had managed to escape. I made Suma switch on his Telecardioscope right then. The outcome of it did not look very bright. Other than the presence of this known figure we were unable hear any heartbeat despite moving the receiver in various directions. It's a different matter if Callenbach is present within the range of one kilometre. But what's he doing there? Is he lying injured? He has got a pistol; he can always fire a blank shot from it to give us a signal. The creature's heartbeat has gone back to fifty. The colour of the light in the Telecardioscope is between yellow and green; that is, this animal is within the range of three kilometres or beyond.

After picking up Callenbach's articles, we returned to the beach to rest and drink some coffee. The moment we came here, what Suma did instantly was to place Callenbach's damaged tape recorder on the sand and turn it on. It played perfectly. Suma's face produced a self-complacent smile as this was a Japanese product! In the light of the setting sun we surrounded the machine and listened to Callenbach's voice.

'This is Bill Callenbach. 14th March, 8:10 a.m. My lone expedition is a success. I've just now seen that creature.

He has come out of the cave and is about fifty yards away from me. He is bigger than a human. Perhaps he is four footed, though he rested on two legs to look around. As I was hiding behind a tree he could not see me. Before I could fit a telephoto lens into my camera the animal retreated inside the cave. From a distance he didn't look to be dangerous. When he walked he looked a bit unwell and old. With great caution I'm heading towards the cave.'

The recording ends here.

Now it's time to return to the camp. We have no idea what the future holds for tomorrow!

16 March, 6:30 a.m.
A dreadful experience.

Incessant barking by Rocket followed by David's scream woke me up at 2:30 a.m. When I came out I saw Rocket, with his face pointed towards the north, barking loudly and at the same time desperately trying to release himself from the leash held in David's hand. The new moon in the cloud laden sky gave almost no light. Hence it was impossible to find out the reason for Rocket's restlessness. Saunders entered our tent to look for a torch and suddenly Rocket pulled at David, who tripped on to the sand, letting go of the leash. Rocket ran towards the northern hillock. Meanwhile, Suma had switched on his Telecardioscope, but it was not showing any result. If that animal has indeed come here it should be within a distance of one kilometre.

It was all quiet and silent; even torchlight could not show us anything as Rocket had vanished behind the hillock. While we were thinking of whether it's safe to go ahead to investigate further, a howl from Rocket chilled our blood. This scream was not that of excitement or wrath. It was an agonized cry.

In the torchlight we saw Rocket return. David raced towards his beloved pet. We, too, ran behind him. When we reached the spot the reason behind his cry became clear; blood was oozing out from a deep wound inflicted on his back. But at the same time it was also evident that the animal hadn't just injured the dog but had got himself injured too. Rocket's mouth was marked by his attacker's blood.

The medicine that has been applied on Rocket's wound will help him recover by tomorrow.

After testing the blood found in Rocket's mouth, Suma informed us that the blood group is 'A.' Just as 'A' group is related to humans, the same group can be identified with some species of monkeys, too. There's no doubt left that this animal belongs to this category. Half an hour later we went and saw his footprints on the sand which was fifty yards away from our camp. Footprints were preceded by palm prints. His paw was marked by five fingers, its size slightly bigger than that of a human.

Now we must be prepared to face this ferocious animal. The island which produces this divine fruit also houses this monstrous monkey. This realization has created a feeling of wonder as well as terror in us.

17 March, 9 p.m.

We're setting out on our return journey tomorrow morning. There's no point in describing my state of mind because after going through this kind of experience, futile expressions like woe, wonder, etc. can't do any justice to describe our escapades. In fact, I've noticed that all my adventures are neither a complete success nor an absolute failure. Just as I have achieved wonderful rewards I have also faced dismal losses. One thing can be vouched for after this expedition—my coffer of experiences has increased manifold with adventures, vast knowledge and wonderment.

Today, we returned to the spot where we had found Callenbach's case for the camera and the tape recorder. Suma turned on his Telecardioscope. Today, too, we could receive the heartbeat of only one being. The rate of the beat was just fifty per minute and the colour of the light on the machine was orange. The animal was away from us by 4.5 kilometres towards the western side. But the animal was not stationary. With the result that Suma had to constantly monitor the direction of the receiver. That the animal is not a fast moving one is what we had learnt from Callenbach's description. Hence, even if he came in our direction, we still had half an hour to roam around. I still can't believe that Callenbach is no more. Maybe he is lying injured somewhere or maybe he is within the range of one kilometre and the instrument can't capture his heartbeat.

Our hope came crashing down within ten minutes. Jeremy Saunders discovered Callenbach's dead body behind a busch of poinsettia plants. By body I don't, however, mean the whole body. A portion of the lower part was missing. It was now proven without doubt that the wretched Callenbach had turned into this savage monster's food.

The movie camera was still strapped to Callenbach's waist. The lens was broken into pieces; its body was badly damaged yet the camera was still there. It took me by surprise to see our Japanese friend's reaction. 'May be an interesting film,' he remarked and removed the camera along with the film from the dead body. We could not bear this bizarre yet poignant scene any more. We ought to bury Callenbach but not now; we need to move on.

Was the cave Callenbach mentioned the one in front of us? Located against the big hillock this dark opening drew attention.

We went ahead. From the camp it had seemed quite rocky. But on nearing it we noticed the presence of a few trees between the rocks. We also realized that these phenomenal fruits were available only in this part of the island.

When we reached the cave, David walked forward and hastened to enter it. David can't resist the lure of a cave. In the last few days, any cavern, large or small, that came our way would be visited by David, who would rush inside with a torch and inspect the inside thoroughly. Of course, he was doing this in the lure of a treasure. Did he ever dream that today would be the day he succeeded in his mission? 'Yo ho ho'—this loud announcement by David was typically a pirate's cry. It seems as if the blood running in David's body is not Munroe's but Brandon's!

The reason for this exclamation was absolutely genuine. We're all familiar with the appearance of a pirate's chest. A decorative ancient chest was indeed lying in one corner of the cave. We couldn't figure out from the outside that the cave was so vast. It could easily accommodate a hundred people. It became obvious that the dacoits of Brandon's group had used this cave as their primary habitat.

David was standing in front of the chest looking wide-eyed at the closed lid. He had gone ahead to open the lid but it was as if some unknown power had turned his pair of hands into stones.

Ultimately, Saunders went up and opened the lid and at that instant David once more let out a cry and fell unconscious. Suma, of course, immediately tapped on

the middle of his forehead with the forefinger of his right hand and revived him. But one must also give allowances for David's loss of consciousness. His childhood desire has come to fruition today; the chest was overflowing with seventeenth-century Spanish gold coins. This was Blackhole Brandon's looted wealth!

Meanwhile, yet another discovery stirred our minds. This, too, was a coffer—though much smaller in size. On a copper plate attached to the box one could still read the clearly written name, Dr H. Munroe.

After opening this chest, other than some ancient pieces of clothes and a doctor's paraphernalia, what we found was an immensely valuable item—Hector Munroe's diary. The diary had commenced from the day after his arrival on this island. How Munroe arrived on this island has also been recorded in this diary. Our hunch had not been exactly wrong. The *Conquest* came under the attack of the buccaneers and was scuppered. It was Brandon himself who rescued Munroe and brought him to his ship. Then they set sail for Jamaica. The ship faced a violent storm. Having lost its direction the ship began to flounder. At this point the sailors were struck by an epidemic. After seven days when it arrived near this island, the ship ran aground some reefs. Apart from Brandon and Munroe, thirty-three sailors somehow managed to reach the coast and save themselves. A sailor by the name of Ragland had discovered the blue fruit. Ragland was unwell at that time. After consuming this fruit he regained his health within an hour. Eventually everyone present in this group ate this fruit and magically got cured. Munroe had named the fruit, Ambrosia, that is, nectar. Whether the birds or animals, too, ate this fruit was what worried Munroe. He writes:

'If not any other animal, I certainly know that monkeys eat them judging by their good health and swiftness. And that's not all; these monkeys are not vegetarian, they eat meat. I have seen them catch and eat chameleons and frogs.'

These observations by Munroe were further clarified by what he had to say next. After eating the fruit in his normal healthy state, he writes—

'Today I tasted something divine. The fruit has the potential to create extraordinary appetite. This morning with much relish we ate deer meat. There's no dearth of fruits and vegetables but that doesn't satiate your hunger. Will this amazing fruit remain only within this island? Won't the rest of the world ever get to know about it?'

Later on there's an intimation that as there was no longer any need for a doctor, Brandon was trying to do away with

Munroe. To save himself Munroe was constantly evading him but at the same time, he writes, he can feel that there's no escape from the pirate's clutches. In the meantime there's food crunch that has set in. After exhausting the deer population, the band of Brandon's robbers was now hunting birds and monkeys. They no longer wished to have fruits or vegetables.

The words Munroe had written right at the end of the diary left a deep impact on my mind:

'I don't know if I did the right thing by sending the letter through a bottle. Whether to define this fruit as something heavenly is raising doubts in my mind now. I can clearly see that within these three months all the humans are about to turn into savages. Am I, too, degrading myself into an animal? The state of this eternal good health clubbed with indomitable appetite—is this a good signal for mankind?'

After we finished reading Munroe's diary, we all sat brooding inside the cave. Suddenly it struck me that we must switch on the Telecardioscope once more.

We turned on the machine but received no result. That meant the animal had now reached within the range of a kilometre. At that very instant I detected a certain smell inside the cave which we hadn't sensed earlier. We were sitting at the entrance of the cave so that we could read

Munroe's diary by daylight. But the odour was coming from inside the cave and it grew more and more intense. It meant that there was an entrance to the cave from the rear side as well. The animal was indeed approaching very cautiously because we could not yet hear his footsteps.

There was now a slight noise. A stone fell down. At that very moment with a blood-curdling roar a stone came hurling out from the darkness of the cave and hit Saunders in the head. Letting out a groan, Saunders lost consciousness and fell to the floor of the cave. And then, much to our surprise, David Munroe picked up the double-barrel gun which had slipped from Saunders' hand, and aiming into the darkness fired two shots.

We caught a glimpse of the animal from the thin light which came from outside and heard his heart-wrenching cry. Rising from four feet he got up on two and lifted up his two hairy hands advanced towards us. Before I could take out my Annihilin gun, producing a sharp, whistling sound, a poisonous capsule from the Sumagun pierced the animal's chest and within minutes he lay flat on the floor, lifeless.

For the first time I saw Suma overcome by excitement. He screamed, 'Just try to grasp the special power of this fruit, Shonku. I could fathom this and hence stopped you from eating it. Once you consume this then there's no escape from a violent death or death by starvation. This creature alone having consumed all other beings of this island was starving to death but having had Callenbach as food had once more aroused his desire to live. But now his hunger has died forever.'

After saying this Suma turned the wrist of his left hand towards the animal and when he pressed a button of his wristwatch a strong beam fell on that animal's face.

'Well, whom you now see as a dead being,' said Suma, 'was beyond four hundred years old.'

'Blackhole Brandon!' David Munroe let out a yell that echoed around the cave.

Saunders has regained consciousness. The four of us were staring at the dead creature. This hairy humongous animal can no longer be identified as a human, but when you see the deep hole in the place of the right eye which now looks even deeper in Suma's torchlight, this itself pointed at his original self.

The shots by David Munroe had first injured him and Suma's poisonous capsule had stopped his heartbeat.

Now, my own weapon eliminated this vicious pirate—Shakespeare's contemporary forever from the face of the earth.

A Messenger from Space

22 October

The renowned English astronomer Francis Fielding has been my friend for the past twenty-two years. Although the majority of scientists across the world have almost given up the hope of discovering any indications of the presence of life on any other planets, Fielding has still kept going. He had installed a self-made receiver with a ninety-five-foot diameter in the backyard of his home and carried on sending radio signals based on the mathematical code of 21-centimetre-shortwave frequency year after year, focused on a specific area of the galaxy. It gave me great joy when I received intimation of his success.

Brentwood, 15 October

Dear Shonku

I strongly feel that all my hard work and efforts over the past twelve years are finally bearing fruit! It's not yet time to broadcast this; I'm disclosing this only to you.

I finally received a response to my message yesterday at 1.37 a.m. from some part of the Epsilon Indi constellation. My message consisted of primary numbers and so did their reply. This makes it clear that some planet in that part of the galaxy is inhabited by certain intelligent species who understand the language of our mathematics and are eager to establish contact with us.

This constellation is situated at a distance of ten light years and hence the radio wave would need ten years to reach them. I had sent my first message twelve years ago. In theory their response should have taken another eight years to reach us. The amazing part of the story is that it just took two years. Do we take it that the inhabitants of this alien planet have found a method to transmit interspace messages at a speed faster than a radio wave? Are they far superior to us and ahead of us in civilization?

In any case, there's no point in worrying over this now. I'm giving you this news as you, too, like me, must be remembering the prophecy imparted by the papyrus of Egypt.

Hope you're keeping well. Will keep you informed with any further news.

With best wishes
Francis

Now I must explain about the prophecy of the papyrus mentioned in Francis's letter.

In the three-and-a-half thousand years of ancient Egyptian civilization there has been mention of the rule of numerous kings, and archaeologists who later dug up their graves have unearthed many amazing items. In order to appease the departed souls of the kings, valuable items like jewels, scriptures, garments, utensils were placed inside their mausoleums. Despite sealing the main entrance of these tombs, these items often got looted by thieves. In 1912, when the seal of the main entrance of the young king Tutankhamen's tomb was found intact, there was great excitement amongst the archaeologists. Cairo Museum houses an array of amazing items that were found in the tomb.

Last March, an American millionaire and archaeologist by hobby, Gideon Morgenstern, travelled to Cairo when he came to know that the police had arrested two thieves and recovered priceless ancient Egyptian objects from them. The robbers confessed that they obtained these articles from a mastaba i.e., a tomb. The entrance to this mastaba was hidden behind a limestone rock in Beni Hasan, situated on the north-eastern side of the Nile.

Immediately Morgenstern obtained permission from the government of Egypt and, at his own expense, organized a group of archaeologists who began the task of digging inside the mastaba. He didn't, however, discover anything of much monetary value. What he did find was, however, both peculiar as well as precious. It was a papyrus document.

Papyrus was used to make paper by the ancient Egyptians. The outer fibres of a papyrus plant were peeled away and the cores of the stalk sliced into very thin strips and then pounded till they were as thin as silver foil. Until now, all papyrus documents discovered had been political documents, or descriptions of some historical episode or the narration of a local fable. But after deciphering, this particular papyrus was found to contain a set of oracles. Many of us know of the French astrologer Nostradamus's oracles. Written almost 500 years ago, among the 1000 quatrains written by him, quite a few have turned out to be surprisingly true. The plague and the great fire of London; the beheading of King Louis XVI by guillotine; the rise and fall of Napoleon and Hitler; and the destruction of Hiroshima—all had been predicted by Nostradamus.

The oracles in the Egyptian papyrus, however, are scientific in nature. Perhaps they had been made by the person who was buried in the mausoleum. Well, whoever had predicted these, the information it provides leaves one awestruck. Almost 5000 years ago, the author of the papyrus foresaw the invention of the steam engine, the aeroplane, the telephone and the television. The papyrus also mentions robots, computers, X-rays and ultraviolet rays. The most interesting thing that's mentioned is that our earth is the only planet in the solar system inhabited by intelligent beings, a fact that has been confirmed and verified scientifically very recently. However, the papyrus also says that besides our solar system, there are innumerable solar systems existing in our galaxy or the universe. It mentions that there are other planets inhabited by different types of living beings but that there is just one other planet in the entire universe that contains beings exactly like Homo Sapiens. But they are far more advanced scientifically. Apparently they visit earth every 5000 years and have greatly helped push our own civilization forward. The author of the papyrus said that he himself had met an inhabitant of this alien planet and learned the power of foretelling events from him.

After persuading the officials of the museum, Morgenstern was able to acquire this remarkable papyrus for his own personal collection. And last May in London, at a special conference attended by a select few noted scientists of the world, Morgenstern presented the papyrus and delivered a lecture on its contents. It had been deciphered by the noted Egyptologist Dr Edward Thorneycroft. But the bottom end of this worn-out papyrus was missing. Perhaps the author's name was mentioned there, but it was no longer possible to decipher. Yet, whatever that has been decoded brings out amazing information. Judging by the time frame of the dates and years described here, it seems the writer of this document had met an inhabitant of this other planet about 5000 years ago. Exactly when and at which location they were to meet again was missing.

My old German friend, Wilhelm Crole, and I were present at this gathering. I'm yet to meet a more sceptical fellow. I have lost count of how many times he whispered close to my ears, 'A humbug, fraud, hoaxster . . .' At the end of the lecture he straightaway demanded to see the papyrus. Respecting Crole's reputation, Morgenstern gave in to his demand. I too examined the papyrus very carefully. It seemed like a genuine article.

Now the question is—the radio wave which Fielding has received from the other planet . . . is it the same presence that has been mentioned in this papyrus?

Unless there's some further progress, nothing can be discerned at this point.

26 October

There is an amazing piece of news in today's newspaper.

Gideon Morgenstern has committed suicide.

He had returned to Cairo; the reason is not mentioned in the paper. The report runs thus. Two days after reaching Cairo, Morgenstern complained to the manager of the hotel saying he was having disturbed sleep because every time he woke up he would see a vulture perched on the windowsill, looking straight in his direction. Initially, the manager treated it as a joke but the result wasn't a pleasant one. An angry Morgenstern tried to throttle him. In consideration of the stature of his guest, the manager did not take any step towards him despite such an unconvincing complaint. When advised to shut his windows, Morgenstern said he couldn't sleep with his windows closed due to his asthma. The complaints continued for two days. On the third day, the room boy took coffee to his room and despite pressing the bell a number of times, got no response. So he opened the door with the master key and found the room empty. Morgenstern's suitcase was still there; the bathroom shelf still contained all his toiletries and on the bedside table lay a parcel with a sticker on top and an open letter. The letter consisted of only one line: 'Nekhbet did not let me live.'

Since time immemorial the Egyptians have worshipped various animals, birds and reptiles in the form of gods and goddesses. Jackals, dogs, lions, owls, snakes, falcons, cats— all of them were objects of worship. Nekhbet was their vulture goddess.

After intensive investigations and threats issued to the doorkeeper, it was discovered that Morgenstern had indeed left the hotel on his own. The police opened the packet to look for a clue. It contained the wristwatch Morgenstern had wanted to send to his nephew in New York.

It must be mentioned here that there have been stories of Egyptian tomb diggers dying mysteriously. For example, during the excavation of Tutankhamen's tomb, the chief organizer, Lord Carnarvon, died after a mosquito bit him on the cheek in his hotel room in Cairo; the bite turned septic which led to blood loss and finally turned into pneumonia that proved fatal.

When Carnarvon expired, his pet dog at Hampshire in London is said to have died suddenly at the same time for no apparent reason. Within a couple of months of these twin deaths, eight more people related to the work at this tomb passed away. None of these deaths was normal.

I'm keen to find out where Brian Dexter is now. Dexter is a very young archaeologist as well as a photographer. He had accompanied Morgenstern during his excavation. It was decided that after completing the work in Cairo Dexter would travel to India. About three years ago he had come to India and had contacted me. With the help of my letter written to the government of India's department of archaeology, Dexter was given permission to take photographs of the Harappan civilization in Kalibangan. He had said he would look me up in Giridih when he visits India this time.

28 October
I just received the most exciting news in Fielding's latest letter.

The signal from the galaxy is now distinct and clear and consists more than prime numbers alone.

Fielding is convinced that the planet where the signal is coming from is the same one mentioned in the papyrus. Judging by the frequency in which the signals are now appearing, it is obvious that the living beings from this unknown planet are delighted at establishing contact with the earth.

Like Fielding, I, too, can feel the same excitement running through my veins. But I still wish we could have seen the missing end portion of the papyrus. I'm positive that the missing part will provide information of when and where this alien is to appear on the earth. Yesterday night, I was sitting on a deckchair with my cat, Newton, on my lap, my eyes fixed on the sky. Generally meteor showers are more frequent in October compared to other times of the year; yesterday I witnessed seventeen meteor falls in only ninety minutes and each time the thought of the papyrus crossed my mind.

30 October

An urgent telegram from Fielding—'Come immediately to Cairo—a room has already been booked in your name in Hotel Karnak.'

I let them know that I'll be arriving on 3 November.

But why do I have to visit Cairo?

God alone knows.

4 November

I reached yesterday though the flight was delayed by three hours. I knew that on arrival at the airport I would see both Fielding and Crole but I hadn't anticipated the presence of a third person. It was Brian Dexter. The moment I spotted Brian I could see the strong effect of the Indian sun on his skin; he was a burnished copper! Apparently while at Kalibangan, Brian had received the news of Morgenstern's death. He promptly returned to London for more details, details that disturbed him, though he insists he doesn't believe in any form of curses. He feels that sunstroke or some kind of related sickness in Morgenstern made his mind go awry. During the excavation of the Beni Hasan tomb, Brian had noticed that Morgenstern could barely stand the heat of the sun.

I asked Dexter, 'Was Morgenstern genuinely interested in archaeology?' Brian said, 'Excess of money often fuels various passions. In addition to this, Morgenstern also had a weakness for fame. Amassing wealth is not enough to carve a decent reputation in America these days. Everyone wants to leave a mark of achievement. Perhaps Morgenstern wanted to earn an enviable reputation by financing this archaeological excavation.'

I wanted to ask a few more questions but Fielding suggested that we continue our discussion after reaching the hotel.

After lunch we went to the first-floor veranda of the hotel for coffee. The scene in front of us was a picture of beauty—a blue stream was flowing by; various boats were moored on the jetty; people from all over the world could be seen gathered nearby. Brian produced a big envelope from his camera bag and handed it over to me. 'Just see if this stuff is familiar to you.'

It turned out to be a photograph of the papyrus.

'I had taken a photo of this the minute I got the document,' said Brian. 'Can you spot any difference from the document you had seen in London?'

Indeed there was! The moment I held this document I had noticed the difference. This was the image of a complete papyrus, with the bottom end intact.

Brian explained: 'The condition of the papyrus was very fragile. This rolled-up document had been lying in one corner of the mausoleum for the last 5000 years. I was the first one to obtain it. The moment I got it, I unrolled it, laid it out on the floor, placed heavy stones on all four corners and clicked a few photographs using a flashlight. Morgenstern appropriated it the instant he saw it. I told him to handle it very gently. Though he said yes to my request I could feel that he had no knowledge of the document's true value. He initially went to Thorneycroft. After Thorneycroft deciphered the script, Morgenstern contacted the curator of the Cairo Museum, Mr Abrahim. I remember that it had been a stormy day. Enveloped by a sandstorm the city had become dark. I think the lower portion of the papyrus somehow went missing at that point.'

'Well, Shonku?'

Until now Crole had kept quiet. Yet from the very moment I met him I had noticed a concealed excitement in him. Crole is well adept at hieroglyphics and I could easily gather that he had already decoded the lower part of the document and hence this excitement.

I said, 'In this portion I can see the mention of the astrologer Menefru. Furthermore, about the visitors from the other planet—when and where they'll arrive are also mentioned here.'

Fielding said, 'That's precisely why I asked for you. The new moon is to appear in two days' time. If that astrologer has not made any mistake in his calculations of the year and date—'

I interrupted and said, 'The mention of a comet in this instance makes everything amply clear. If Halley's Comet appears every seventy-six years then it must have appeared exactly 5000 years ago, during 3022 BCE.'

Crole agreed. He sounded greatly excited. 'My calculation also tallies with yours. The papyrus scroll revealed that the astrologer too had talked of a comet when he had met the Wiseman from the other planet. It is possible it was 3022 chiefly because then Egypt was under the rule of Menes, perceived as the beginning of Egyptian Golden Era. Everything's fallen into place, Shonku!'

Dexter said, 'But can one completely rely on this? Can't this shift by a year or two?'

Taking a long drag of his cheroot, Fielding said, 'I feel there's no mistake in this because the day before I arrived here I received a signal from Epsilon Indi. It indicated that during the next new moon their agent will arrive on earth and the exact location of this visit is about 200 kilometres towards the west of here.'

'Which means in the desert?' asked Dexter.

'Isn't that natural?'

'But in which language did you receive this code?' I inquired.

'In the telegraphic code,' said Fielding. 'Morse.'

'That means they have maintained a connection with earth over the last 5000 years?'

'That's not very surprising, Shonku. Remember, their civilization is far more advanced than ours.'

'In that case they may also know English.'

'Nothing is impossible. But it wasn't possible for them to know whether I was an Englishman; hence they used the Morse code.'

'In that case where's the location?' I asked. 'After all, they won't come and meet us in this hotel.'

Fielding smiled and said, 'Of course not. We need to go to Baoyiti—it's 230 kilometres in the south-west direction. There is a road but it cannot be described as a highway. But that shouldn't pose any problem. You have already seen Crole's car.'

Yes, indeed I've seen the car. I had travelled from the airport to this hotel in his car. It's a strange car—almost a mobile hotel. It is also quite sturdy. Crole has coined the term Automotel for his car.

'Dr Thorneycroft is arriving tomorrow morning,' said Fielding. 'He too will join our group.'

I had no knowledge of this. But the eagerness on Thorneycroft's side is justified. After all, it was he who had decoded the papyrus.

'I hope you're carrying your Annihilin with you?' asked Crole.

I assured him that on expeditions like this, I always carry the gun on me. They're all familiar with this amazing pistol that I had invented. However big or powerful a creature, if you aim the gun at him and pull the trigger it will immediately disappear. In total, I have had to use this weapon about ten times when faced with acute danger. Judging by the descriptions of these aliens from the unknown planet in the papyrus, they don't seem to be violent in nature. But as we are clueless about the mission of this present group, where's the harm in a bit of self-defence?

The four of us made a pact that apart from us not a soul was to know about the forthcoming expedition.

When we got up and started moving towards our own rooms, we came across the hotel manager, Mr Nahum, walking towards us. I must mention that it was from this very Karnak Hotel that Mr Morgenstern had disappeared. Mr Nahum informed us that there had been no further news of Mr Morgenstern. Hence, one had to assume that Mr Morgenstern had gone out of the city and committed suicide by jumping into the river Nile.

'I hope no more vultures have been seen since then at the window?' Crole asked with a smirk.

If the gesture of biting one's tongue as an act of abashment had been in vogue in the Egyptian culture, Mr Nahum would have surely done that. But instead he stepped close to us and whispered, 'I've never heard of anyone at all noticing any vultures in and around our hotel. But I can't promise that you won't see any cats or dogs! Ha ha.'

We decided to set out immediately after lunch. We have no idea of what the future holds, but I am really happy to be in Egypt. If you sit quietly for a couple of minutes, the surroundings of the contemporary Egypt fades away, replacing it with ancient Egypt. Added to that is the thrill that aliens from an unknown planet will arrive in the land of Imhotep, Akhenaten, Khufu and Tutankhamen. The very idea is so enchanting.

5 November, 10 a.m.

Two incidents within a gap of a few hours have perturbed us quite a bit. We still haven't got over the shock.

I had decided that I would get up at five in the morning and take a walk by the Nile. It is my longstanding habit of taking a walk by the river Usri in Giridih every morning. In any case I always wake up by 4.30 a.m. But today I didn't wake up as a normal course. There was a sudden loud banging on my door.

In haste I wrapped myself in the purple kimono I had received as a gift in Japan and when I opened the door I found Dexter standing there. His eyes were bulging out, and he was panting as if he had just completed a marathon!

'What's the matter?'

'A snake—there is a snake in my room!'

Uttering these words, he stumbled into my room and flopped on to the sofa. I knew Dexter's room was three rooms away from mine. The other two were staying on the floor above. Hence he had to come to me.

Having reassured Dexter, I left him and ran into the passage. Not a soul could be spotted on the long carpeted corridor decorated in Egyptian patterns. That's not unusual as it was 2.30 a.m. I needed to take action right away.

After taking out the Annihilin pistol from the suitcase I raced towards room number 176. Not that I was fully

convinced of what Dexter said. Yet one should be well prepared for any emergency.

The door of his room was ajar. After entering it I realized that the only difference between my room and his was the painting hanging on the wall.

When I turned my eyes towards the left I spotted the snake. A cobra. It was climbing down the leg of the bed towards the carpet on the floor, half of its body still resting on the bed. Though not as deadly poisonous as its Indian counterpart, it is indeed venomous. In the ancient times this snake was also worshipped as a goddess in Egypt.

With the help of my pistol, in absolute silence, I rendered the snake invisible.

Dexter was still traumatized. For one who had complete scepticism in the curse of Menfru's angry soul, the appearance of this snake has converted him into a firm believer! My mind was telling me something else; therefore I dissolved a drop of my Nervigour (a tonic invented by me to steady the nervous system) in water and gave it to the troubled young archaeologist and patted his back.

This did not fully solve the situation. I took him along with me and only when I showed him there were no snakes in the room did he look relieved.

One would have had a showdown with the manager the next day, but as the snake's body, which was our evidence, had already been annihilated by me, we avoided pursuing the issue. Since we were anyway to leave the hotel that day, I did not broach the topic.

The next incident took place in the Hotel's Pyramid Room during breakfast. Thorneycroft's plane was to arrive at six in the morning and hence he would reach the hotel by 7.30. At 8.00, when we were at breakfast, the manager himself informed us that Thorneycroft had arrived. He was in an ambulance.

While coming out of the airport he had fallen and suffered a head injury. Two Swiss tourists, with the help of the police, had called for an ambulance. There's no doubt that this was a case of a mugging. His wallet containing 300 pounds was missing.

Fortunately the injury was not very serious. One was afraid that he would have to be dropped from our trip but Thorneycroft paid no heed to such a thought. He said he had been expecting something like this. 'I know your cogent mind will not agree to such notions but I fully believe in curses. If you knew ancient Egypt as much as I do, then you too would agree with me.'

5 November, 2.45 p.m.
We will set off in half an hour. In the meantime, another event has taken place and I'll note it down now.

Fifteen minutes ago, Mr Nahum showed me a peculiar thing.

It's a small pocket diary. It's obvious that the diary had got soaked in water. Whatever was written inside has all been washed away; even the printed matter could hardly be read. No doubt remains, however, about the owner of the diary. Attached to a page with a gem clip was a photograph. Despite being discoloured, there was no trouble identifying that person. It was Morgenstern's wife, Miriam. The police had traced it eleven kilometres from Cairo inside a fisherman's hut near the banks of the Nile. The seven-year-old child of a fisherman had found it stuck in mud near the river.

Though Morgenstern's act of suicide was a very irresponsible one, I couldn't help but feel rather compassionate towards him.

There's a knock on my door. This must be Fielding telling us to step out for our rendezvous with the aliens!

5 November, 6.30 p.m.

On our way to Baoyiti, eighty-three kilometres from the south of Cairo, we stopped at a roadside cafe at Al Fayyum for coffee and walnuts.

Thorneycroft is much better now. Dexter looks grim. One has to keep a strict eye on him and he has been told not to go anywhere without us. Crole is cleaning out different parts of his camera. He has three different models of Leica. One of them has a large telephoto lens attached to it. He plans to capture on his camera every incident that will follow, beginning with the arrival of the spaceship. Dexter is openly contemptuous of all those who go ecstatic about 'Unidentified Flying Objects'. He said, 'Many images by people have appeared in numerous newspapers and journals but the hoax becomes apparent because each time the flying object is shown in the form of a disc. Is this convincing? Must they always appear in this shape just because the spaceship belongs to another planet?'

Fielding winked at me and said, 'Suppose our spaceship too resembles a disc?'

'In that case I'll drown all of these cameras including all paraphernalia in the waters of the Nile,' said Crole. 'I haven't come to this land of sand and stone looking for a disc.'

A certain thought had been hovering in my mind for some time; I couldn't help but discuss it now.

'Has it ever crossed your mind that if we journey back to 5000 years, quite a few interesting facts might turn up? We are all aware that the Golden Age of Egypt started 5000 years ago. If we go back 5000 years in time we see that people had already begun venturing into agriculture and were farming their own produce. Five thousand years before this humans were for the first time shaping bones and ivory into weapons, blades for spears; fish-hooks etc. and at the same time were creating paintings inside caves. Thirty thousand years ago we observed that the shape of the human skull

196

had transformed into what we see today. Many chapters of ancient history are still unclear to us, yet what we observed in this pattern of five . . . isn't that quite amazing?'

Everyone agreed with me.

Crole said, 'Perhaps they might have a systematic description of the world's history—right from the arrival of the Homo sapiens to Egypt's Golden Age.'

'It can be a possibility,' said Fielding. 'If they ask what we desire, then I shall ask for that record. After we obtain this, is there a need for anything else?'

Having paid for the coffee and walnuts we left.

Today is a new moon day.

For the rest of our journey we need to look up at the sky.

6 November, 6.30 p.m.

I call myself a scientist as I have a decent flair for various disciplines of science, but I have never claimed to be a specialist in any field. The other four members of this group belong to specialized areas, though they are not equal in age, experience, calibre or reputation. But the fact remains that between Fielding, Crole, Thorneycroft, Dexter and myself right now, no difference can be distinguished. Compared to the Arctic Ocean, is there much of a difference between a local pond or the Ganges?

I'm now trying to recount coherently the series of incidents which took place yesterday.

After coming out of the café at Al Fayyum, we set off in the car, driving through the rocky desert for ten minutes when a horrible event took place. But before I talk about that I must describe in detail the interior design of Crole's 'Automotel'.

In the front of the car, two people can sit next to the driver. Right behind the front seat is a narrow passage. One side comprises a bathroom and a storeroom and on the other is a kitchen and a pantry. After you come out of the passage there are bunks on both sides—upper and lower. If there's an additional passenger he can easily fix up a bed in between the bunks.

Crole was driving the car and I was sitting next to him. Behind us on the lower bunks were Thorneycroft on one and Fielding and Dexter on the other.

We started our journey at 6.45 p.m. There was still some light in the sky at that time. Both sides of the road were lined by sand and stones. Though the area was more or less flat, occasionally we noticed limestone hills or a group of hillocks, some of which were quite high.

All this while, I kept remembering the face of our hotel manager, Mr Nahum, and something began to bother me. His behaviour was far too smooth to be natural; it was as if he were part of some intrigue.

We had just begun to spot a couple of stars in the sky when there came a sudden scream. This was followed by the sound of an explosion that made Crole lose control over the steering wheel, landing the car in a ditch near the road.

Both sounds had come from the rear of the car.

When I ran down the passage and reached the rear I saw Thorneycroft holding a revolver and Dexter standing pale-faced against a door, looking down at the floor. And Fielding, with his face distorted with pain, was sitting on the floor, with some sort of liquid sprayed over his spectacles.

Dexter was staring at yet another cobra, its head smashed. This breed of cobra was different from the one I had encountered the previous night. This cobra is native to Egypt too but it's called a spotting cobra. Instead of striking with his fangs he sprays his victim with poisonous saliva. If not death, then blindness is inevitable. Fielding had escaped thanks to his glasses. And Mr Snake had been killed by Thorneycroft's weapon.

We now stopped the car in order to take care of Fielding. A drop of the poison had touched the corner of his left eye; I applied my Miracurol ointment on that spot.

Matters were now reaching a crisis point. I felt it had nothing to do with any curse whatsoever; somebody was clearly up to some mischief. The snake must have been slipped into the car through the window when we were drinking coffee at that cafe. The one who accomplished this task must have come from Cairo.

When we started our journey dusk was on its way. Baoyiti was another 100 kilometres from here. The map indicated no roads beyond this point but if need be the car could proceed on a flat road.

After driving for another ten minutes we came across both humans as well as animals.

A fifteen-year-old boy was approaching us with a stick in his hand, followed by a herd of donkeys. Spotting our car, he slowed down his pace, raised his hands above his head and began to wave them.

'Eestop, eestop, sahib! Eestop!'

Left with no choice, the road being blocked by the animals, Crole stopped the car.

What was the matter? In the glare of the headlights, the eyes of the boy were shining and the herd of donkeys looked restless.

He signalled us to come out. 'Permit, Sahib, permit.'

That the boy was terribly excited was evident from his heavy breathing and his expression. But surely there could not be a pyramid here?

He gestured towards our left.

'But those are rocks—limestone rocks. Where's a pyramid there?'

Yet the boy repeatedly pointed us in the same direction.

'Crole asked, "Is it behind the hills?"' The boy nodded his head to say that it was indeed so.

I looked at Crole questioningly. Meanwhile the three others had also joined us. I explained everything to them. Fielding said, 'Ask him how far away it is.'

When asked once more, the boy again repeated that it was behind those hillocks. It was pointless to further interrogate him about the distance as I have noticed that farmers all over the world are devoid of any idea about distance. In other words the pyramid could be two kilometres from here or even twenty.

'Here.' Thorneycroft took out some small change from his pocket, handed it over to the boy and patted him on his back, indicating that he should now leave us.

Looking happy the boy continued on his way with his herd chanting, 'Permit permit.'

We drove on. The sky was now dotted with lights but we were yet to spot a moving beam. We were all scanning the horizon; I know that all three pairs of eyes belonging to those sitting at the back were glued to their windows. Only poor Crole couldn't take his eyes off the road.

When we emerged from behind the hills, we did indeed see a pyramid. How far away it was or what size it was could not be fathomed but no doubt was left about its shape. There was certainly a pyramid behind those rocky limestone mounds.

Even if one hasn't seen most Egyptian sites, this much can be understood: this was an unlikely location for a pyramid and for it to emerge out of the blue was not customary either.

Crole suggested that however bad the road was one must go and take a look at it. There were still about eight hours for the spaceship to land.

Cautiously, the Automotel began to proceed towards the pyramid, travelling across sand and uneven road.

After covering another hundred metres or so, I realized the pyramid was much too small as compared to those in the renowned pyramid complex of Egypt. Its height wasn't more than thirty feet.

When we got closer, we noticed that the pyramid was not built of stone but of some metal which gleamed a shade of copper in the Automotel's headlights.

Crole stopped the car and switched off the headlight. All of us stepped out. Fielding began to proceed towards the pyramid.

We followed him.

Crole whispered into my ears, 'Keep your hand on your gun. This may be our spaceship.'

Such a thought had crossed my mind, too. However, though we had been scanning the entire skyline for hours, we hadn't seen the spaceship land.

Fielding paused and raised his arms. I understood why. I too could feel some heat in my body. It was obvious that the heat was emanating from the spaceship.

But why was there such complete silence?

Why was there no light?

Why hadn't we heard any noise of their landing?

Is the heat being generated because they want us to come near them?

But that wasn't so. The heat was now reducing at a remarkable speed.

We once again started moving towards the pyramid, one step at a time. Above us, we could see the galaxy covering the entire sky. The night sky in any desert area is a subject of great wonder to me.

'1-3-7-11-17-23 . . .'

Fielding had started mumbling the prime numbers. In awe we saw countless spots of light appearing on the pyramid. In reality these were small holes—the lights inside the spaceship were being turned on and we could now see those lights through the holes inside the pyramid.

'41-47-53-59 . . .'

It was a human voice but it did not come from any of us. The source was from within the pyramid.

Breathlessly, we watched, listening and trying to comprehend this entire scenario.

Now the voice spoke again:

'After a gap of 5000 years we have once more descended on your planet. Please accept our good wishes.'

Fielding had switched on his cassette player. Dexter and Crole were holding their cameras ready. But nothing worth photographing had happened yet.

More words were spoken in perfect English. The pronunciation was flawless.

'We learnt about the existence of your planet some 65,000 years ago. Then we understood that there was not much difference between your planet and ours. Only after discovering this detail did we journey to your planet for the first time and ever since we have been making trips every 5000 years. Each time we came with the same mission in mind. We wished to push human civilization a bit further. Far beyond the atmosphere of the earth, a satellite of ours has been keeping a close observation over your people for the last 65,000 years. Whenever we visit, we do so only after ascertaining the exact condition of the earth. We do not come to cause any harm. We have no self-interest in mind. We do not want colonization. We come only to solve problems faced by humans and after offering our aid we will return. Modern Homo Sapiens, in a way, are our creation, including the special design of your brain. We have taught you agriculture, architecture, mathematics, astronomy and medical sciences.

'However, we had no control over how man has utilized this knowledge. We never thought it was appropriate to go beyond giving some hints and explaining principles for advancing civilization further. We never taught man the techniques of war, colonization, class difference and superstitions—these are all your own creations. That people are now marching towards destruction is chiefly because they haven't learnt to be selfless. If they were not selfish, then they would have been capable of solving their own problems. What we have come to bestow now will help the human race enhance their lifespan. However, before we explain it further, we would like to know if you have any questions to ask.'

'Yes, we have,' shouted Crole.

'Then please ask.'

'Whether you look like us humans or not is what I'm curious about,' said Crole. 'If the atmosphere of your planet is like ours, then I guess there can be no harm done if one of you steps out.'

Crole was ready with his camera.

The reply came.

'That's not possible.'

'Why?' asked Crole, curious.

'Because this spacecraft contains no living body.'

All five of us were rendered speechless for several seconds.

'There's no living being inside?' asked Fielding 'Does that mean—?'

'Let me explain. Within a single year there was a devastating earthquake followed by a collision with a huge meteor which led to the disappearance of all beings on our planet. Now what is left are a few laboratories and some equipment—one of which is this spaceship. Ten years before this turmoil was to occur, and knowing about its impending arrival, our scientists pre-planned all the arrangements for this expedition to earth. This journey was possible due to instructions delivered by the machineries. I myself am a machine. This is our last journey.'

Now I asked a question.

'May I know the aim of this last journey of yours?'

The voice from inside the pyramid replied: 'We're leaving with you the solutions to four problems. One—the ability to change the weather according to your own free will. Two—the capacity to cleanse the polluted air of a city. Three—instead of electricity, the use of solar power for various activities. Four—the habitation of people on the seabed with a possibility of food production undersea. At the rate in which the population is expanding, in the next 500 years it will no longer be possible for anyone to exist on land . . . Other than these four offers, for the enhancement of human knowledge we are donating you the historical account of the last 65,000 years of human race.'

'Are these solutions and descriptions available in written form?' asked Fielding.

'Yes. But to document this we took help of miniaturization. Since the mishap on our planet seven years ago, our wavelength with the earth has weakened. I hope in these few years you have considerably progressed in the art of miniaturization?'

'Yes, indeed we have!' uttered Crole. 'The calculator which we use for complicated arithmetic is not more than the size of a human palm.'

'Very well. Now notice that a door will open in the spacecraft.'

We saw that about a couple of metres above the ground a triangular door was sliding open along the wall of the pyramid.

The mechanical voice continued:

'Inside the spaceship there's no other furniture apart from a table. You will find some equipment lying there in a transparent box. This contains the solutions to the four challenges and also the history of the human race in the last 65,000 years. Any one of you can enter the spacecraft and take possession of the article. The spacecraft will immediately leave for its return journey thereafter. But mind you, these solutions or remedies are for the benefit of the entire human race. If this object falls into the wrong selfish hands then ...'

The voice stopped.

As we stood rapt, a shadow had appeared from the darkness and rushed into the spaceship. Within seconds it stepped out and disappeared as quickly into the darkness.

And then we saw the triangular door close and the pyramid leave the soil of Egypt with a thunderous screech. All five of us explorers watched dumbfounded as it turned into a square piece of light and then disappeared amidst the countless stars in the galaxy.

All this seemed to happen in a split second. We only came back to our senses when we heard the noise of a car starting and being driven away. The car was not ours. It sounded like a jeep.

'Come along!' Crole's command sounded like a whiplash. He was running towards his Automotel.

Within a minute our car too began to race through the rocky desert.

In which direction had the jeep gone? It had to hit the road at some point.

Suddenly, there was an ear-splitting noise of a collision and Crole's glaring headlights finally picked out the whereabouts of the jeep. The jeep's driver had been driving at a reckless speed without the lights on. As a result it had smashed into a boulder lying on the road.

Crole very carefully drove his car and parked it a metre away from the jeep. All of us stepped out of the Automotel.

The jeep had turned turtle amid the sand and the boulders and beside it lay the blood-spattered dead bodies of two men.

One was a local fellow, probably the driver, and the other—we recognized him in the light of Thorneycroft's torch—was the American tycoon and aspiring archaeologist, Gideon Morgenstern! In an instant the mystery of the snake and the vulture were solved. There was definitely a pact between Nahum, the manager of Karnak Hotel, and Morgenstern. Now it was clear as daylight that Morgenstern's death was not due to the curse of some ancient Egyptian god but a curse showered from a particular planet located in a particular spot in the galaxy.

'What's in his pocket?'

Crole took out a fragile piece of paper from his pocket. Needless to say, it was the missing portion of the Manefru papyrus.

I noticed something else.

A blue light was shining through the fingers of Morgenstern's clenched fist.

Fielding went up and prised his fingers open.

Was this the product that contained the solution to the human race's four major crises along with its 65,000 years of history?

Between the forefinger and thumb of his right hand, Fielding held a shining blue pebble the size of half a pea.

Giridih, 27 November

It speaks volumes of the faith my friends have in me. They felt if anyone could figure out exactly how such an enormous amount of information could be packed within this amazing stone, it was me! For the last two weeks I have run endless research and experiments on this stone in my laboratory, yet I haven't been able to unravel its mysteries. I need some more time as our science hasn't progressed to such a height yet.

At this moment the stone is adorning my right hand, embedded in a ring. And when I go to bed at night, I look at the radiant blue halo that reflects from this celestial gem, inspiring me to always carry on the crusade against human ignorance and superstition.

Nakur Babu and El Dorado

13 June

One event this morning has upset my entire work schedule. The work was no big deal really: I was writing an article for the noted Swedish journal *Cosmos* about my numerous discoveries and inventions. I've never taken on such a task earlier despite several requests from various journals across the world because of the sheer lack of time. In the recent past, however, I've deliberately cut down on my own research. I am beginning to feel that staying in a city like Giridih and working in my own laboratory with limited equipment one cannot produce much work but nowadays I also strongly feel that there's no need for me to produce any more work. I must admit though that in a number of countries, the amazing range of work created by many young scientists using the latest equipment under the aegis of different scientific organizations and universities are indeed commendable.

But for what I have produced with limited monetary support and ordinary equipment, the scientific community of the world has always given me full credit. Yet, at the same time, within this very scientific fraternity there are some who don't recognize me as a scientist at all. To them I'm some sort of magician or witch doctor, that I've mastered the art of mumbo jumbo in order to hoodwink the scientists and earned my reputation merely on such powers. Of course, I've never let this upset me. I'm well aware that I possess the saintly qualities of serenity and temperance. In one word, I'm a very peace-loving person. In the West I've met many learned researchers who, on the least provocation, loudly bang their hands on tables, and when there's no table at hand they thump their hands on their knees. The biochemist Dr Heilbroner, while trying to explain his latest discovery, once slapped my shoulder so hard in excitement that I cried out in pain.

All said and done, I'm being given a good chance to explain one issue in this article—namely, the reason why I haven't allowed my inventions to be used across the world. My justification is very simple. Out of all my products which are most powerful and beneficial for mass consumption— like the Annihilin gun or the Miracurol medicine, the Omniscope, or the Microsonograph or the memory revival instrument, Remembrain—none can be mass-produced in a factory. They are all handmade products and can be created by one and only person. Trilokeshwar Shonku.

This morning, as usual, after completing my morning walk by the river Usri, I returned home, had coffee and went to my study. Just as I had filled ink into my fifty-year-old Waterman fountain pen and was about to start writing, my man Friday, Prahlad, came in and informed me that a gentleman had come to meet me.

'From which country?' I asked. This was a very normal query as eminent personalities from all over the globe have visited me in Giridih. Three weeks back, a world-renowned entomologist, Professor Jablonski from Lithuania, had come here to meet me.

'I did not inquire,' said Prahlad, 'but he is clad in a dhoti and khadi kurta and he spoke with me in Bengali.'

'What did he say?' My attitude might seem unwelcoming but I have to confess that I simply had no time to chat with any Tom, Dick or Harry.

'Well,' Prahlad said, 'he said, "Ask your master if he can take a break from his writing for Kismiss and spare ten minutes for me." He has something to tell you.'

Kismiss? Could he mean *Cosmos*? But how is that possible? Not a soul here knows that I'm writing for *Cosmos*!

I got up from my desk. There would be no peace of mind till I solved this problem of 'Kismiss'.

When I entered the drawing room, I saw a man nervously clutching the folds of his dhoti in his hands and sitting all bundled up in one corner of the sofa. I've yet to come across a more innocuous person than him. Not so much at first glance, but when you look at him again you do notice the distinct quality of the pupils of his eyes: whatever life force the man has seems to be concentrated on his pupils.

'Namaskar, Tilu Babu!' His hands, still holding on to the edges of his dhoti, now reached his chin as he folded them in greeting. 'I apologize for interrupting your *Cosmos* write-up. I've come here with a great desire to exchange a few words with you. And I know you will fulfill my wish.' It was not just the reference to *Cosmos*, but the use of the name Tilu which aroused great curiosity in me. Only my father who, sixty years ago, had called me by this name. As I grew older, the need for a pet name was lost. I was transfixed.

'My name is Shri Nakurchandra Biswas. I live in Makorda (a town very close to Calcutta). For the last few days you have been appearing in front of me. But seeing you like that and in real are not the same thing.'

'What do you mean by I have been appearing before you?' I was forced to ask.

'This phenomenon has started since the last one and a half months. People from distant lands or events taking place in different areas appear before me. At times these events are often not very distinct, yet, I see them. I've heard of your name and have seen your pictures in newspapers. One day, when I was trying to recall your image, you promptly appeared before me.'

'This has been occurring over the last one and a half months?'

'Yes, about a month and a half. One day it was raining heavily and the clouds rumbled. It was in the afternoon. I was sitting on a cot; there were three kittens playing in the courtyard in front of the veranda. As I sat on the veranda enjoying tamarind pickle, I suddenly saw about twenty yards away from behind the tree of Mitra's house something like a fireball rolling in the air. You'll not believe this, Tilu Babu, this ball arrived right before me. It looked like a glowing football. I saw it coming near our tulsi tree in our courtyard; I've no recollection of what happened after this. When I came back to my senses, the rain had stopped. The three kittens were dead. Yet I had remained unscathed. A coral tree and a wood apple tree behind our house were both charred.'

'And the rest of the people in the house?'

'There was no one at home other than my grandmother. My younger brother was in school; he is a primary schoolmaster in Makorda. My mother is no longer alive; my father was playing chess in Nani Ghosh, our neighbour's house. Grandmother was unwell. She was lying down in a room at the rear side of the house. Nothing had happened to her.'

Listening to the description it seemed to me he was talking about 'Ball Lightning'. Once in a while, one gets to hear of this, when electricity appears in the form of a ball which floats in the air momentarily and then explodes. If this electricity passes close to a human and one observes that this person has undergone a distinct change then there's nothing much to be said. One has heard stories of a deaf person beginning to hear after being struck by this ball of lightning and of a blind man's vision being restored. My query was, how powerful was this gentleman's potential?

Before I could begin questioning him further, an answer was suggested to me.

Nakur Babu suddenly began to murmur, '3-8-8-8-9-1-7-1.' I noticed he was looking fixedly at the cover of the American weekly *Time* kept on the table. The image on the cover was that of the American millionaire, Petros Sargsyan. Staring at the picture Nakur Babu continued to speak, 'I can see a trunk in this man's house—on the right side of his bed, made by the Croskey Company—it contains cash—wads of hundred-dollar notes . . .'

'And the number you quoted, what was that?'

'That's the code to open the chest. The lid has a set of wheels around which the numbers 1–9 are carved. The wheel rotates in both directions. When the numbers are matched the chest is unlocked.'

Apprehensively he added, 'Please don't get me wrong, Tilu Babu. Talking about such matters to a busy man like you would amount to wasting your time—'

'Certainly not,' I interrupted him. 'A power like yours is a unique phenomenon. It's a great fortune for a scientist to meet you. All I want to know is—'

'I'll tell you all. You want to know, after I encountered the ball lightning experience what special powers I've acquired, isn't it?'

His deduction was accurate. I answered, 'Exactly so.'

Nakur Babu said, 'Do you know my problem? I don't treat these as "special powers"! A person who laughs or cries or yawns or snores—does he treat these as special powers? It's as normal as breathing. Whatever I'm doing, I don't think of these as special powers. For instance, let's look at your table. Can you tell me what's kept on it?'

Following this gentleman's suggestion I looked at the Kashmiri table kept in one corner of the room.

An object was placed on the table which I had never noticed earlier. It was a brass figurine—though it was not very clear. It was as if the object was vibrating, and the figure looked translucent. As I was looking at it, it disappeared.

'What did you see?'

'The brass figure of a meditating Buddha. But it wasn't solid.'

'That's what I was trying to tell you. I still haven't mastered this exercise. This statue is at present in the drawing room of the lawyer Shibratan Mallik's house. I saw it there once. At this point I imagined it to be present on your table, but it didn't appear entirely.'

I was telling myself no one on earth till now (with the exception of the Chinese magician Chee Ching) has been able to hypnotize me. But to an extent Nakur Babu was successful. This was indeed a kind of hypnotism. This was one of the many powers of Nakur Biswas. Hypnotism, telepathy, clairvoyance—this gentleman seem to be in full possession of all these three qualities.

'I first heard about you from this Shibratan,' said Nakur Babu. 'That's when I thought, why don't I take a trip to Giridih? Because not only do I get to meet you, I can also caution you about something.'

'Caution?'

'Please don't mind, Tilu Babu, and also pardon my impertinence. I'm well aware that you not only belong to India, your fame is known around the world. You are invited from all over the world and you often accept these invites. But in case you accept an invite to visit São Paulo, I request you to be particularly careful.'

São Paulo is Brazil's biggest city. 'Till now I've not received such an invitation,' I said. 'What's happening in São Paulo?'

'Sorry, sir, but I can't tell you anything beyond this. As of now things are still not very clear to me. To be frank, I've no idea where São Paulo is. Out of the blue I saw before me one long white envelope on which your name and address were typed. On one corner of this was a stamp with the mark appearing—"São Paulo"—and immediately my heart trembled. And thereafter I noticed a luxurious room in which a huge, pot-bellied foreigner sat staring at you. I didn't find that man very pleasant.'

Having sensed that he had crossed the limit of ten minutes Nakur Babu tried to get up. I asked him to sit down. I possibly can't let him go without offering him a cup of coffee. Moreover, I needed to know how to contact him in future.

Hesitatingly Nakur Babu sat down. I asked, 'Where are you staying now?'

'I've checked in to Manorama Hotel, sir.'

'For how long will you stay?'

'Till I have accomplished my mission I guess . . .'

'But I must have your address.'

He curled up in embarrassment. In that pose he said, 'I can't believe you're actually asking for my address.'

I had to tell him firmly that his humility was now crossing the limit. I said, 'You ought to know that it'll be a cause of great regret if any scientist after an interaction with you for only ten minutes is unable to keep in touch with you.'

'If you write "Care Of Hargopal Biswas, Makorda", I'll receive the letter. Everyone knows my father there.'

'Suppose you get a chance to travel abroad, will you?'

This question had been hovering in my mind for quite some time. There's a marked tendency amongst scientists abroad to scoff at all supernatural abilities or incidents. It wouldn't be a bad idea to present Mr Nakurchandra Biswas in person before them. I myself do not belong to this group of sceptics. I do not treat this ability of Nakur Babu with disbelief or scorn. We still know very little about the human brain. My grandfather, Botukeshwar, could remember everything he heard. He only had to hear or read an epic only to recall it perfectly. Yet he was also a full-fledged family man and rarely preoccupied with literary or religious activities. Can any scientist abroad be able to explain how this was possible? No, they can't, because they still haven't solved even half the mystery of a human brain.

But when Nakur Babu heard my question he behaved as if I'd said something absurd.

'I, go abroad?' he said, rolling his eyes. 'What're you saying, Tilu Babu? And even if I was inclined to how could I possibly go?'

I said, 'When a conference is organized abroad, many organizations, often send two tickets to the participant and also bear the cost of hospitality. Some take along their wives and some their secretaries. I, of course, always go alone but if you agree to come along—' Nakur Babu all at once got up protesting vehemently.

'That you have given me a thought is a boon for me. I don't wish for anything more.'

I joked, 'However, if ever in your act of clairvoyance you foresee yourself going abroad, then please let me know.'

Nakur Babu seemed to enjoy my joke and picked up the edges of his dhoti as he stood up to leave, saying, 'Please accept my warm regards. And do give my blessings to Newton.'

21 June

I have sent off the article I'd written for *Cosmos*.

So far, I haven't heard from Mr Nakurchandra Biswas. Unless he himself writes to me, how else will I get news of him? At the same time, it won't be right to exhibit too much eagerness from my side. Hence, despite knowing his address I haven't yet contacted him. But in the meantime I've informed two of my friends, Saunders and Crole, about his exceptional powers. They both have shown great eagerness and interest in the topic. Crole said it won't be a problem to raise funds to bring over Mr Nakurchandra for a demonstration. In fact, by making a few appearances on television he may return home with a decent income. I've let them know that the moment I receive any signs of interest from this resident of Makorda I'll inform them.

24 July

Since the last month, in connection with my article, I've received 177 letters from various members of the scientific fraternity. They are all laudatory in nature. One of these comes from the proprietor of a major American Corporation, Solomon Blumegarten. He has let me know that he is ready to buy patents for three of my inventions. For this he is willing to pay me 75,000 dollars. The three inventions are—Annihilin gun, Miracurol pills and the Omniscope instrument. Even though I'd mentioned in my article that these inventions cannot be mass-produced in a factory, Blumegarten is not ready to accept that. He feels that if a human hand can produce anything there's no reason why a machine can't reproduce that very thing. You can't argue on such matters through letters. Hence, I've let them know that purely on personal grounds I'm not ready to sell my patent rights.

I wonder how he reacted when he came to know that even the amount of 75,000 dollars could not tempt me.

17 August

An unexpected letter. Written by Mr Nakurchandra Biswas. The contents as well as the language of the letter are unanticipated. Here's the entire correspondence—

After paying one billion bows at Trilokeshwar Shonku Esquire's feet I humbly beg to say:

Sir
I'm well aware of the fact that you have remembered this worthless creature. Very soon the letter from São Paulo will

arrive in your hands. For obvious reasons you will not be able to refuse this invite. You may recall, you had appealed to me with the request that I could travel abroad with you as your very dutiful servant—as your secretary. At that time I hadn't agreed to that proposal but after returning to my humble abode I've eventually realized that if I am not present in person beside you, you'll find yourself in deep trouble. Since the last few months, having worked tirelessly, I've taught myself shorthand following the method of Pitman. In addition to this, I've read a number of books and acquired basic knowledge of Western etiquette. Therefore, I'll be eternally grateful if you please let me know in a letter your decision about taking me with you as an attendant as soon as possible. You're a subject of pride in India as well as the world. But above everything else you're a son of Bengal. We all pray for a long, healthy and safe life for you.

Yours sincerely,
Shri Nakurchandra Biswas, your obedient servant

Now, my question is—can I trust the reason mentioned for this change of mind to come along with me for a foreign trip? Or is there some intrigue involved? Is this fellow in reality a shady character? Are the emotion and language of the letter mere pretence?

These issues arise chiefly because this fellow is genuinely in possession of such amazing acumen. But there's no point in worrying about this now. To start with, let's see if the invite comes or not at all. Only then can action follow.

3 September

Nakur Babu has amazed me. The invite has arrived. What really surprised me even more is that there's no way I can refuse this offer. São Paulo's famous Butantan Institute is organizing a three-day science conference which as a matter of course will consist of talks, lectures, discussions, etc. In addition to that, on the last day of the conference, the institute will honour me by conferring a doctorate degree on me. Clearly, that article in *Cosmos* is responsible for reviving interest in my achievements once more in the scientific world. The officials of this conference do not just desire my presence, they propose to exhibit a collection of all my inventions, including the relevant documents related to them. In this connection, they stated, the government of India is ready to work in cooperation with the Brazilian embassy in Delhi. The institute has informed me that the hospitality won't be limited to only three days. They'll arrange for another seven days of stay in Brazil so that I can travel around the country properly. They will bear the cost of travel and accommodation for two persons.

I informed them via telegram to confirm my participation. I also added that I'll be accompanied by my secretary, Mr N.C. Biswas.

A letter, of course, has been posted to Makorda. The conference starts on 10 October. I think I'll be able to arrange everything within this one month.

I've also given this news to Saunders and Crole. As renowned scientists, I'm sure both of them will be invited to São Paulo but I thought it was important that I let them know about Nakur Babu. I've also informed them that on this trip we cannot get too involved with Nakur Babu's activities. However, Crole himself is very enthusiastic and an authority on supernatural matters. I'm sure Nakur Babu won't object to offer a few demonstrations for Crole's benefit within the confines of a hotel room.

I don't know if my not-too-distant crisis is for real or not. I've got this sneaky feeing that Nakur Babu could not resist the temptation of a free trip to a foreign land. I've written to him saying that he must arrive at my place at least three days before our journey. I must run a check on his sense of social grace. There's no problem on the issue of language. I think he will somehow manage to communicate in English, and if for some reason he has to speak in Brazil's language—Portuguese—I would be around to help him with that. With my interest in the history of Portuguese in India, from the age of eleven, I'd picked up the language from the local padre in Giridih, Father Robello.

2 October

Nakur Babu has arrived. I noticed quite a remarkable

change in the appearance of this man within the last few months. He said this was a result of yoga. In the meantime he went to Calcutta to get himself two suits tailored, along with a few shirts, ties, shoes and socks. As he had always used a neem twig to brush his teeth, he had to now buy a toothbrush and toothpaste as well. The suitcase which he had brought along apparently belonged to the lawyer, Shibratan Mallik.

'Won't you be visiting the jungles of Brazil?' he asked while having lunch with me. I said, 'They said they'll offer us seven days to see the country. Visiting a forest, I'm sure, will be part of this package.'

'After a search in our Shri Guru Library, I found an old book with pictures of Brazil by Baroda Banerjee. It mentions the forest and tells you that it has a certain breed of snake which is double the length of our python.'

In all, Nakur Babu was in his element. Till now he hasn't shown any signs of his powers. To be frank, he hasn't broached that topic at all.

Both Saunders and Crole have written to say they will be going to São Paulo. Needless to add, they are both very keen to meet Nakur Babu.

10 October, São Paulo, 11.30 p.m.
After attending the first session of the conference followed by a dinner in the house of the chief organizer of the

conference, Professor Rodrigues, I returned to my hotel. This magnificent hotel is located in one corner of the city and beats many famous hotels of the world hollow. All the invitees to the conference are staying in this hotel. I've been allotted a grand and well-furnished suite—number 777. My 'secretary' Nakur Biswas is also staying on the same floor—in a single room, number 712.

Along with the officials, Crole and Saunders too had gone to fetch me from the airport. Right there I introduced Nakur Babu to them. The instant he was introduced to Crole, Nakur Babu looked at him for a few moments and said, 'Alps—Bavarian Alps—1932—you had two young men climbing, climbing—then slipping, slipping, slipping—then—eeks—very sad!'

I saw Crole's jaw fell in shock. Not being able to contain himself any more he loudly blurted out in German: 'My foot had slipped. To save me both Herman and Karl lost their lives!'

When I translated this in Bengali to Nakur Babu, he said in Bengali: 'The scenario emerged right before my eyes. I didn't want to talk about it. What a tragic incident of his life.' Needless to add, I didn't have to say anything to Crole after this. I know Saunders has reservations about the phenomenon of supernatural powers. Initially he didn't comment on this. On our way from the airport he sat next to me in the car and asked, 'Did you know of this incident of Crole's in his youth?'

I shook my head to say, 'No.'

During dinner today, I met Prof. Rodrigues's secretary, Mr Lobo. Most people here have a wheatish complexion and their hair and pupils are black in colour. Mr Lobo too was no exception to this. He was a very sprightly man. He was more or less adept in English and within hours we were getting along very well. I told him that after the conference is over we'd like to venture into the forest of Brazil. 'Of course, of course!' said Mr Lobo, though his tone suggested a slight hesitation. They probably want to show us only modern Brazil. In today's seminar I lectured in English. My secretary has taken down the entire address in shorthand. I know in today's day and age it is much safer and easier to record a lecture on a tape recorder, but as Nakur Babu has taken the effort to learn Pitman's shorthand I thought it best to put that to use.

The exhibition of my inventions along with the necessary documents was also inaugurated today. The items which had hitherto been kept inside my cupboard in Giridih away from the public gaze were suddenly on display in another hemisphere of the world—in the city of Brazil in a public domain. It made me feel strange. To be very frank, it's not that I wasn't afraid, though the Brazil government has arranged for very good security. Armed police were put on duty in front of the exhibition as well as at the main entrance of Butantan Institute. So there was no need to fear.

12 October, 6.30 a.m.

A chain of events took place yesterday.

After lunch, I went out with my foreign friends and my secretary to explore the city. After a bit of shopping we returned to our hotel and Nakur Babu soon retreated to his room. I've noticed that he stays with us only when absolutely necessary. He doesn't linger a minute beyond this. Crole and Saunders, after having coffee with me in my room, also eventually retired. We decided we would meet in the lobby after an hour and proceed together to attend a local music concert.

Brazil's coffee is superb. So I poured another cup for myself but just then the phone rang. After saying 'Hello', a rough voice from the other side asked:

'Is that Professor Shonku?'

I acknowledged my identity.

'This is Solomon Blumegarten.'

I remembered the name. It was the same man who had written to me in Giridih and proposed to buy the patents of three of my inventions.

'Do you recognize me?' he asked.

'Yes, indeed.'

'May I come up to meet you once? I'm calling from the lobby of the hotel.'

The problem with me is that under such circumstances I can never say 'no', though I know talking to him will be of no use. So I decided to ask him to come up.

Wiithin a few minutes he arrived. I don't think I've ever met a man like him. Thank goodness there was no third person present in this room. If there was, he would have burst into laughter seeing this humongous man next to the miniscule me.

It was impossible to talk to him while standing and looking up at him. After the customary handshake I said, 'Please sit down, Mr Blumegarten,'

'Call me Sol.'

A mountain moved away from my sight. He took his seat.

'Call me Sol,' he repeated. 'And I'll call you Shank, if you don't mind.'

Sol and Shank. Solomon and Shonku. Was there really any need to get so familiar? Yet I also know that in such a situation I'd no choice but to say 'yes'. I said, 'Tell me, Sol, what I can do for you?'

'I've already told you in my letter. I've come to offer the same proposal to you. Today I went to see your exhibition. If you don't mind—by concealing these amazing inventions from the entire world—you're being extremely selfish.'

I said, 'Are you that intented in human welfare? I strongly feel you're looking more at the business prospect of these inventions, isn't it?'

Solomon Blumegarten knitted his bushy eyebrows till they almost covered his eyes before returning to normal position.

'I'm a businessman, Shank, so I'll look at the business side—what's so surprising? But not by denying you! I'm ready to give you one hundred thousand dollars for buying the patents of those three inventions. I'm carrying my chequebook with me. If you prefer cash I'm ready to give that too—just that you might have a problem carrying so much cash.'

I shook my head. I repeated what I'd already mentioned in my letter—that none of these inventions can be replicated with the help of a machine.

Blumegarten looked straight at me for a while, gravely suspicious. He then roared.

'I don't believe you.'

'Then what can be done!'

'I can double my price, Shank!'

O dear! How could I convince this man that I was perfectly happy. I need no more money. Even if I get a larger price I won't part with my rights.

He was about to say more when the doorbell rang.

On opening the door I saw that it was my secretary.

'Well.' Sounding hesitant, he walked into my room.— 'Tomorrow morning's programme—?'

After saying these words his glance fell on Blumegarten. Nakur Babu looked embarrassed at having disturbed us. What a strange situation. Many people would feel awkward in the presence of the burly Blumegarten. But Nakur Babu doesn't seem to have lost his bearings; on the other hand, he seemed to have gained something.

'Did you want to know about tomorrow's programme?' I asked him just to ease the situation.

The words that came out of Nakur Babu's mouth were totally irrelevant in the present situation. Not removing his eyes from Blumegarten, in a near whisper, he said, 'El Dorado.' Then he left the room looking bemused.

'Who was that man?' Blumegarten asked the minute I closed the door.

I said, 'My secretary.'

'Why did he mention El Dorado?'

The puzzlement on Blumegarten's face looked a bit unnatural to me. I answered, 'He has read up on South America and therefore to speak of El Dorado is not surprising.'

Who doesn't know the legend of the gold city, El Dorado? In the sixteenth century, the army of Cortés from Spain arrived in South America, defeated the locals in battle and established Spanish rule in this area. Then the Spaniards came to know about El Dorado, the city of gold, from the local tribes and ever since it has attracted avaricious explorers like a magnet. Infatuated by the thought of El Dorado, even Walter Raleigh from England arrived there with a fleet of ships. But El Dorado has always eluded explorers. Be it Peru, Bolivia, Colombia, Brazil, Argentina—El Dorado could not be found in any of these

South American countries. I noticed that Blumegarten seemed transfixed, his eyes focused on the table lamp. So I was compelled to say, 'I need to go out in a while; in case you don't have anything else to say then . . .'

'Indians know magic,' Blumegarten mumbled, ignoring my words.

I smiled and said, 'If that was the case would India suffer such poverty? Even if they know magic they surely do not know the magic to improve their own status.'

'You're one such prime example,' said Blumegarten, jeering. 'A person of that land who refuses to take money even after it is pushed into his hand. That country is bound to remain poor. But . . .'

Blumegarten once more lapsed into silence, looking preoccupied. I too remained helpless; I was unable to find a way to get rid of this man.

'I'm talking of magic chiefly because,' said Blumegarten, 'at the very instant the thought of El Dorado crossed my mind, the name was mentioned by the gentleman. With the chief mission to look for El Dorado, 200 years ago, my forefathers, over three generations journeyed to South America from North America. In my youth I've been here twice. Peru, Bolivia, Guiana, Ecuador, Venezuela—no country was left unsearched. In the end, when I arrived in Brazil and was travelling through a forest I fell so ill that I was compelled to let go of my El Dorado dream and return to my country. While taking this trip to Brazil after so many years I'm constantly thinking of El Dorado and today . . .'

I made no comment. Blumegarten got up. He said, 'I'm staying at the Marina Hotel. If you change your mind please let me know.'

When I told Saunders and Crole about this encounter they were both very annoyed. Saunders said, 'You're absurdly polite. Which is why you have to suffer the impertinence of such people. If he turns up next time, please call us and we'll tackle the situation.'

The next event took place at midnight. When I checked the clock later I realized it was 2.15 a.m. I got up to the sound of the doorbell. In this foreign land who could come to see me at this unearthly hour?

On opening the door I saw the esteemed Mr Nakur Biswas standing there. His face was pale and he looked alarmed.

'Please pardon me, Tilu Babu, but I couldn't help coming.'

I didn't like the look on his face. So I said, 'Do please sit down and then we'll talk.'

After sitting on the sofa he said, 'It has been copied.'

Copied? What had been copied? At the dead of night what was he talking about?

'I don't know the name of the apparatus,' Nakur Babu said. 'But I saw it clearly before my eyes. A box-like object with a light inside it and a glass case on top. A sheet was inserted inside it, and after a knob was turned a copy of that original sheet came out.'

I realized he was talking about a Xerox machine.

'What paper was copied?' I asked.

Nakur Babu was breathing heavily. A panic-stricken look appeared on his face.

'What was printed?' I once more inquired.

Nakur Babu now looked up. He looked frightened.

'All the formulae of your inventions,' Nakur Babu said in a near whisper, eyes wide open.

I couldn't help but laugh.

'You've come to tell me so at this time of the night? How can the formulae come out of the exhibition room? They are—'

'Doesn't cash get stolen from banks? Don't documents get stolen?' Nakur Babu said in a tone of rebuff. 'And this is an in-house person. Why should the security stop such a person?'

'An insider?'

'An in-house person, Tilu Babu. Mr Lobo.'

I felt Nakur Babu was speaking utter rubbish. I inquired, 'Did you see this in your dream?'

'It's no dream!' Nakur Babu said, raising his voice considerably. 'I saw everything vividly about ten minutes ago. Mr Lobo entered with a torch in his hand—using the key he himself opened the exhibition room. The guard was standing still. Lobo went straight towards a particular table—where your papers are kept below a glass case. Opening the top he took out two notebooks. He then went out of the other door, proceeded towards a corridor, climbed up the stairs and entered an office on the first floor. That's where the machine is kept. What's the name of this machine, Tilu Babu?'

'Xerox,' I answered, trying to keep my voice under control. I could not really explain it but I had begun to believe Nakur Babu. But Mr Lobo?

'I'm deeply sorry for disturbing your sleep, Tilu Babu,' he said again in his typical hesitant voice, 'but I couldn't help sharing this news with you. But as I'm present here I'll try my best to see that no harm comes to you. It's such a help if you get to know well in advance what is about to happen. Having arrived at such a new place I was unable to gather my wits. With the result I couldn't come to know of Lobo's action—I could only figure out that you'll face a problem in São Paulo.'

Nakur Babu once again apologized before leaving and I too went back to bed, laden with worries.

Even if I don't possess supernatural powers like Nakur Babu, I can jolly well follow that it's not possible for someone like Lobo to do such a thing of his own free will. There's someone behind him. A wealthy man.

I can think of only one person.

Solomon Blumegarten.

12 October, 11.45 p.m.

Today the Butantan Institute conferred a doctorate degree on me. An engrossing programme, followed by moving speeches by four different scientists across the world, including Prof. Rodrigues, finally wound up with my own vote of thanks. In all, I was very pleased with myself. During today's dinner, thanks to my two friends as well as at Prof. Rodrigues's request, I took a sip of champagne for the first time in my life. This too was an event indeed.

Yesterday, my mind had turned bitter after what I heard from Nakur Babu about Mr Lobo. But today his warm behaviour makes me wonder if Nakur Babu has made a mistake this time. I peeped into the exhibition room to see if all my papers were still intact.

By the time I returned to my hotel it was 11 p.m. But the moment I entered the hotel a scene took me by surprise.

The hotel lobby is well-furnished with many sofas. On one such sofa I saw my secretary, Mr Nakur Babu, sitting with the pot-bellied Solomon Blumegarten on one side and an unknown foreigner on the other side.

The second our eyes met, Nakur Babu got up to greet me with a beaming smile.

'I was conversing with them.'

Blumegarten stood up.

'Congratulations!'

While greeting me, Blumegarten hurt my hand as usual with his hearty handshake but he raised his eyes and said, 'Who have you brought here as your secretary? He is an exceptionally gifted person. Looking straight into my eyes he disclosed all details about my life!'

While I was wondering how these two could have met, Nakur Babu himself gave away the answer.

'When I went to the counter to send a postcard to my friend Jogen Bakshi's son, Kanailal, they were standing behind me. Seeing me, Blumegarten Sahib came forward and introduced himself. He said, that having heard the name of El Dorado on my lips he was curious to find out how much I know about El Dorado. I said—I'm an illiterate man—no education—I had read about El Dorado in a Bengali book. While engrossed in the book the city wrapped in gold appeared before my eyes. But he—'

Nakur Babu had to put a stop to his spiel. Judging by the expressions on both Crole and Saunders's faces it's obvious that they were also eagerly waiting to get all the details. I translated and explained to them what Nakur Babu had said so far. Then all three of us settled down on a sofa nearby and I introduced Blumegarten to my friends. The name of the other foreigner was apparently Mike Hachette. From his behaviour I could gather that he was either Blumegarten's bodyguard or some sort of toady.

This time Blumegarten himself said, 'Your man Biswas is a real wizard. If I hand him over to Myron he'll produce a goldmine out of him overnight, and your man will own a Cadillac in three months' time!'

When asked who this Myron was, Blumegarten raised his eyes and exclaimed, 'Holy smoke!—haven't heard of Myron? Myron Enterprises! There's no other impresario bigger than him. Countless singers, dancers, magicians have all attained success due to the support of Myron Enterprises. Morever, Nakur Babu is a genuinely talented man.'

My head was reeling. At the end of the day Nakur Babu will earn his reputation by exhibiting his supernatural powers on a stage? But that was not to be!

'And he knows where El Dorado is!'

I glanced at Nakur Babu. I wanted to probe this matter further. I said, 'Hey Mister, have you told this sahib that you know where El Dorado is?'

'I've told them whatever I know,' Nakur Babu answered with folded hands looking like a convict on trial. 'I've said that El Dorado is located in Brazil. It's towards the northwest from where we are now. There's a deep forest in the middle of a plateau surrounded by hills. The city is inside this forest. No one knows of this city. There's no human presence. It's a ruined city but when the sun shines even now the gold dazzles. There's a golden gate; a gold pyramid; gold pillars scattered everywhere; even the doors and windows of houses are made of gold. As gold never perishes, everything is still intact. Whatever human presence was there vanished long ago. Once there was a heavy monsoon; soon after the forest was invaded by a deadly insect which led to an epidemic. Please believe me, Tilu Babu, I saw each of these images appearing before my eyes just like a movie.'

After translating this bit to Crole and Saunders I told Blumegarten, 'So finally you now know the whereabouts of El Dorado; now prepare yourself for an expedition there. We're now a bit tired, thus please pardon us. Come along, Nakur Babu.'

The grim expression that appeared on Blumegarten's face would have invoked dread in anyone's mind. I decided to ignore it. Nakur Babu too got up.

The four of us settled in my room. Nakur Babu wanted to retire to his room but I said I needed to talk to him.

After I had apologized to my friends for speaking in Bengali, I told Nakur Babu, 'Look, Mister, I'm telling you this for your own good—the fact that you possess such uncanny power need not be disclosed to one and all. You have had only limited exposure so far. You're not that good at judging people but I can vouch for this: in case you fall into the clutches of Blumegarten that'll be the end of you. I'm requesting you—don't ever do such a thing on a whim without my knowledge.'

Nakur Babu looked thoroughly ashamed. He said, 'Please pardon me, Tilu Babu; I've indeed committed a blunder. As I've never been abroad and being a provincial man . . . perhaps that's how I didn't know where to draw a line. By warning me you've really helped me.'

Nakur Babu left.

Crole puffed his pipe and blowing smoke into the room said thoughtfully, 'In case El Dorado is present in real, don't we too need to see it?'

As I've told you before, Saunders is a staunch sceptic. In a standoffish tone, he said, 'Hey, my dear German scholar, over the past three hundred years countless people have been searching all over Latin America in pursuit of their dream of gold but could find no trace of El Dorado and you're getting provoked by a few words from this gentleman? If this humungous Jew being taken in by this tall talks goes into a jungle and becomes the victim of a jaguar I've no problem with that. But I'm not having any of it. I don't want any kind of change in our chalked out plans. And I believe that Shonku too shares the same view.'

I nodded my head in agreement. Our plan was to catch a flight after breakfast to go to the north, to the city of Brasilia, the capital of Brazil. After staying there for a day we would board a mini plane to go towards the northern part of the Xingu National Park to reach the city of Posto

Diyauyarum. The rest of the journey will be on the river. We will go to Porori village on a boat by the river Xingu. In Porori live the Chukahamai, an ancient tribe of Brazil. Few of them still exist and till recently, they had belonged to the Stone Age. We will be accompanied by a specialist from Brasilia called a sertanista. In the local language, the word means a forest specialist. These sertanistas are very keen to establish relationships with this tribe; among other things they know their language very well.

After leaving Porori we will go further north to see the Von Martius waterfall and then we return to Brasilia and fly back to our own destinations. Our trip should be over within seven days but the government of Brazil is ready to extend their hospitality for another three days.

It was now 11.30 p.m. Both Crole and Saunders got up. That Crole begged to differ became apparent when before leaving he stood in front of the door and said, 'I'm surprised, Shonku! That you cannot make out a person so close to you. The look on the face of your secretary was completely different. When he was describing El Dorado in the lobby, I couldn't take my eyes off him.'

Hearing this, Saunders winked in my direction and gestured with his hand, as if he was holding a glass just to let me know that Crole had had too much champagne in tonight's party.

It's past midnight. The city is quiet. Let me go to bed.

13 October, Hotel Capitol, Brasilia, 2.30 p.m.

We arrived here a couple of hours ago. By 'we' I mean my two friends and I and Mr Lobo. Mr Lobo will stay with us all throughout this trip. At least I have not noticed any lack of courtesy in him.

Inadvertently, one ends up talking about Nakur Babu. In plain words, he has jilted me and it's obvious that it's in the greed for money.

Today in São Paulo my room boy brought me a letter along with my morning coffee. It was in Bengali and the writing was familiar to me. Compared to the previous one I have to admit the language this time was comparatively informal. This is the letter.

Dear Tilu Babu

Please pardon this worthless creature. I couldn't resist the offer of five thousand dollars in hard cash. Over the past four years, my grandmother has been bedridden with an incurable illness. I lost my mother at the age of eight and a half. Ever since, I've been brought up by by grandmother. I heard that this country has come up with a new medicine for this disease. Medicine is very expensive. Thanks to Blumegarten's generosity, I'll have the fortune to return home with this miraculous medicine for her.

This morning we are flying off in Blumegarten's personal helicopter. Our aim is to reach a forest area

situated 300 miles northwest from São Paulo. El Dorado is
located in the midst of this forest. Without my advice and
help, Blumegarten can never reach this destination. Out of
mere compassion I have agreed to give directions. After my
mission is accomplished I'll meet you. I'm aware of your
itinerary.

May God bless you. By God's grace if I am ever of some
use to you I'll be most obliged.

Your humble servant
Shri Nakurchandra Biswas

After inquiring at the hotel reception I found out that
Nakur Babu had indeed left early this morning at 6 a.m.

'Was that pot-bellied man with him?'

'Yes, sir, he was.'

Saunders looked much more annoyed than I was. He
was angry not just with Nakur Babu, but with me too. He
said, 'For people like you and me it's best we stay away
from matters related to the supernatural, spiritual and the
mystical.'

Crole had been looking rather downcast ever since
he heard about Nakur Babu's defection, but for a different
reason. He said, 'If your fellow is saying he will meet us
again then it's clear that El Dorado is not very far from our
destination. In that case why can't we all go there, too?'

Both Saunders and I didn't pay any heed to his remark.

Though Brasilia is Brazil's capital, there's no way you can compare this city to São Paulo. As soon as we arrived at our hotel, we met Mr Heiter, the sertanista i.e. the forest expert who would accompany us. Even though he was quite young, he looked experienced. In addition, his even temper and restrained behaviour marked him as an ideal person to coordinate with tribals. Today Crole asked him about his views on El Dorado. Hearing this question he raised his eyebrows and said, 'In today's day and age we are talking of El Dorado? It has been declared a myth long ago. El Dorado is not just a city; it's also a person. The word Dorado denotes both a city as well as a human figure in Portuguese. The tribals in ancient times used to worship a special person as a symbol of the sun and he was referred to as El Dorado.'

I've never seen someone look as disillusioned as Crole.

Tomorrow morning, our journey begins. What Nakur Babu has done is indeed wrong but I can't help admitting that I'm also responsible for this and this is something I can't deny. It was I who first invited him to come with me.

16 October, 4.30 p.m.
In a well-furnished canoe we have travelled almost thirty-three miles by the river Xingu. Other than the five of us—that is, Crole, Saunders, Lobo, Heiter and I—there are two South American Indian boatmen. Two more boatmen

carrying our luggage and provisions are travelling by another canoe. After choosing a clean patch we have now set up camp by the riverbank. Near the camp we have fixed two hammocks in three trees nearby. Saunders and Crole have occupied two and are currently arguing about the well-known anaconda snakes of Brazil. One gets to know through accounts by travellers that on certain occasions they can acquire huge forms. According to Crole, it's not surprising if they are as long as twenty feet. Saunders is not convinced by this. I must mention that none of us has seen an anaconda other than in a zoo. I've no idea if we will have the fortune to come across one in this trip. Even if it's not to be I'll have no regrets. There's no comparison with the beauty that we have seen in Brazil's jungle, which is replete with creepers, vegetation, insects, birds and animals. Even if the forest is deep and dark there's no dearth of colour. We have observed lantana flower bushes, colourful butterflies and dazzling birds of the parakeet family. While we took the boat ride we were not allowed to touch the water as it's full of the monstrous piranha fish. Yesterday, we spotted the carcass of a crocodile; apart from a portion of his head there's no presence of any flesh; it was all bones. The flesh has gone into the piranha's belly.

Many areas of Brazil have still been unexplored by people from the outside world. During the last few years, however, quite a bit of the forest area has been cleared to add land for cultivation. In addition to this, the Brazilian government continues to create highways by cutting forest land and by flattening mountains with dynamite. On our way here, too, we heard blasts. At midnight, we were all woken up in our camp by an ear-splitting blast. The resonance of the sound was so high that Crole's beer glass broke into pieces. As I had a suspicion in my mind, this morning I asked Heiter if there was any volcano nearby. Heiter only nodded his head solemnly.

17 October, 6 a.m.

A strange incident occurred last night.

To protect myself from mosquitoes and the annoying barracuda flies, I had brought along some cream which I had prepared at Giridih. All three of us had applied it and had gone to sleep by 9.30 p.m. in our respective tents. Though there's nothing like the stillness of the night—the chirping of crickets and the cries of the jaguars can be heard all through the night—one is so tired that one falls asleep in no time. But we were all suddenly awakened by a loud scream.

When both Saunders and I rushed out of our tents I saw that Crole too has come out of his and so had Mr Heiter.

But where was Mr Lobo?

Crole took out his torch and swung the light in different directions till we finally spotted him. Pulling a distorted face we saw him come out, limping towards us from behind a busch twenty yards away. He was crying out the name of Jesus in Portuguese.

Screaming out 'I've been bitten in my leg, I'm no more!' Mr Lobo rushed into Saunders's arms.

There was a spider bite on his right foot. Lobo had gone behind a bush to relieve himself. His gold wristwatch was a bit loose and it had slipped off his hand to the ground. While looking for it with a torch his feet had landed on a spider's den. The bite was definitely poisonous but not lethal. But looking at Lobo's reaction, one wouldn't have thought that.

As I was applying my medicine on his wound with the help of Saunders's torch I suddenly caught Lobo's peculiar expression—it was a strange mix of terror and guilt. He was also looking directly at me.

'What's the matter?' I asked him.

'I've sinned. Please forgive me.' He uttered these words in a grief-stricken voice.

'What sin are you talking about?'

Mr Lobo held my feet with his hands. His lips were quivering; his eyes full of tears.

Both Crole and Saunders stared at him.

'That night,' said Mr Lobo, 'that night after bribing the guard I entered the exhibition hall and took out all your documents and notes. And then . . .'

He was in great pain, yet he seemed desperate to talk to me.

'Then I replaced everything after xeroxing those papers.'

Now I asked him, 'Then?'

'Then I handed over the copies to Mr Blumegarten. He gave me cash . . . loads of cash . . .'

'Enough. Say no more.'

Mr Lobo let out a deep sigh. 'I feel so relieved after confessing. Now I can die in peace.'

'You won't die, Mr Lobo', said Saunders in a dry voice. 'By the bite of this spider you are wounded, but not killed.'

Mr Lobo's wound will definitely heal but the damage he has done to me is irreparable.

Not a word by Shri Nakurchandra was out of place.

Can we then infer then that El Dorado exists for real?

18 October, Hotel Capitol, Brasilia, 10 p.m.

I must write down all about the unexpected, unforgettable ending of our trip to Brazil as we are leaving for our own countries tomorrow morning. I've to admit that Saunders's reasoning and scientific outlook has for the first time received a big blow. He has relented to admit that not all things have scientific explanations. I feel this will be all for the better at the end.

Now let me come to the point.

Yesterday morning, in a canoe, all of us, including the bandaged Lobo, set off for Porori, the area inhabited by the Chukahamai tribe. We needed to travel for fifty kilometres. The more we travelled, the richer the array of trees, fruits, flowers and butterflies appeared. Everything seemed more exciting despite the underlying hint of terror in our expedition to this exhilarating land.

I know both Saunders and Crole share the same opinion. Their eyes were glued to the banks of the river, hoping to spot an anaconda. I had no hope of the same. After covering a few miles, we had to bring our boat to a halt. Three men had appeared on the bank of the river. They waved at Heiter to draw his attention and spoke with him in an unknown language. I know in this community there's a prevalence of a language known as Gay, which Heiter is well familiar with.

After speaking with them, Heiter turned to us. 'They are local Indians. They are forbidding us to visit Porori.'

'Why?' All three of us questioned together.

'They are saying for some reason the Chukaihamas are in a state of great agitation. Yesterday a group of Japanese tourists had gone to Porori. The tribals killed two of them using poisonous spears.'

I know that these prehistoric communities often hunt using spears whose tips are laced with a dangerous poison, kurari.

'Then what's to be done?' I asked.

Heiter said, 'For the moment, let's camp here. You all wait while I go further in a canoe to figure out what's been happening.'

'But can you guess the reason for this sudden aggression?' asked Saunders.

Heiter said, 'My conjecture is that this is related to the blast we heard the day before yesterday. If any natural calamity occurs they treat it as God's curse and go berserk.'

With not much choice we disembarked from the canoe.

I could clearly see that this was not quite the ideal place for camping. In general, up to a point near any river the forest remains thick. If one proceeds further it starts thinning. But in this region even if you look further you see no signs of the forest growing sparse.

Around twenty yards from the river we found a comparatively open space and decided to rest there. As we had no idea about how long we needed to wait, we decided to set up camp, keeping Lobo's condition in mind. Despite signs of recuperation at regular intervals, he was sounding delirious, muttering the names of Jesus and Mother Mary. Perhaps he assumes after we return to the city we will lodge a complaint against him. He was not all wrong because even if I'm prepared to pardon him, both Crole and Saunders are determined to chop off his head. And if they find Blumegarten they will boil his flesh, look out for a cannibalistic tribal in Brazil and invite them for a gala feast. They feel his meat will feed twelve people.

All three of us were exhausted. After hanging some hammocks on the trees in the clearing we were gently swinging in them while occasionally listening to the hoarse calls of churiyangi birds when suddenly Saunders exclaimed in surprise. The two boatmen present with us also let out a shriek.

Ten to twelve yards away from us, a snake slithered down from a top branch of a huge tree directly moving towards us. I don't think I've read such a description of a snake away from fairy tales or myths.

I know the name of this snake but under normal circumstances, out of sheer, wonder the name, as a reflex, would have come out my mouth. But in reality there was then no question of using my voice. Terror coupled with dizziness had gripped me, a feeling which I later found out had been experienced by both Crole and Saunders as well.

This humongous anaconda was climbing down from a height of twenty feet and was about to touch the ground even while the other half of him still rested on the tree. Which means his length was not less than sixty feet and the width was such that a person cannot hold him with even both hands.

While I was trying to figure out how much of my feelings were awe and how much fear, a familiar voice sounded, and the anaconda disappeared in front of our eyes.

'Hope your curiosity is now fulfilled?'

We had no idea when a canoe had appeared behind us from which Shri Nakurchandra had disembarked.

'Let me introduce you,' Nakur Babu said, coming towards us and pointing in the direction of a gentleman.

'This is Mr Blumegarten's pilot, Mr Joe Hopgood. He brought me here in his boss's helicopter. We had to take a boat ride for the last one and a half miles.'

Crole was unable to remain quiet any more. 'He made us see that snake!'

I said, 'I did tell you I got an idea of his power while I was in India.'

'But this is incredible!'

Nakur Babu blushed in embarrassment. He said, 'Tilu Babu, please explain to them that I can't take any credit for it. The entire credit goes to—someone's divine intervention.'

'But El Dorado?'

'I've already shown that to the gentleman from the helicopter. I showed it to him just as I showed you the snake. There were a few pictures drawn by Madan Pal in Baroda Banerjee's book. These were pictures of snakes, El Dorado and the works. The pictures are dull and boring. The images of the gold houses looked warped and crooked. That man saw El Dorado just like these images and said, "El Dorado is breathtaking."'

We were enthralled listening to Nakur Babu. 'And then?'

'What was to follow? The city was amidst the forest. How can a helicopter land there? We landed on this side of the forest. Master went inside the forest along with his two armed security guards and as promised I came here to meet you. I know what you're thinking—how did Mr Hopgood agree to bring me here? Isn't it? An agreement was made with Mr Blumegarten that the moment he gets to see El Dorado in real, he'll hand over 5000 dollars in cash to me. I'd told Hopgood that I'll give him 2500 dollars if he takes me to meet you here. Just see how he has kept his promise— what a generous heart he has! Moreover, Blumegarten had also promised that once he gets to see El Dorado he'll return your documents. Here are those papers.'

Nakur Babu took out a fat bundle of papers from his coat pocket and handed them over to me. I was so stunned that I remained speechless. The next question was put forth by Crole.

'But when Blumegarten realizes that there's no El Dorado in real, then what?

Hearing this, Nakur Babu let out a hearty laughter which made a few macaws fly off the trees nearby. 'But where's Blumegarten? Is he still alive? He entered the forest at 5.30 p.m. Six hours later at 11.33 p.m., due to a meteor fall an entire forest measuring an area of three and a half miles simply vanished. I had foreseen this whole event thanks to your blessings, Tilu Babu! I am also grateful that I have enjoyed the company of someone of your stature. Moreover, thanks to you, I could purchase an expensive medicine for my grandmother, but how can I let this enemy live?

After arriving in Brasilia, I noticed that half of the front page of the newspaper was devoted to this news—in a deep forest in Cuiabá, thirty kilometres from the south of the Santiam Highway, there was reported the apparent fall of a meteor weighing twenty lakh tonnes. Fortunately, this area was devoid of any human habitation. The presence of any flora and fauna has apparently vanished into oblivion.

Shonku's Expedition to the Congo

Dear Shonku

One person in our group is down with kala-azar (black fever) and therefore I'm sending him off to Nairobi. This letter is being sent via him and he will arrange to post it. After reading this letter you'll understand why I'm writing to you. I couldn't help but give you this news. Not all will believe this, let alone the scientists. You have an open mind; you have encountered many varied experiences. Hence I can confide only in you.

Are you familiar with the word Mokèlé-mbèmbé? Perhaps not, since I personally heard of it only after reaching the Congo. The locals say Mokèlé-mbèmbé is a humongous creature. The description suggests it to be an animal from the prehistoric era. Apparently it has been spotted in a forest in Congo. When I first heard of it, naturally my curiosity was aroused. But even after staying here for a couple of months, when I could not spot it, I did not give the matter any further thought. Three days ago I came across a monstrous-sized footprint on the banks of the river Lipu. This footprint is not the print of any animal known to us. The size of the print suggests the body to be huge, certainly as large as an elephant. But I still haven't seen the real animal. Hopefully I'll get to see it in the near future. If so, I'll let you know.

I'm now staying next to the Virunga mountain range north-east of the Congo forest. I feel no one from the civilized world has stepped into this region before. I strongly feel your absence. If possible do come over to this place. It is beyond me to describe the beauty of this ancient forest. Perhaps your poet, Tagore, could. Geetanjali *is still my constant companion.*

I'm yet to trace that Italian group. The locals say they must have turned into prey for this Mokèlé-mbèmbé.

Hope you're doing well. May God bless you.

Chris McPherson

I met the geologist and mineralogist Chris McPherson three years ago in London. At that time I was holidaying as a guest at my friend Jeremy Saunders's house in Sussex. After fixing up an appointment over the telephone, McPherson came to meet me carrying a first-edition copy of *Geetanjali*. The book had been signed by Tagore himself. McPherson's father was a schoolteacher. He had got it autographed by the poet. The father's devotion to Tagore now runs in the son. I bought him three more books by Tagore.

After returning to my country, I've occasionally received letters from him. He had informed me about his trip to Congo. Last year, when the Italian group under Prof. Santini's guidance had gone missing in the forests of Congo, I fear the team under McPherson must have faced the same fate. I haven't heard from McPherson since I received this letter four months ago. The International Geographic Foundation under whose sponsorship this group had gone to Congo haven't heard from them either. Yet through radio contact they had been in touch with each other.

Three expedition groups are known to have vanished from the jungles of Congo. Two years ago a group from Germany disappeared. I knew some of the people in that group. I had met the leader of that group, Professor Karl Haimendorf, seven years ago. He was a multifaceted scientist, simultaneously excelling as a geologist, physicist and linguist as well as being a daring explorer. Even at the age of sixty-five, he had possessed extraordinary physical strength. I remember attending a science conference where, due to a clash of opinion, Haimendorf had cracked the chin of a colleague of his with just one blow.

His group consisted of three more members. Of these, I'm familiar with the work of the noted professor in the field of electronics, Professor Ehrlich, and the inventor and physicist Rudolf Gouws. I've never met the fourth man, the engineer Gottfried Helmsman.

This group too had gone missing within four months of their arrival in the Congo.

Ever since receiving this letter from McPherson, my mind has been fascinated by the primitive forests of Congo. One wonders what mysteries that forest holds! In fact, how true is the reality of Mokèlé-mbèmbé? Dinosaurs had reigned in our habitat 150 crore years ago, yet within the last 70 crore years this breed had simply vanished from the earth. Till now scientists have not come up with any valid reason for their disappearance. Both varieties had existed—carnivores as well as herbivores. Do they still exist in some unexplored part of this world? Suppose they still exist within the forests of Congo? Would it be a very unreasonable act to go to Congo in order to search for them?

Fifteen days ago, I wrote to two of my friends, Saunders and Crole, suggesting a trip to Congo. The chief mission of the journey would be to look for McPherson's group. Saunders informed me that he knew the chief of the International Geographic Foundation, Lord Cunningham, very well. It would be easier if the foundation sponsored this trip. Saunders is extremely keen on this expedition.

That Crole would be equally enthusiastic is something I could predict very well. The richness of the Congo remains unmatched to any other region of the world, in its range of animals as well as minerals. On one hand there are elephants, hippos, lions, gorillas, chimpanzees; and on the other hand there's huge mineral wealth in gold; diamond, uranium, radium, cobalt, platinum, copper. But Crole's intention was not just this. For quite some time he has been inclined towards the supernatural. He is familiar with hocus-pocus, mumbo jumbo and the magical practices of various countries. He has even come with me to Tibet to pursue his interest in these matters. Since the last one year he has taught himself the art of hypnotism and attained mastery in it. As Africa is a rich storehouse of such matters, it's natural for Crole to be so enthusiastic.

Or, in other words, all three of us are more than eager to go on this trip. We're awaiting the decision of the International Geographic Foundation. There's no reason for the organization not to offer us the sponsorship as our chief mission is to look for McPherson and his group.

21 April

Good news. I've received a telegram today. The International Geographic Foundation has agreed to bear all costs of our expedition. Saunders has done wonders. We have decided to set off by the first week of May.

29 April

Another person has joined our group. Actually not one, but two. David Munroe and his Great Dane, Rocket.

I have already recounted the adventures we all faced when accompanied by David Munroe and his dog, when we went to what we call Munroe Island, in search of Hector Munroe, one of David's ancestors. David is a sensitive young man but crazy about adventure. He is extremely well read and in addition to this, even if not too easily noticeable, he is courageous and a physically strong man. When he heard about the expedition from Saunders, he immediately let him know that he was keen to accompany us to the Congo. It appears that he is very knowledgeable about the subject of Africa's forests—in particular, Congo's tropical rainforest. He says if we don't take him with us, his life will be in vain. I saw no reason to reject him.

We are all assembling in Nairobi. It's there that we'll decide on our itinerary.

7 May

This morning we arrived in Nairobi. There are certainly no signs of the ancient African civilization near and around the hotel we are staying at.

It's a neat, tidy and flourishing modern city. The habitat, architecture, roads, shops—all strongly bear the influence of the western world. Yet I know that within five miles of the city there stretches the wilderness—which they refer to here as the savannah—where a wide variety of animals roam freely. On the south of the savannah stands the snow-capped Mount Kilimanjaro.

Now I must introduce Jim Mahoney. In appearance—with his thoroughly tanned face and a lean, wiry and straight figure—this forty-five-year-old son of Ireland is a typical White Hunter. In order to conduct an expedition into these African forests one can't do without the help of a hunter. The hunters are knowledgeable about local languages and dialects; they understand the nature and the environs of the forests; and only they know the ways to save themselves from the attacks by ferocious animals. It was also Mahoney who arranged for the six Kikuyu tribal coolies to carry our luggage and other supplies needed for the expedition.

We met him over coffee at the hotel. When we asked Mahoney about the disappearance of the three groups of explorers, puffing at his pipe and exhaling smoke, he said, 'What can I say about the number of dangers hiding inside a Congo forest? Adjacent to the forest lies a series of volcanoes towards the east. Mukenku, Mukubu, Kanagoraui. Beyond Rwanda, after crossing Kivu, the forests appear adjacent to these volcanoes. In the recent past, no one's heard of an eruption but you never know when they might explode. Moreover, numerous cannibals inhabit these regions. One must also consider the usual dangers associated with a forest. Not just ferocious animals, but fatal diseases too lurk in Congo's forests.

The point is, everything depends on exactly where you intend to go.'

Saunders replied, 'One member of the lost group we're trying to trace was afflicted with kala-azar four months ago and was admitted in a hospital here. In due course, he recovered and returned. But we found out from the hospital officials that the group was moving in the north-east direction alongside the Mukenku volcano.'

'Would you like to go in that direction?'

'Wouldn't that be wise?'

'Well . . . to reach that spot you need to walk for almost 150 miles as the helicopter can't go there. It won't find a flat surface to land. The Geographic Foundation has provided us with two big helicopters. We'll travel in one and the other will be used by the porters with the luggage.'

David had been looking restless for a while. Now, he broke in with a question.

'Do you know of Mokèlé-mbèmbé?'

Much to our surprise Mahoney burst into a loud guffaw.

'Where have you heard this story?'

I couldn't help but mention that in the recent past I'd read about this humongous animal in a number of journals on Congo.

'These are all tall tales. Don't pay any heed to those,' said Mahoney. 'There's no sure estimate of how many thousands of years old these mythical creatures are. I've known this forest for the past twenty-seven years and I've never spotted any animal other than the familiar ones.'

Munroe persisted. 'But I've read its description in an eighteenth-century diary written by a French padre in the British Museum. The explorers he was accompanying had located huge footprints in African jungles. These were as big as an elephant's footprint but did not belong to an elephant.'

'You'll hear of many such creatures,' said Mahoney. 'Have you heard of kakundakari? Just as there's the illusory yeti or snowman in the Himalayas, there's also the legend of the kakundakari in the African jungles. It's supposed to be a furry biped, bigger than a gorilla. I have been hearing of this creature since I started hunting here but in the last twenty-seven years I have never known if anyone's come across it, ever. But yes—there is an object which is supposed to be found in these areas but one is still unaware of its exact location—I'm in possession of such an object.'

Mahoney put his hand into his trouser pocket and fished out something which he placed next to the coffee cup on the table. It was a transparent stone which could easily fit into the palm of your hand.

'Please observe those blue veins,' remarked Mahoney.

'Is it a blue diamond?' I asked.

'Yes,' replied Mahoney, 'almost 700 carats. This was found in one of these jungles. Possibly some place in the same direction where we'll be heading soon. I was once feasting with a pygmy family and one of them showed it to me. In exchange for two cigarette packets he gave it to me.'

'But it deserves an exorbitant price,' Munroe said with great admiration, taking the stone in his hand.

I said, 'Not quite. As a gem, a blue diamond is not so expensive. But I've read somewhere that in the field of electronics its demand has risen considerably.'

We all took turns at examining the stone before handing it back to Mahoney.

8 May, 10.30 p.m.

On the border where the primitive forests of Congo begin, in a somewhat open space, we set up our camp. Our tents are made out of my own invented plastic—'Shankalan'—light yet strong. There are five tents in all. Three of these are being shared by the five of us. David and I are in one; Crole and Saunders in the second and Jim Mahoney in the third. The other two are being shared by the porters. I'm writing sitting inside a mosquito net. The mosquito menace is perennial. Since I always carry my creation which kills all ailments—Miracurol—I've no fear of any disease. We'll enter the real forest tomorrow. But let me note down the events of today.

At 8 a.m. we left Nairobi in a helicopter. After crossing Kenya we arrived in Rwanda and landed in Rwamagana airfield for refuelling. Thereafter, we left Kivu Lake behind us and after flying for another half an hour we landed in an open space and began to walk northwards. From the sky above we had seen this deep forest akin to a dark green carpet spread west and northward. The horizon showed the greenery to be absolutely dense. The area of the tropical rainforest is spread across 2000 miles. The civilized world is yet to invade many parts of this forest.

After dropping us off, the helicopter departed. We'll stay connected to Nairobi via radio. After our expedition is over the helicopter will once more return to take us back. We have a stock of food and basic supplies for a month.

From where we got off, if you look northwards, the erect peaks of the volcanoes can be spotted above the trees and foliage. It's the habitat of the mountain gorillas. At present we are in a valley, about 1000 feet above sea level. Here one finds elephants, hippos, leopards, several breeds of monkeys, okapi and pangolin and members of the reptile family like crocodiles. Several narrow rivers flow through this forest but the current is so fast it's dangerous to navigate them. Hence, there's no choice but to walk.

After having a snack of tea and biscuits, we set off at 10.30 a.m. We needed to proceed towards the north. We had to scale a mountain and then climb down to enter the denser part of the forest. The forest is not that thick; we could see the sky occasionally through the leaves. Among the trees here are mahogany, teak, ebony and sporadically one can see some bamboo groves and creepers. We were prepared to face the sudden appearance of any ferocious animal. Mahoney has a double-barrel gun with him; Crole and the leader among the porters, Kahindi, are both carrying a rifle each. Kahindi is such a pleasant man. He speaks in broken English though his native language is Swahili. It was a matter of great surprise to him when he heard I knew Swahili. This language is indeed very interesting. They say, 'Chai taiyari', which means the tea is ready. Like in Bengali, many words from Arabic, Persian, Hindi and Portuguese have been absorbed into the Swahili lexicon.

We were all walking single file, led by Mahoney. We all seem to share a suppressed excitement. I don't know anyone in that Italian group which has gone missing. But Crole knew Haimendorf very well and Saunders and Chris McPherson have been friends for a very long time. It's only Munroe who knows no one except us, yet his excitement exceeds ours. Added to the feeling of adventure, we are walking down the same path traversed by the great explorers Livingston, Henry Morton Stanley and Mungo Park, a fact that is thrilling him to no end. He has mentioned this to us a number of times.

I must tell you about his dog. When I first saw Rocket, I had found him to be an amazingly well-trained dog. But this time I find his level of intelligence as well as his discipline much superior. Not that we can't locate any animals at all—we're often spotting monkeys hanging from branches of trees—but Rocket is completely indifferent to this. Even if his gaze moves in that direction, he never veers from the path.

After walking for a couple of hours, Mahoney stopped, raised his right hand and asked us to stop too. Along with the porters we all paused in our tracks. Only Kahindi came forward and stood beside Mahoney.

There was a bit of an open space ahead of us and about fifty yards away we could see smoke billowing from behind the bushes and trees towards the sky. Between the trees one could also see movements of some life. Not of animals but of humans.

'Kigani cannibals,' whispered Mahoney. 'Take cover behind the trees.'

When I heard a clicking sound, I realized Mahoney had released the safety catch of his gun. Kahindi too was ready with his pistol. I didn't turn to see what Crole was doing. We all spread out and stood behind the tree trunks. There was no sound other than the noise made by the crickets.

We stood in this position for ten minutes. The spiralling smoke gradually vanished. Was something about to happen?

Yes, something did happen. Several dark-skinned men emerged from behind the bushes and trees. They carried bows and arrows, their bodies were painted with white stripes, and the faces, other than the eye sockets and the lips, sported a thick layer of white paint. It looked as if a skull had been placed over a body. Glancing at David on my right I saw him trembling but looking agog at this group. It was easy to comprehend that the trembling was not out of fear but thrill.

The cannibals were proceeding in our direction. I noticed that Mahoney's gun was still lowered. And so was Kahindi's.

The cannibals noticed both of them and stopped.

Then their gaze spread out in different directions. They had seen us too. The tree trunks we were standing behind were not broad enough to conceal us completely.

It was as if the entire forest was waiting with bated breath. I could hear my own heartbeat.

After staying in this position for about a whole minute, the cannibal group walked past us and, in their own slow, rhythmic motion, vanished into the forest.

David Munroe was the first one to open his mouth. 'But they didn't eat us!'

Mahoney laughed. 'Why must they eat you? If your stomach is full and someone offers you a plate of meat would you eat it?'

'Did they come here after eating?'

'That's what I think.'

'Human flesh?'

'This can be validated only when we proceed further.'

We resumed our journey once more. After passing through some more bushes and trees we once again came across an open space. On our left was a thatched hut. Mahoney said this was a farmer's hut. We had noticed some cornfields while coming here. But it was obvious that this hut was now devoid of any human presence.

'Look at this.' Mahoney pointed to the ground with his finger.

Next to an extinguished fire lay a few bones; needless to add, these were human bones.

'We have left behind the habitat of Kiganis,' Mahoney said. 'They had come out to gather food.'

'Such uncivilized culture still exists in Africa?' queried Saunders.

Mahoney replied, 'The government did try to reform them but it wasn't totally successful. But I'm not ready to call them uncivilized. Perhaps I can reword it by saying that their eating habits are somewhat different from normal people. Cannibalism is present amongst many animals. And I've heard that human meat is very tasty and nutritious. It's just that they mark themselves by painting their faces. The notion of nefariousness associated with them is completely wrong. They know how to laugh, how to enjoy, and they help each other.'

In the evening we located a suitable spot to camp. After this nothing worth recording happened. Tomorrow we will walk by the foothill of the Mukenku volcano and then enter the deep forest.

9 May, 9 p.m.

Due to incessant rain we spent the whole day inside the camp. In the evening when the rain had stopped for a moment, a group of Bantus appeared near our camp. This particular tribe is scattered all over the forests of the Congo. A witch doctor also accompanied this group. With the help of Mahoney, Crole exchanged a few words with them. African witch doctors often take on the role of fortune tellers. Dr Witch has warned us that we will soon confront acute danger. We should never trust a red person. We will come out of this danger through a ball resembling the colour of a new moon. For our good luck, Dr Witch has left strands of elephant hair for us, which we had to twirl these round our wrists.

Crole has spent the entire evening trying to decode the words imparted by the witch doctor.

10 May, 10 p.m.

Today I'm in a state of deep misery.

We have found proof to show that Chris McPherson is no more in this world. Today was an eventful as well as a fearful day. I'll try to put everything down cogently. I still can't fathom the strange terrain we have landed in. I can see signs of restiveness among our Kikuyu porters. What if they abandon us? Kahindi has tried hard to pacify them. Hope this works.

Today was a clear day. So we set off early in the morning and reached the foothills of Mount Mukenko. The presence of volcanic ash in the soil marks the history of past volcanic eruptions. It's apparent that these volcanoes have erupted several times.

After climbing six-and-a-half thousand feet up all along the mountain, we lunched on tinned meat, cheese, bread and coffee around 3 p.m.

The ancient forest of Congo was spread out right below us. I'd never seen such an array of greenery. It was not hot at these altitudes but one knew that once we descended the slopes the temperature would increase and so would the humidity. It was quite cloudy and we did face sporadic rain on our way.

After climbing down a few thousand feet, we finally noticed a gorilla group. About twenty yards away on the right side of our pathway we saw around ten young and old gorillas huddled among the branches of trees. I've had the fortune to see gorillas in their natural surroundings earlier too yet I could not help but stop with the others to look at them.

The revolver held in Crole's hand was rising but when Mahoney noticed this, he rebuked him in whispered tones.

'Have you lost your senses? Are you planning to kill all of them with that one gun? Please put it down.'

Crole's hand came down.

The gorillas were watching us intently. One of them—perhaps their leader—left the group and came towards us, stood erect and began to beat his chest intensely with both hands, creating sound similar to drumbeats. This could be easily decoded—this is our territory, do not come in this direction. We all know that gorillas apropos of nothing will never attack a human.

But so what if we knew this, the dog didn't! Rocket was hell-bent on charging at the gorillas. Letting out a loud bark, he leaped. His chain was in David's hands but due to the dog's sudden dive, the young man almost lost his balance and fell on the ground. A dreadful incident followed. The gorilla ground his teeth, let out a sharp cry and came charging at us.

In moments of crisis my nerves and the reflex of my body work automatically. Before any of the three guns carried by the members of our group could be raised, at lightning speed I took out the Annihilin gun from my pocket and, aiming at the gorilla, I pressed the trigger. In an instant the animal disappeared.

Mahoney or Kahindi did not know about my unique invention. Therefore it was no surprise to see them standing there, mouths wide open in shock.

'Whoa—what did you do?' Mahoney asked, stupefied.

The reply came from Crole.

'This is one of Professor Shonku's many amazing inventions. A machine for mere self-defence.'

With a glazed look still on his face, Mahoney nodded in my direction. I said, 'I don't think the other gorillas will trouble us any more. Let's proceed.'

Without saying a word Mahoney took my hand in both of his and shook it with great respect. We continued our journey.

Needless to add, the act of climbing down was much faster than going up. After reaching the valley, we entered the dense forest at around 4.30 p.m.

This primeval forest was a completely different world to us. You're taken in by surprise the moment you step in. You can never ever forget its ambience. The girth of each tree is well beyond 50–60 feet and they tower majestically at 100–150 feet. When you look up you cannot see the sky. When you see these surroundings you experience a feeling of great reverence, just the way you react when you enter a medieval cathedral. The most interesting thing, however, is that despite the wide variety of creepers you can hardly see any weeds. The ground was clear, so we faced no difficulty in walking.

Mahoney said, 'As we don't have any specified destination to follow let's move in any one direction. At the same time we need to be alert about watching any signs about the missing group.'

The ground was not even, and there was a slope at one angle. We were still walking along the edges of the volcano. It was a riot of colour despite the darkness: a wide range of butterflies were flying around, flowers too grew in profusion and at regular intervals strange birds of the parakeet family could be spotted flying from tree to tree, calling to each other.

Meanwhile, Rocket began to bark once more. He was pulling at his chain, which was in David's hands. The dog seemed very keen to go in one particular direction.

We came to a halt. David's 'Stop it Rocket' produced no result. The dog dragged David behind a huge trunk surrounded by liana creepers.

On following the dog, we realized the reason for his agitation.

A dead body was lying on the roots spread around the tree. A substantial portion of his flesh had been eaten by some animal but it couldn't be ascertained whether the death took place due to the animal attack. It was not difficult to see that the body didn't belong to any tribal, judging by the shoes worn and the wristwatch strapped on his hand.

'This is the deed of an elephant,' Mahoney said. Possibly because the bones of the ribcage had been smashed to pieces.

I saw Kahindi shaking his head.

'No, tembu, Bwana. No tembu, no kiboko.'

That is, neither an elephant nor a hippo.

'Then what do you have to say to this?' asked Mahoney with annoyance.

'Mokèlé-mbèmbé, Bwana! Baya asana, baya sana!'

Baya sana—very bad.

Mahoney looked furious. 'I'll kick you out if you speak such rubbish.'

'But I know! I've heard it roar.'

'What nonsense are you uttering, Kahindi? Please speak up! What have you heard?'

'I once headed the porter's group of the Bwana Santini community.'

Till now, Kahindi had concealed this fact. He was also part of Italian group which had gone missing.

Kahindi finally spoke up. The Santini group had set up their camp at night around the foothills of Mukenku. It's more towards the north from the area we are at present. At midnight Kahindi woke to the sound of a growl. When he left the tent and came out he saw a pair of eyes glowing in the darkness about five or six feet above the ground. Kahindi fled. After running for about a few miles he then walked on to return to the civilized word. He had recounted this experience to many but the sahibs did not believe him. Kahindi's own view is that everyone present in that group had lost their lives after being captured by that demon.

'Then why did you come with us?' questioned Mahoney. 'Or were you planning to escape from our group, too?'

Looking sheepish, Kahindi said, 'I'm here to earn my bread, Bwana. I would have run away again if I'd encountered the demon once more—but now having seen Bwana Shonku's weapon I feel safe. I promise I'll not run away this time.'

'Then you must share this assurance with your porters too. Once they have joined us there's no way they can leave us. I'm telling you this once and for all.'

There were more disturbances in store for the day. After discovering the white man's body and listening to Kahindi's confession we proceeded onwards and within ten minutes came face to face with a group of pygmies.

I'd no idea that pygmies, who are only about four feet to four-and-a-half feet in height, wander around so silently. We had no indication of their presence before we faced them. And the moment we ran into them they surrounded us. Mahoney raised his voice and said, 'Do not fear; they are harmless. But their curiosity is limitless.'

Each pygmy carried a bow and an arrow with a leather bag for quivers. The brown spot on the edge of the arrow was a sign of poison. I was aware of this fact. I've read in books that they hunt only to satisfy their hunger; they are not at all violent in nature. Mahoney went ahead and started speaking with them in Bantu. A few of them came close to Rocket. Several hunter dogs or wild dogs roam Africa but clearly no one had seen a Great Dane before.

While Mahoney was engaged in conversation I suddenly noticed that the pygmies had started taking out various stuff from their bags. How strange! All these items belonged to the civilized world! Binoculars, compass, camera, clock, fountain pen, shoes, flask—how did the tribals acquire these articles?

After finishing his talk, Mahoney turned towards me and said, 'They have discovered quite a few dead bodies of white men in this region in the last few months. I'm sure you can guess where they got these objects from.'

Now there's no doubt left that all three groups are no more.

Meanwhile, I froze in fear when I saw a pygmy take something out of his bag.

It was a book—and it was very familiar to me.

When I went forward and extended my hand in his direction, the pygmy silently placed the book in my hands.

I told Mahoney, 'Will you please ask them if I can take this book?'

The pygmy readily agreed. I put it inside my pocket. It was a first-edition copy of *Geetanjali*. I was numb. What more clinching proof that McPherson is no more?

'Can they give us some information regarding this giant animal?' I asked.

Mahoney said, 'No. I've asked them about it. But they said they've only seen something strange flying in the sky.'

'A bird?' asked Saunders.

'No, it was not a bird. Neither was it a mechanical vehicle, as it didn't produce any sound.'

The pygmies left. Worried, we continued our journey.

We camped at seven in the evening. We could hear the sound of a river with strong currents. We have to cross that tomorrow.

The mystery thickens. God knows what our future holds.

There's lightning and a thunderstorm outside, in addition to strong winds. Perhaps it is about to rain.

10 May, 11.45 p.m.

What a terrifying experience! Even now, I can barely hold my pen steady in my shaking hands.

Last night, after writing my diary, when I was about to lie down I heard a scream.

David and Rocket immediately sprang up. The three of us instantly rushed out of our tents. Crole, Saunders and Mahoney were all already outside. The scream had come from the porters' tents. It was pitch dark outside. The campfire had gone out in the rain.

The scream had now turned into a groan and along with it one could also hear the sound of drumbeats—as if someone was beating a huge hammer on the ground.

Saunders and I had both come out with torches in our hands; when we focused our light through the curtain of rain a terrifying scene appeared before our eyes.

The porters' tents were smashed and flattened—as if a steamroller had come and destroyed them.

The third tent was about to receive the same treatment—a gigantic animal was approaching it, eyes glowing in the darkness.

It was the most ferocious carnivorous animal of the prehistoric dinosaur era—the Tyrannosaurus Rex.

'Your gun, Shonku, your gun!' Saunders and Crole both screamed together. Mahoney had meanwhile shot twice at the animal, with no effect.

I had to go into my tent to get my Annihilin and it was a matter of a few seconds yet within that span of time I saw David's powerful Great Dane return to the tent trembling, his tail between his legs.

As I stepped out a dazzling blue light followed by lightning and an ear-splitting sound momentarily blinded and deafened me. I could not press the trigger of my Annihilin.

In the next flash of lightning I saw that the Tyrannosaurus had changed his route and was receding away from us.

'It's been struck by lightning!'—shouted Mahoney.

'But still it could not subdue him,' I said. 'What an extraordinarily powerful animal!'

Three of our porters have been crushed to death by the dinosaur. Kahindi along with other three porters were spared as they had come out after they heard the screams.

We returned to our respective tents. But thank goodness the rainfall was not as intense as the sound and fury of the storm outside. We couldn't possibly have withstood nature's vagaries after this horrifying incident.

I've distributed my Somnolin pill to everyone. If we do not sleep well we won't possibly be able to cope with the demands of tomorrow.

Mokèlé-mbèmbé, after all, is not a myth!

13 May, Nairobi

There's no doubt left that this expedition to the Congo is perhaps one of the most dreadful in my entire oeuvre of adventures.

Such an assortment of unexpected, breathtaking events take place only in stories—that too not in many stories. I never imagined that one day we could actually return to the civilized world. That is my great fortune and nothing else. Of course, along with it I must give full credit to the amazing courage and presence of mind that my teammates showed.

On May 10, the first thing we saw in the morning were the footprints of the Tyrannosaurus Rex.

The footprints had travelled northwards. Now the point was: which way should we head?

Mahoney was consulted. He said, 'We were heading north in any case, so there's no point changing our minds. After all, we can't turn back; if we proceed it has to be ahead. And there's no point in thinking about the animal. If he still has any grudge towards us he'll chase us in any case—wherever we go. I feel he is slightly injured because the lightning struck him. It'll take a while for him to regain his strength.'

After hearing this, David Munroe said with great gusto, 'We will follow his footsteps. In the twentieth century, if we get to see the Tyrannosaurus in the light of day, we need not try to accomplish anything else for the rest of our lives.'

We set off at 7 a.m. I had a feeling that loads of mysteries were yet to be solved. As we were short of three coolies, we distributed some of the stuff amongst us. Kahindi is still with us as a result of Mahoney's warnings. But I seriously wonder how long he will stay.

Though it was a clear day, the forest still remained shrouded in dense darkness. Our path presumably followed the beast's footsteps, which kept appearing at irregular distances. It looked as though he was limping.

After walking for ten minutes, we heard the sound of water rushing and soon reached a river. It wasn't wider than fifteen yards. The water too was only knee deep. Hence, it wasn't difficult to cross it on foot. That the animal too had crossed the river was evident as we located its footprints on the opposite side.

After another quarter of a mile, the surface of the earth changed. Once more it was back to volcanic ash and pieces of rock. Again we had come closer to a volcanic region. The forest was no longer so dense. The opaque covering of leaves above us had thinned, allowing light to peep in.

Now the footprints faded and eventually vanished. There was no way we could find out where the animal had gone.

'Let's go straight on,' Mahoney said.

But we couldn't go further.

Like magic, from behind shrubs and bushes, appeared a group of khaki-clad locals who immediately surrounded us. Each of them held a bow and arrow. And they were all aiming at us.

Mahoney instantly picked up his gun, but in a flash from his left an arrow appeared and hit the butt of his gun, which fell to the ground.

And then the archer himself picked up the gun and said something in Bantu. Mahoney turned towards us and said, 'They want us to follow them.'

'Where?' I asked.

'Wherever they take us.'

'Who are they?'

'They are Bantus, but not Bushmen exactly. One can make out that they are following someone's orders. Unless we go with them we can't find out who this person is.'

We had no choice. When there are at least fifty people pointing arrows at you then there's no question of not obeying them.

After walking for five minutes against the mountainside, we reached a clearing that was obviously man-made. Trees had been chopped off in all directions. On one side of the clearing stood a wonderful wooden cabin on wooden stilts. It could be called a forest bungalow.

Under the direction of our captors, we proceeded towards the cabin. Was there any human presence inside it?

Yes, indeed there was.

First it was only a voice and then the owner of the voice came out on to the verandah of the cabin.

'Good morning, good morning!'

The face was replete with a bushy red beard and moustache and it wasn't difficult to recognize the man.

He was the renowned German scientist Professor Karl Haimendorf.

'Welcome, Professor Shonku! Welcome, Herr Crole!'

With a clap of his hands he dismissed the Bantu group.

'Come along, all of you, let's go upstairs.'

We followed Haimendorf up the stairs into the cabin. There were two other white men present, men I knew well—Dr Gouws and Professor Ehrlich. After the introductions were over, Haimendorf said, 'Another member of our group, engineer Helmsman, is a little preoccupied with his own work. You will get to meet him later.' Then he turned towards me and said, 'I received the information that you are visiting this area. We are in touch with Nairobi via radio and with Kisangani as well. And via Kisangani I'm in touch with my own country. As a result we get to know what's happening all across the world.'

I said, 'But the people outside don't know that you all are still alive.'

Haimendorf let out a hearty chuckle. 'If this news is allowed to reach them they'll definitely know. Perhaps we didn't let them know.'

'Why?'

'It'll create problems, in our work.'

I decided to say no more. It's obvious that some venture was in progress, though I've no idea about the nature of the work.

This time Saunders asked a question. 'If you are in touch with the outside world then you must have heard about the arrival and the disappearance of the Italian and the British groups in the forests of the Congo as well.'

'Yes, indeed, I heard about their coming. But then I did not receive any further news about them. '

'Have you any knowledge of a prehistoric animal living in your vicinity?' asked Crole.

Elmendorf's jaw dropped. 'A prehistoric animal?'

'The Tyrannosaurus Rex, to be exact.'

'Have you seen him?' Haimendorf asked.

'Not just seen him . . . the animal attacked our camp. Three of our porters were crushed under his feet.'

'How strange,' said Haimendorf. 'He hasn't appeared in this locality.'

A native servant served us coffee, and we sipped it cautiously, still bemused by the presence of Haimendorf and his team. Soon, Haimendorf got up and said, 'I deeply regret bringing you over forcefully but it was essential that we meet. When I heard you had come here, I couldn't let go of this opportunity. Now let's walk around. I'd like to show you this place. I think you'll find this interesting.'

Haimendorf, Gouws and Ehrlich started off. Forming a line we followed them down the wooden staircase. The sides of the bungalow had been cleared of all bush and the trees had been spruced up. However, there were still signs of volcanic ash on the ground. During a volcanic eruption the lava flow is perhaps the least of the problems; far more dangerous is this ash and associated poisonous gases. A lava flow is slow and a man can easily run and outpace it in order to save himself.

We were walking along the sides of the dormant volcano. On the eastern side, the mountain range, we noticed a huge wall had been built on one portion of which was a huge wooden door. It was shut.

'We are using this natural cave as a working space,' said Haimendorf. 'The cave is almost forty yards deep. There are two more such caves, both in use. Nature seems to be blessing our work.'

'What if nature creates havoc?' asked Crole.

'What do you mean?'

'There's no guarantee that these volcanoes won't ever erupt?'

'If we see such signs we have our ways to escape,' Haimendorf said mysteriously.

Walking further we reached the entrance to a tunnel. The moment I entered the tunnel a thought crossed my mind, and this was echoed by the words spoken by Haimendorf.

'This is a kimberlite pipe,' said Haimendorf. 'The stones which you notice on the wall have diamonds embedded in them.'

In the scientific world there are a number of theories regarding the origin of diamonds. One theory states that 1000 miles underground, due to tremendous pressure and heat, carbon crystallizes into diamond. These diamonds are brought up with lava and other melted minerals during a volcanic eruption and become embedded on the walls of the tunnels.

Haimendorf was speaking. 'One ordinary hundred tonnes kimberlite pipe yields hardly thirty-two carat diamonds. That is, one fifth of an ounce. But with one strike of a crowbar in this tunnel, we won't be surprised if we get 500 carat diamond.'

It's obvious that the tunnel is being dug here. Crowbars are lying on the floor, lights are fixed up against the entire wall of the tunnel, and a trolley is lined up on the ground—to take the supplies outside.

'Is this a blue diamond?' I asked, pointing to a stone in the wall.

'So you keep yourself quite well informed,' answered Haimendorf with a crooked smile. 'Yes, this is a blue diamond. A particular brand of blue diamond–Type II-B. It has no value as a gem. But this variety of diamond has revolutionized work in the field of electronics. I believe that there's no other place in the world which contains such an endless supply of diamonds. There are many such pipes available here where the work is on in full swing. If you can control the locals well they produce good work for you. In my mine both the labourers as well as the police are black.'

We came out of the tunnel. The afternoon was now ebbing. We took the same route by which we had come. When we reached the shut door we had seen earlier, Haimendorf unlocked it and ushered us inside.

It was like Aladdin's cave. In the presence of such a variety of tools and machinery you hardly felt you were within a mountain. A laboratory, restroom, conference room—they were all there.

'You must be surprised to see so many items,' said Haimendorf. 'In today's day and age if you're connected to the city then receiving supplies is never a problem.'

Now four armed men appeared at the door. By their uniforms, it was clear they were from the police.

Apart from Crole, all of us settled down on a sofa. Crole looked very restless; he roamed around the room looking at everything. He came to a halt in front of a machine and asked, 'Are you operating some device through remote control? I can see a switch full of various instructions.'

In a dry voice, Haimendorf said, 'Helmsman is an able engineer. Morever, Gouws has earned his own reputation as an inventor, even if he is not Professor Shonku's equal. If to reduce a man's hard work is the main aim in the field of electronics, we indeed try out our experiments on how one can conduct various external jobs while sitting at home. I came to know of your arrival in this direction while sitting inside this cave.'

On one side of the cave I saw four TV screens placed in a row. When Haimendorf got up and pressed four buttons, we could see four different scenes from the forest.

'We have fixed cameras against the trees across many areas of the forest,' said Haimendorf.

Crole finally sat down.

Now we noticed a distinct change in Haimendorf's face. The easy, friendly expression was now replaced by a grave and solemn one. He paced up and down, cleared his throat and said, 'I'm sure you can make out that the work we are pursuing here demands utmost discretion. Other than the four of us, our fellows based in Kisangani and Nairobi, our local employees, the sponsors of our expedition who are based in Germany and the few of you, no one else knows anything about the blue diamond mines. You've come to know because you'd come too close to this area and I was obliged to tell you. But I'm sure you're aware that I'll not allow this news to be carried out by you.'

Haimendorf stopped talking. There was pindrop silence in the cave. Mahoney was grinding his teeth but somehow managing to keep calm. The rest of us sat like stones, looking straight at Haimendorf. It was Crole who broke the silence. 'Karl, will you tell them about your own role during the reign of Hitler? In the Buchenwald concentration camp what kind of torture was carried out on Jew prisoners by a young physicist—'

'Wilhelm!' Haimendorf growled. Crole now fell silent as he had already let the cat out of the bag. In horror I looked at Haimendorf. Those cold, cruel eyes, the icy, steely voice—how accurately they all matched up to my idea of a former Nazi.

Another white man entered the cave. He was six feet in height with black, bushy eyebrows, a head full of unruly black hair and thick glasses. This must be Helmsman I thought. Looking at Haimendorf, he gently nodded his head as if indicating that the work had been completed.

'Sanga, Mobut!'

At Haimendorf's shout two black men came forward. He issued orders in Bantu and the guns in the hands of Mahoney and Crole were immediately taken away. It was pointless to protest as the other two guards were aiming at us with their arrows.

Now Haimendorf looked at me. 'Professor Shonku, I've a request for you.'

'Tell me.'

'I need you to be part of my group.'

I was speechless for a moment at this absurd proposal. Pausing a little, Haimendorf once again began to speak. 'I've heard of two amazing discoveries made by you from Gouws. One is a pistol and the other, a pill. A cartridge is not just expensive to produce; if the aim is not definite it's impossible to kill an animal. We don't have any first-class hunters among us. Just the other day a herd of elephants created a great deal of chaos for us. I have heard that your pistol always works when its trigger is pressed. In the same way your pill too works like magic, I'm told. African diseases are peculiar. Soon after arriving Ehrlich contracted malaria and Helmsman fell ill with sleeping sickness. German medicines are no less effective but unlike your medicines they are not always a sure hit. I need you chiefly because I require these two products. In addition to this, I may also need your advice occasionally. Do not fear, you'll live in great comfort. We always honour our esteemed guests. We have done so in the case of another person too.'

I had this great urge to take out my pistol and make this disgusting man vanish, but I also knew that these archers would immediately kill all of us.

I said, 'There's no question of my leaving this group.'

Haimendorf did not seem convinced. He said, 'I agree, I do not have such extraordinary talent to match your genius. What's the real strength of Type 2-BW diamond? Will this help to improve an electronic revolver?—Unlike others, it's you who can easily work on this. Needless to say, we'll suitably recompense you for this.'

I found my voice. 'Please forgive me as I've no wish to help you in any way.'

'Is this your final word on the matter?'

'Yes.'

Looking in my direction for a few moments, Haimendorf opened his mouth.

'Very well.'

All this while, I had been aware of Rocket's restlessness and whining. Was it the sounds of monkeys and apes? On my way here I'd noticed some colobus monkeys on the trees. The shrill scream which I now heard from outside, was it coming from a monkey?

'Gentleman,' said Haimendorf. 'Now the time has come to bid farewell to you all. We have work to do. I don't wish to waste my time by talking, especially when it's not going to yield any fruitful result. Our guards will drop you back at the appointed place.'

He walked to the instrument Crole had been examining earlier. 'You may leave now,' said Haimendorf.

We all exited the cave, all except Haimendorf. The sun had by now receded behind the mountain, bringing darkness all around.

Four local men were aiming their arrows at us. I could feel our end was near. Something needed to be done right now. There was only one way.

The advantage of my pistol is that it doesn't look like one. In desperation I took it out of my pocket and, aiming at the archers, pressed the trigger. In an instant three of them vanished. I wasn't as quick with the fourth one: his arrow whizzed by my left ear, taking along a tuft of my hair and hit the door of the cave, before the archer vanished.

Rocket still seemed very restless. The colobus monkeys were jumping about and screeching loudly on the trees.

'Mein gott,' screamed Crole. 'Look at that!'

Twenty yards away towards the east from between the rows of trees, charging towards us, was the Tyrannosaurus Rex! In the dusky light we could see his eyes gleam like a blazing fire, and its mouth was stretched up to the ears, showing rows of sharpened teeth.

I took out my Annihilin from my pocket but instantly realized that the pistol would not work on this beast.

Because it was not a living being! It was a robot, created by the Haimendorf Company. This prehistoric animal was a mechanized being!

The engineer Helmsman was controlling it from within the cave.

Crole too had figured this out and in an instant he rushed back into the cave.

The mechanical beast was now moving quickly towards us. We all retreated into the cave for refuge.

Inside, we witnessed a dramatic scenario.

Helmsman's left hand was on the controls of the machine and his right hand was holding a gun aimed straight at Crole. But Crole's behaviour was peculiar. In a gentle voice he was calling out Helmsman's name even while slowly approaching him, one step at a time.

'Helmsman . . . Helmsman . . . Helmsman . . . Please put down the revolver, Helmsman . . . Drop the revolver . . .'

To our amazement, Helmsman's right hand came down gradually.

'Now please stop the movement of your animal, Helmsman, stop the animal and do not let him come here.'

Helmsman's left hand now went towards a button.

It all became very clear to us. Crole had hypnotized Helmsman. Outside the sounds of the beast approaching had come to a halt but our legs suddenly began to shake.

The ground was trembling. All the equipment inside the cave was shaking. Rocket was barking loudly.

An earthquake—and it would not be surprising if a volcano too now erupted. Birds and animals often get to know of an earthquake well in advance due to their sixth sense. Now I could understand the reason for Rocket's restlessness. The screeching noises by the monkeys were probably for the same reason.

We ran out of the cave. Ten yards away the Tyrannosaurus lay lifeless, his body vibrating in the earthquake. Human cries could be heard from all directions. We were about to run when we heard a very familiar voice.

'Shonku! Shonku! This way—Shonku!'

I turned—another shock on this already eventful day! From afar Chris McPherson was waving to us desperately. Just behind him was a hot-air balloon, the colour of a bright yellow sun. Solving this mystery could wait—we needed to escape first.

We ran in his direction.

'Don't let them come!' McPherson shouted, pointing behind us.

Turning I saw Haimendorf, Ehrlich and Gouws racing in the direction of McPherson.

In a split second, Mahoney's blow knocked the first two down. Saunders's blow stopped Gouws in his tracks. Kahindi had definitely fled with his other teammates. Now there was no time to think of them.

Within seconds the five of us including Rocket tumbled into the hot-air balloon and drifted off the mountain. As we rose, we could see Mount Mukenku erupt, emitting fire from its crater. Streams of lava were flowing down the mountainside. The sky and the wind were wrapped up in smoke; with each explosion countless stones were being thrown out of the crater and scattered all over the earth. We could see all kinds of wild animals—big and small—escaping the area to save themselves from this natural calamity.

Soon, everything receded. The sounds of the explosions were getting fainter as we drifted away in the evening breeze. The sun cast one final illuminating glow before finally setting. Amidst the eternal foliage of Congo's ancient forest, a speck of tiny orange flame reminded us of the sudden awakening of the sleeping Mukenku.

Finally McPherson spoke.

'I saw you from a distance but didn't know how to establish contact. At last I got the opportunity thanks to this catastrophe.'

I asked, 'But why did they capture you?'

McPherson said, 'This gas balloon belongs to us; it's not Haimendorf's. As we had to work within the volcanic region we carried this along with us. This is the best option for a getaway in times like this. But there's another reason too.'

'What was that?'

'The doctorate I got in geology was on the subject of the blue diamond. That is why Haimendorf detained me. Or else, like the others in my group, I too would have been crushed under the feet of that mechanical demon. Of course, such a death would have perhaps been better than this slavery.'

David asked, 'Who invented this amazing beast?'

'The plan was hatched by Haimendorf. The form was created by Gouws, Ehrlich, Helmsman and fifty Bantu craftsmen. Few in this world can match up to Bantu craftsmanship. This demon was produced chiefly to keep investigators and explorers away.'

We were now travelling towards the east. We would begin our descent the minute we spotted a city.

There's one thing I still had to tell McPherson. 'We've lost everything, but fortunately my pocket has retained one thing. Take it.'

The first edition of the English *Geetanjali* containing Tagore's own signature was now returned to its original owner.

A few facts of this story have been taken from *Congo*, a novel by Michael Crichton.

Shonku and the UFO

12 September

The subject of Unidentified Flying Objects has created a huge uproar around the world in the last twenty-five years. Numerous societies have surfaced all across the globe simply to study UFOs. The members of these societies are convinced that UFOs carrying aliens from distant planets regularly strike the earth but soon disappear. Countless photographs said to be of UFOs have regularly appeared in various journals. Ninety per cent of these images that are published depict the UFO as an upturned saucer, hence the name flying saucer. This fact itself makes the entire phenomenon highly dubious to me. There are after all so many shapes; why on earth should all the UFOs have the same form? All the rockets and spacecraft sent from earth do not resemble flying saucers! I myself once encountered one such UFO in Egypt which was in the shape of a pyramid. Thus all the stories of flying saucers appear to me as a laughable hoax.

So much for flying saucers! Very recently, images of UFOs have come out in two newspapers—one from the city of Oxelösund in Sweden and the other from Leningrad in Russia. It's clear that both the photographs are of the same spacecraft (if at all it's a spacecraft) and neither of them remotely resembles a flying saucer. This spacecraft has a complicated design and is not easy to describe; hence it's difficult to recognize this object as a spacecraft. It was spotted in the sky of Sweden on 2 September and in Leningrad the following day. It was also sighted in other parts of Europe but could not be photographed. These sightings have generated a lot of excitement among the UFO experts.

Almost a decade ago, I had tried to establish contact with alien civilizations via radio signal and achieved considerable success. However, I had to abruptly put an end to this work due to a special reason. Let me explain.

Ten years ago an international conference was held at Geneva where the main subject under discussion was how to establish contact with extraterrestrial civilizations. I published a paper there on the subject talking about my own experience in this field. Most of the scientists who were present there greatly appreciated it. They were all amazed at the extent of my achievements working in a city like Giridih and using only very basic instruments.

A pleasure cruise across the Lake Geneva was arranged for the delegates on the following day. Tables were arranged for lunch across the deck of the luxury steamer. A gentleman joined our table with my permission. He was a tall, lean man of about fifty-five. His jet-black hair and his pale, emaciated face were a complete mismatch. He introduced himself as Rodolfo Carboni, a Milan-based physicist. After the initial introductions, he produced a big bunch of foolscap sheets and placed it on our table with force.

'What is it?' I asked, taken aback.

'Just read the heading on the first page and you'll understand,' replied Dr Carboni.

The heading amazed me. The title was identical to the subject of my own paper.

'Are you working on the same line?' was my startled question.

Carboni replied, 'Yes. Exactly. I had established radio contact with the inhabitants of the planet which is located around the solar system of Alpha Centauri. There is no difference between your research and mine. I was supposed to read this paper. As you read your paper first I refrained from reading mine, as it would have been mere repetition.'

'But why? It would not have harmed your reputation or undermined your achievement in any way. On the other hand, it would have reaffirmed our line of argument that alien civilizations do exist.'

'No.' Carboni shook his head. 'It wouldn't have gone down well. I would have been accused of plagiarizing your work. Your international reputation, your fame plus your good luck would have favoured you. The fact that your own country is poor and backward would have attracted more support and sympathy. Nobody knows me here. Why should they believe my word?'

Saying these words, Carboni picked up his papers and left the table. I was very upset. Had he read the paper first this situation would not have risen. I know such envy does not help anyone but the sad fact is that many scientists just waste their talent feeing envious of others. I can easily name at least four such scientists who have created a lot of problems even for me, thanks to the green monster.

I knew nothing about this Carboni. That evening I got some information about him from my longtime friend Jeremy Saunders. And I decided to discontinue any further endeavour to contact alien beings.

Carboni was apparently an architect by profession. The Italian government had decided to establish a sports stadium in Turin and had invited designs from the best architects in the country. Carboni too came up with a design. His uncle was a member of the Italian cabinet. With his help Carboni's plan got approved. However, the stadium developed a dangerous crack midway during the construction. Carboni's design was rejected and another architect was assigned the contract. Carboni's reputation suffered a huge blow. He had to quit his profession. He attempted suicide twice but failed.

Subsequently he resurfaced as a physicist after a mysterious eight-year hiatus.

After listening to Carboni's personal history I felt a deep sympathy for him. There's no dearth of subject matters in the field of scientific research. I wouldn't really become penniless if I gave up my own work on this subject. I decided to convey my decision to Carboni in writing. He could jolly well continue with his work and need no longer treat me as his rival. Carboni didn't bother to reply. His name has now crossed my mind due to the current spate of news about UFOs. Is he still continuing with his research? Has he managed to establish any contact with this particular spaceship?

17 September
An old friend of mine visited me. Our friendly neighbourhood Nostradamus, Mr Nakurchandra Biswas. I've already talked about his extraordinary psychic powers. He lives in Makorda and almost every three months he comes to meet me. He possesses the unusual power of reading minds, clairvoyance, conducting past-life regression, enjoys the the power of premonition and fortune telling and can even foresee the future. Moreover, he has the capacity to imagine a situation or events which he can make others experience as well. A number of rare talents indeed! Science still can't explain these phenomena but I strongly feel it will be able to in the future. I shall be

eternally grateful for the way he saved me from a perilous situation in Brazil. He is half my age but I can't help but greatly respect him for his unusual powers. He is a thorough gentleman, though he appears to be a simpleton. In reality, he has ample presence of mind as well as chutzpah. I've seen enough evidence of this.

He arrived at 7 a.m. and respectfully touched my feet. Then he sat down across me on the sofa. I instructed Prahlad to prepare another cup of coffee, folded away the newspaper and asked, 'How are you, sir?' Embarrassed he said, 'Please don't call me "sir". You're almost as old as my father.'

'Fine. I shall remember that. Tell me, how are you? What keeps you busy these days?'

'I'm fine, sir. Trying to catch up with my studies. I can hardly afford to buy books. However, the advocate Mr Chintaharan Ghoshal has kindly allowed me to use his library. My father, you know, practises homoeopathy. He cured Mr Ghoshal's gout. So out of gratitude he has permitted me to use his library during the afternoon. Sir, he owns 7000 books, covering almost every subject under the sun.'

'What subject are you studying now?'

'I am reading chiefly history, geography and travelogues. You see, when I get to see events unfolding before my eyes I can perceive that they belong to another age. If I have knowledge of basic history and geography, I can easily identify those scenes. Thus I'm trying to gain knowledge of those subjects. If I describe these events to you, I'm sure you would readily explain them to me. But I don't wish to disturb you in any way for such small matters. After all you're a very busy man.'

'Are these studies helping you?'

'Yes, sir, to a certain extent. Two months ago, on 19 July I witnessed a grisly scene. A gown-clad, bearded and bejewelled person was seated in a room and a big salver covered with an embroidered cloth was produced before him. When the cloth was removed it revealed the freshly-severed head of a human being.'

'Does this relate to Aurangzeb?'

'Yes, sir. The book I read suggests so. The head belonged to Aurangzeb's elder brother, Prince Dara Shikoh.'

'Yes, I too know of this event.'

'But sir, I don't always understand each event that I see. For instance, I saw a clock the day before yesterday.'

'A clock?'

'Yes, sir. But it was no ordinary clock. I've never seen an illustration or image of such a clock in any book.'

'Will you be able to produce the same scene before me?'

'Why not, sir. But you need to give me three minutes' time.'

'Yes, of course. Take your time.'

'Please concentrate on that flower pot. I need to close my own eyes.'

It didn't even take three minutes. I could soon see an image on the opposite wall which appeared through a curtain of muslin. It was a magnificent water clock, designed and manufactured by TsuTsung in the city of Kaifeng city in China in the eleventh century. This amazing clock had been created in the memory of Emperor Tsen Jung.

The scene disappeared within a minute. When I described the clock to Nakur Babu, he looked elated. 'That's exactly why I visit you so often. You possess such encyclopaedic knowledge.'

Such platitudes would have normally irritated me, but not when they came from Nakur Babu.

Out of curiosity, I couldn't help but ask him, 'Do you read the newspapers?'

Nakur Babu very shyly shook his head.

I said, 'Then you may not be aware of the UFO-related news.'

'What's that news?'

From the stack of newspapers I looked for the newspaper dated 3 September. I showed the photograph of the UFO to Nakur Babu. He reacted instantly. Looking amazed he exclaimed, 'My God! I saw this very thing the other day!'

'Where did you see it?'

'I was resting on the verandah after lunch and looking at a squirrel dancing around a drumstick tree when suddenly the atmosphere all around me turned hazy. I could not see anything at first. It took me a while to understand that everything was covered in sand. Hence the smoky effect. When the sand finally settled, I saw it—it was really massive—standing on the sand bed. Its metallic body was shining brightly in the sunlight.'

'Did you notice anyone there?'

'No, sir. Not a soul. The spacecraft didn't seem to be occupied. Then again, who knows? But the area appeared to be a desert. I could see snow-capped mountains at the back. I saw everything clearly.'

Nakur Babu was with me for another ten minutes. At the time of leaving he said he could feel that he would have to meet me again soon. 'Please do not mind, Tilu Babu. I feel so worried every time I apprehend any signs of danger for you.'

'Are you foreseeing any such thing?'

'Not immediately but when I saw you in the room today, my heart skipped a beat, as if I were seeing you imprisoned in a room.'

'Are you taking good care of yourself? This world has enough scientists like me. But you're too precious. The kind of power which you possess is a very unusual thing. It should not be allowed to go to waste.'

'Sir, I understand your sentiments. I consume Brahmi leaves (waterhyssop herb) regularly.'

'Good. But if you ever feel that your power is on the wane then please let me know. I can give you a medicine which might help you.'

'Which medicine?'

'It's called Cerebrilliant. It helps one stay alert to keep the senses active.'

Nakur Babu mentioned that if need be he can come over whenever his presence is required. All I have to do is drop him a postcard.

25 September

One terrible piece of news has distracted my mind from any interest in UFOs.

The Parthenon, one of the best instances of Greek civilization, has been destroyed. This is unbelievable. Does the Parthenon really stand no more? It had been designed and built over the Acropolis hills at Athens by legendary Greek architects and sculptors like Ictinus, Callicrates and Phidias. It was originally a temple dedicated to Goddess Athena. One is always overwhelmed by its beauty while standing in front of it. And now it is history.

Yet the news is true. The media has helped spread this news like wildfire all over the world, casting everyone to despair. Nobody really knows the truth behind this terrible disaster. The incident took place at midnight. The Athenians woke up with a jolt from their sleep to a loud explosion. Naturally everyone rushed out of their homes. That was the second night of the waning moon. Those who were residing around the Acropolis saw with horror that their beloved Parthenon was gone. Only millions of marble fragments were strewn all over the place. It is being investigated whether any powerful terrorist group is behind this explosion. But nobody knows anything for sure.

I just can't write any more. Let me wind up here.

27 September

A strange letter arrived today which has rekindled my interest in UFOs.

My German friend, Wilhelm Crole, is touring China on an official invitation. He had earlier informed me about this. His main purpose was to tour around the Xingjian province of China and to visit the ancient Buddhist temples and relics. Crole left Beijing for Xingjian along with a group of Chinese archaeologists. The same area had once been visited by the famous traveller Sir Aurel Stein at the behest of the Archaeological Survey of India. The area was then known as Chinese Turkistan. Sir Aurel Stein uncovered an amazing Buddhist monastery in the town of Tun-huang, located on the southeast side of Taklamakan Desert. Recently, Chinese archeologists have found an ancient scroll that describes another eighteenth-century monastery which could be lying buried below the sand of the Taklamakan Desert. An archaeological team is carrying out the digging around the Khotan town in the Taklamakan region. Crole's letter, of course, is not related to this archaeological expedition although he is part of this team. He writes:

Dear Shonku

You have possibly read in the newspapers about a story on a UFO. I feel this particular UFO could be operating somewhere in the same locality where I'm working at present. During the last three days I've spotted it twice in the sky. On the first day it was seen flying towards the west. The next day it zoomed in from the west and then disappeared behind the Tian Shan mountain located in the east. I feel it's our duty to enquire into this. The Chinese government has agreed to provide us with helicopters. But I do not want to go by myself. I feel we three musketeers must be together for such an expedition, as in the past. If you're not too busy then please let me know through a cable. I'm sounding out Saunders as well. The sooner we move the better. You're a well-known figure in the scientific community. Perhaps they are not that familiar with Saunders but it doesn't really matter.

Waiting for your return cable.

Yours
Wilhelm Crole

I remembered the descriptions provided by Nakur Babu. A rocket in the middle of a desert! With a snow-capped mountain as the backdrop. If it is the Taklamakan Desert then it's quite possible that the Tian Shan mountain located in the north is the snow-capped mountain seen in the vision.

I'm already feeling excited about the expedition. I've visited so many places but I've never made it to Chinese Turkistan. The descriptions provided by Aurel Stein and Sven Hedin have only whetted my curiosity even more. Marco Polo's travel account also describes the thirteenth-century Chinese Turkistan. During Marco Polo's visit Kublai Khan, the grandson of Genghis Khan, was ruling over China. The account of the Taklamakan Desert given by Marco Polo is quite frightening. The inhabitants of the UFO wouldn't have possibly found a better place to hide themselves.

Nakur Babu had wanted to be kept informed. I've a strong feeling that his services would be required in this expedition. Crole has already witnessed some of his magical powers in Brazil and so may not object to his accompanying us. I must send a cable to Saunders and a letter to Nakur Babu right away.

1 October

Saunders has agreed to accompany us. He'll, of course, travel directly from London. Nakur Babu too has agreed to come but I have a reason to quote his letter verbatim below as it's very special.

> *Thousand bows to Trilokeswar Shonku Esq*
> *Most respectfully I beg to say—*
> *I'm overjoyed that you have recalled me prior to your journey to China. You must be told that the UFO that is visiting the earth has come here with a harmful mission. I apprehend that it would cause great suffering to a sensitive person like you, sir. I'm still clueless as to how I can offer you any help. I shall feel highly honoured if I can join you in this expedition—as in the last one. The question of refusing does not arise as the request comes from none other than you. Just let me know when I am required to arrive in Giridih.*
>
> Yours faithfully
Nakurchandra Biswas

I must inform Nakur Babu to make arrangements for heavy woollen clothes as this place gets extremely cold in October.

9 October, Khotan

The two pieces of information that I received from Saunders have depressed me to no end. Normally, I feel so charged up every time I visit a new place but not this time. Instead, sorrow has almost paralysed me.

In the last four days, two of the most well-known symbols of human civilization have been demolished . One is the Eiffel Tower in Paris and the other is the massive temple complex in Angkor Wat in Cambodia. Almost thirty-three years ago I remember standing spellbound in front of this stupendous Buddhist monument.

The incident in Paris occurred around the new moon night. The entire city woke up to the sound of the Eiffel Tower cracking down the middle. As the area in which it stands is sparsely populated, only three loitering drunks were killed in the incident. Almost every Parisian broke down in tears when they saw the beloved symbol of their country razed to the ground. Investigations of the iron fragments have revealed that the tower snapped due to the use of an extraordinary powerful ray on it. A large number of people are blaming the disaster on the presence of the UFO, though it could not be seen in the Paris sky because of cloudy weather.

Angkor Wat was destroyed in the evening and since it's located inside a tropical forest, there were no eyewitnesses. Details are still not available. What is clear is that the entire complex has now turned into a heap of rubble.

The Chinese archaeologist Dr Sheng is a gem of a person. He is forty years old but looks younger. He has made arrangements for our stay in Khotan and is likely to join us in the hunt for the UFO. Judging by the looks on Saunders and Crole's faces, they are both extremely worried. At dinner Saunders said, 'If the unknown spacecraft is responsible for these series of devastations, they must be in possession of a very powerful weapon of mass destruction. How can we match them? After all it's not possible for us to use a nuclear weapon against them. We don't even know where this rocket or spacecraft is located. And God alone knows how much more destruction is being planned. Therefore . . .'

When I saw Cole agreeing with Saunders, I had to put forth my own view.

'If you believe that we should throw up our hands against this bunch of rogues who are determined to destroy the best symbols of human civilization one after another, then please count me out. If need be I shall go alone to the Taklamakan area. I do not know what opinion Dr Sheng has to offer, but—'

Strangely enough, Dr Sheng extended his right hand to shake mine and said, 'I know these monuments have been built with the blood, sweat and tears of labourers during our feudal rule. We cannot underestimate their greatness. We have always protected our ancient monuments and we are doing everything to preserve our ancient Chinese artefacts. We're continuing with our archeological expedition to dig out further evidence of our ancient culture. We should and must try to put a stop to this chain of destruction.'

Attired in several layers of woollens, the almost inert Nakur Babu now opened his mouth. In Bengali he said, 'Tilu Babu, I've a feeling that our victory in this battle is certain. Therefore there's no reason for us to step back.'

Nakur Babu had met with a minor head injury at the Makorda railway station when he was hit in the head with a steel trunk being carried by a coolie. That injured spot is now covered by sticking plaster. I was afraid that this may have affected his mental powers. Now I found his firm views rather reassuring. But when I translated his words into English to my friends they looked a bit sceptical. They were not quite convinced.

We agreed to fly towards the north across the Taklamakan Desert in the direction of Tian Shan mountains tomorrow morning.

10 October, 8.30 a.m.

Our six-seater helicopter is flying over the endless sand dunes of the Taklamakan. I'm trying to write my diary. Marco Polo had mentioned in his account that it would take a year to cross this desert horizontally. Even at the narrowest points it would take a month to complete the journey. From our altitude I can see that the Venetian traveller wasn't wrong. All the major towns like Khotan, Kashgar, Yarkand, Cherchen and Aksu were established around different oases and waterbodies. The inhabitants of Xingjian province are Uyghur Muslims whose mother tongue is Turkish. South-west of Xingjian lies Kashmir; Afghanistan is located further west, followed by Soviet Russia and finally on the extreme east is Mongolia.

During our helicopter ride Dr Sheng kept describing the regions visible below and sharing with us the ancient history of the Sino-Turkistan area.

Today both Crole and Saunders look their normal selves. I had known that in the morning sunlight much of their fear and apprehension would disappear. I also know too well that they are actually very brave as well as adventurous. But the main hurdle in this present expedition is our almost total ignorance about our enemies. Our knowledge of alien civilization is next to nothing. What kind of people are they—if at all they are people! If they are responsible for these recent destructive orgies why are they so angry at human civilization? Does this also imply that they are angry with humans in general? We know absolutely nothing. I can't deny that I too am apprehensive. Will our forthcoming encounter be one sided? Are we willingly walking into a death trap?

Nakur Babu is looking a little low today. When asked he replied that he was quite all right and his head injury has almost healed as well. Yet I wasn't fully convinced. All the more because he suddenly asked, 'Where are we heading, Tilu Babu?'

The question puzzled me quite a bit and when I looked at him for a minute he suddenly came back to his senses and burst out laughing, 'Oh! Of course, that unknown UFO, isn't it?'

I think a dose of my Cerebrilliant medicine will do him good.

We can now see a mountain range towards the north. But before that lies a large lake. Sheng said this is Baghsar Noal, i.e. Baghsar Lake.

In the interim we have had some coffee and biscuits. The name of our Chinese pilot is Tsu Shi. He does not know English and Dr Sheng is interpreting for him. I can hear the pilot bursting into Chinese songs every now and then. I can hear his singing from the cockpit even over the sound of the helicopter rotors.

Crole was just bringing out a mini chessboard from his pocket to play a game of chess with Saunders when suddenly Sheng pointed a finger towards the window, looking very excited.

4:30 p.m.

We have landed. Low stony hills surround us on three sides. None of them is above sixty to seventy feet in height. Sheng had located four deep holes from above and decided to land there. We examined the holes closely and were quite sure they had been caused by the weight of the four legs of the spacecraft. The horizontal distance of the holes proved that the rocket or spacecraft was a massive thing, almost the size of a big house. But we have no inkling about its present whereabouts. Tsu Shi flew the helicopter all alone over an area of about 250 sq km to do a recce but without any result.

We have pitched three plastic tents behind a fifty-foot-high boulder. The ground is sandy but quite plain and firm. It is strewn with small and medium-sized boulders. We have no idea how long we have to wait and we also know we need to have ample patience. We should in no way give up on our mission.

The biggest challenge would be if the spacecraft indeed lands here: how are we expected to act then and what sort of reaction should we expect from them? Crole said, 'Those who can destroy the Parthenon should simply be finished off with your Annihilin gun. There's no need to talk to them.'

I'm quite confident that my Annihilin gun is capable of finishing any alien creature. But it's quite possible that these aliens are friendly. Perhaps the destination is being organized and carried out by somebody else. This series of incredible attacks is quite puzzling. I'm still not willing to believe that some aliens have landed on earth with the chief mission of destroying the best works of human civilization.

When I shared my thoughts with Saunders his reaction was: 'Since we do not propose to talk to them we will never know the reason behind their arrival. But why take any risk? I go with Crole's proposal. To finish them off at the very first opportunity.'

I see their point of view yet I cannot agree with them. As a scientist I can't let go of this unique opportunity of meeting the inhabitants of an alien world. In the entire history of the human race, this is the first instance of human-alien interaction and I don't wish to lose out on this rare chance. I did encounter an alien spacecraft once in Egypt. But it was uninhabited. I have a feeling that it won't be the case this time. So we can't turn back for fear of losing our lives.

Sheng too shared my view. Perhaps more so because the rocket has landed on Chinese soil. He too feels that if the aliens had a malicious game plan they would have first attacked humans rather than destroying those cherished monuments.

Then Nakur Babu suddenly blurted out, 'They are absent.'

'Who?' was my baffled response.

'Aliens from the other planet.'

'They are? What does that mean? absent?'

'They were present. Inside the UFO.'

'Then where have they gone?'

Raising his eyebrows slightly, Nakur Babu quietly said, 'Below the ground.'

'Below the ground?' echoed both Saunders and Crole, startled.

'Yes, below the ground.'

'Then who is in the rocket? Or is there no rocket at all?'

'No, the rocket is indeed present,' said Nakur Babu. 'But it contains no alien being.'

'What does it have then?'

'There are machines.'

'Computers?' queried Sheng.

'Yes, computers and—'

'And . . .?'

The four of us were intensely curious.

But Nakur Babu shook his head with great disappointment and said, 'I've lost it . . .'

'You lost what?' I asked.

'I saw a vision. But it disappeared. My head is still—'

I'd given him a fresh dose of Cerebrilliant this noon. Perhaps it still hasn't fully worked on him.

Nakur Babu fell silent.

The sun had set long ago. It's getting darker as well as cooler.

Where was this sound coming from?

Everyone has heard that noise. I can't write any more.

11 October, 9 p.m.

We are imprisoned in the spacecraft. All five of us. Tsu Shi was sleeping inside the helicopter. So he is not with us. We've no idea if he can arrange for our release. I too don't know how long we have to remain in this captive state. We are feeling like utter fools, totally confused. Let me explain in detail.

Yesterday, within minutes of hearing a humming noise like that of thousand bees together, a spacecraft appeared from out of the clouds. It looked similar to the ones we have seen in newspapers but was emitting a mild orange glow. How could a black-and-white photograph capture this! From the front the UFO looked like a giant helmet. There were a number of portholes all along the outer shell and a number of horn-like arms extended from it as well. I'm sure they have a role to pay. The spacecraft moved in our direction, possibly targeting their earlier landing site. We were watching from behind a boulder, trying very hard to conceal ourselves. Yet we knew for sure the aliens in the spacecraft must have spotted our helicopter even though they may have missed us. We had no idea how they'd react to our presence.

But the rocket made a touchdown on exactly the same spot as it had previously, completely ignoring our existence.

With bated breath we waited for almost ten minutes. But there was no response at all from the aliens. Now what was to be done?

Sheng was the first to suggest that we move towards the spacecraft. After all, how long would we wait? My pocket contained the Annihilin. Crole and Saunders had a revolver each. Nakur Babu and Sheng had no weapons. But did it matter? Meanwhile, both the Europeans had popped nerve-soothing pills and readily agreed to our suggestion.

We climbed across the boulder and crossed the even area to move in the direction of the spacecraft. The spacecraft looked very sleek indeed. The design was a masterly combination of technology and art.

Out of the blue Nakur Babu said, 'The UFO has selected such a strange place for landing.'

I said, 'Yes, indeed. This place on the edge of Taklamakan Desert near the Tien Shan mountain range is the most ideal place for hiding.'

'No, I didn't mean that.'

'Then?'

Before Nakur Babu could speak further, Crole whispered, 'The door is opening.'

Indeed. A door had opened up at the corner of the spacecraft. A stepladder, made of an element resembling aluminium, was unfolding on the ground.

'Won't you go in, sir?'

These words came from Nakurchandra Biswas. I noticed no sign of fear or worry in him.

'Is it safe to go inside?' I couldn't help but ask him.

'The question of safety or danger does not arise here.' Nakur Babu said in response. 'Our entire point of coming here was to examine the UFO. So how can we stand outside it when it's welcoming us with an open door?'

Now Sheng said, 'Let's go in.'

Crole and Saunders too nodded and the five of us trooped in one by one. I had the Annihilin in my hand and both Saunders and Crole were holding their revolvers.

I led the team and walking in through the door entered an oval-shaped room. It was dark outside but there was a bright but soft blue light glowing inside the room. We couldn't see the source of the light. There was a round glass or plastic window on the opposite side. Other than this there were two round doors on each end. But they were closed. The room was furnished with only ten stools. They were transparent but looked like they were made out of a hard substance. There was nothing else. We could not make out if any living being was present in the rocket.

Was this rocket run by a robot or computer? The controlling mechanisms should be present in the other two rooms.

While we were standing clueless we heard a sound, and when I turned around I realized that the entrance had closed.

Crole immediately pounced on the door and tried his best to reopen it using its handle but nothing worked. There must have been a button or switch to control the door which was not present in this room. The person who had pressed this button to lock us up had done so with a definte purpose.

'Welcome, gentlemen!'

We all jumped when we heard a human voice speaking in English. Sheng indicated a hole on the left wall. The voice had emerged through it. My heart beat rapidly.

Why did the voice sound so familiar?

Once more the voice spoke.

'I'll meet you shortly. You need to wait. Although there's no open window in this room you'll face no difficulty in breathing as there'll be no lack of oxygen. But no smoking, please. Also, you'll not feel hungry or thirsty while you're here. So relax.'

The voice stopped. Well, he didn't sound that hostile or sinister! If he was a human did that mean the rocket hadn't arrived from another planet?

I just couldn't think any more. Crole and Saunders sat on the stools and were wiping sweat from their faces.

Absolute silence once more. We all put back our weapons inside our pockets.

How long do we need to wait? What's in store for us?

12 October, 6 p.m.

Let me recollect and describe the entire hair-raising adventure we experienced in this UFO (correction: it's now no longer unidentified) which has arrived from the nearest star, G2 Alpha Centauri.

Once more we heard that familiar voice sitting inside that round room.

'Listen, gentlemen, even if you can't see me, I can watch each one of you. This rocket has specialized instruments for observation. So I now know that you all have firearms in your pockets. Now please drop those weapons in that round hole on the opposite wall. I'll then talk about what will happen.'

I immediately pulled out my Annihilin from my pocket but noticed that Crole and Saunders were still sitting motionless. I signalled them to follow the instructions. Still there was no reaction from them.

'I'm waiting,' the voice boomed.

Once again I signalled. Saunders, in an impatient and hushed voice, whispered, 'Why must we fear a charlatan? This is no UFO!'

All at once I noticed an unexpected change in the atmosphere of the room. We suddenly found it difficult to breathe. Why so? Saunders and Crole were now bending forward with their hands on their chests. Nakur Babu too was gasping. Sheng's face looked distorted with his tongue hanging out. Oh lord! Will this be the end?

'Drop the guns. Do not act like stubborn fools. Your life is in my hands.'

'Please, please give them away!' Nakur Babu spoke in a choked voice.

Carrying my Annihilin I stumbled towards the hole. The two Europeans struggled to walk but managed to drop their revolvers into that hole. Finally, I also dropped my Annihilin.

Immediately the atmosphere of the room returned to normal.

'Thank you.'

We remained silent. We could now breathe properly and went back to our seats.

Now the door slid open sideways and from the middle someone emerged. I had seen him ten years ago in the Lukung steamer at Geneva.

It was the Italian physicist Dr Rudolfo Carboni.

Saunders and Crole were also familiar with him. They too exclaimed in surprise.

Carboni looked even paler and thinner than when I had met him. His jet-black hair was now greying. But his earlier morose look had now been replaced with a newfound self-confidence, as if he was enjoying unlimited power and did not care a damn about anything.

'Well, gentlemen,' Carboni continued without moving from the door. 'I must warn you in the very beginning that I'm armed so don't try to attack me.'

I looked at Saunders as I knew him to be a very short-tempered person. I've seen him lose his cool a number of times. He was possibly gnashing his teeth and trying hard to restrain himself.

I had to pose a question to Carboni.

'Are you the owner of this spacecraft?'

'Well, yes. For the time being.'

'Time being? Who owned it earlier?'

'The ones I've maintained contact with for the past fifteen years. You too had contacted them. They are the inhabitants of a planet revolving round Alpha Centauri. They'd given me prior notice about their arrival. I was ready for them.'

'What was the language you were using with them to exchange ideas?'

'In the beginning we used the mathematical language and later sign language. I thought of teaching them either English or Italian but that was not to be.'

'Why?'

'They were indisposed shortly after their arrival.'

'Illness?'

'Yes. Influenza. They couldn't escape the virus. They were three in number. All died. I of course had the antidote for the flu but chose not to use it.'

'Why?' I asked, surprised.

'Because I found no good reason to save them. They were utter fools.'

'Fools?'

'Not from the technological point of view. They were far ahead of us in this area. But they came here as our friends to do us good. I did not support their outlook. Nonetheless, they died too soon, before they could produce anything. I arranged for their burial below the sands of Taklamakan Desert. They provided me with the instructions of running this rocket before they died. It is extremely easy. The whole thing is computerized. It's only a matter of pressing buttons. There's a robot here but it is dormant now. I don't know how to control or run it. But there's no need for it either. Now I'm the ultimate authority.'

'May I have a look at the instruments that are running this spacecraft?' I asked. 'You can appreciate that as a scientist I have a natural curiosity.'

'Come with me.'

We walked through the round door into the next room.

It was huge. The rhythmic sound that we had heard in the earlier room was even clearer and louder now. It was as if someone was beating a giant drum from afar. There was a big glass window opposite the door. Possibly this was the front side.

The instrument panels were located on two sides of the window. There were rows of switches and buttons and geometric signs marked against each of these, indicating their individual uses. A headless transparent body was standing in one corner of the room. Undoubtedly this was the robot. The two hands of the robot had six fingers each. Instead of eyes there was a yellow lens on his chest. There was nothing else present other than this. What was most striking was the simple and the uncluttered appearance of the robot.

But the question was: how was Carboni proposing to use this robot?

I asked Carboni this.

Carboni replied, sporting a crooked smile. 'Well, I still have some work left on this earth. Having accomplished that, I'll take a long journey through space. After the rocket leaves the earth's gravitational field it will travel at the speed of light or 3,00,000 km per second. It will take me ten years to reach Alpha Centauri, the origin of this spacecraft.'

'What then?'

'Nothing in particular. I've no attraction left for the earth, nor do I fear death—I tried to commit suicide twice. It hardly matters if I die on the way.'

'You just said you're left with some mundane work left to be done. What is it?'

'I'll show you. You all need to be seated; let me start the rocket engine.'

We sat down. Carboni went to the next room and closed the oval door behind him.

Within half a minute we started to rise very fast. We could see the entire Taklamakan Desert and the Tian Shen mountain range. Then we began moving westwards.

It was difficult to guess the speed of the rocket but the way the ground below was changing its scenario we guessed the rocket was zooming ahead with a far greater speed than that of an average jet plane.

It was 9.30 p.m. when we started. Within fifteen minutes we had gained such a high altitude that it was impossible to guess our whereabouts.

I do not know about the others, but I felt a bit dizzy after a while, but the pressure in my ears made me realize that the rocket was descending.

Within a minute we emerged from the clouds and could see a snowy mountain range. Which range was this?

I received my reply through the hole from the opposite wall.

'The mountain range below is the Alps.'

'Where are you taking us?' asked Crole in an irritated manner.

The answer: 'To my motherland.'

'Italy?'

There was silence after this.

The spacecraft crossed the Alps and slowly descended. I could see the city lights. One luminescent spot disappearing fast to reveal another.

The rocket's speed decreased further. So did the height. We were passing over a large metropolis. On the west was a massive waterbody. Could this be the Mediterranean Sea?

'Rome!' cried out Saunders. 'There's the Colosseum!'

Yes, Rome was clearly visible now. All five of us were now huddling around the window.

Then we suddenly heard the booming voice of Carboni.

'Listen. Listen to how the so called civilized humans ruined me. The Turin stadium, while being constructed according to my design was, damaged due to certain errors created by some corrupt architects who conspired against me. The entire blame fell on me. My reputation was completely ruined. This alien spacecraft has given me the opportunity to avenge that insult. You will shortly witness such an incident.'

I froze with apprehension. So it was Carboni who was responsible for the destruction of the Parthenon, the Eiffel Tower and Angkor Wat. But what on earth was he going to destroy today?

I understood within seconds.

The spacecraft was hovering over the world-famous St Peter's Basilica. It contained the tour de force by the sculptor Michelangelo.

'My God! Do something!' shrieked Saunders. Crole was swearing in German at the lunatic Carboni. Sheng looked miserable. Nakur Babu seemed to have lost his miraculous powers.

As a last resort I raised my voice and said, 'Can't you show any respect towards these grand creations? Are you that mean and despicable?'

'What creation are you talking about? I do not give a damn for anything but scientific creations.'

'But you told us that the inhabitants of this spacecraft originally came here as our friends. So how come they carried such destructive weapons on board?'

A rasping laughter could be heard from the next room.

'Do you think they had kept these weapons with this mission in mind? They used them only to destroy stray asteroids or meteors and to avoid collisions. I'm using them for a different purpose.'

The rocket now veered towards St Peter's Basilica. No ray could be spotted but we saw the moonlit church falling into bits pieces all over the ground.

Crole was shaking with rage. He could barely speak.

'D-don't you know that there's a weapon to destroy your own rocket?'

Again we heard that hysterical laughter.

'Don't you know what will happen if this spacecraft is destroyed? Can't you guess why I allowed you all to board this spacecraft? I'm not so sure about the Chinese or the Indian government but when the others get to know that the world's three pre-eminent scientists are present in the spacecraft, who would dare order its destruction? In this case you too would be finished.'

I had to admit that Carboni had played his trump card rather well. Crole and Saunders both looked completely devastated.

The rocket, after completing its act of destruction, rose again and took a 180-degree turn.

'Now I shall address Shonku,' said Carboni. 'The rocket will now move towards your country. If any Indian are asked about the proudest and greatest possession of their country, eighty per cent would come up with the same answer. I hope I do not have to explain further. Thousands visit India every year to see this monument.'

The Taj Mahal? Was Carboni referring to the Taj Mahal? Was he planning to destroy Emperor Shahjahan's greatest creation?

I couldn't restrain myself. 'Is there no end to your destructive orgies? Don't you have any feeling or respect for the greatest and the best creations of your own race? Does art have no appeal to you?'

'Why just single me out? The works of art have no value. Art is worthless. What use do these monuments have for us? Does it really matter if the Taj Mahal is ruined or saved? What's the worth of the Parthenon or St Peters? There's no point in hanging on to the past.'

How does one argue with a raving lunatic? Yet if he was not restrained, he would continue with his catastrophic acts.

'Tilu babu—'

I suddenly noticed Nakur Babu looking rather listless and weak. I was concerned.

'What's happened?' I asked him.

'Can you give me another dose of that medicine?'

'Are you feeling feverish?'

'No.'

'What is the problem?'

'My head is reeling.'

The medicine was with me. I offered him another dose of Cerebrilliant. But under the trying scenario what could this poor chap do anyway? He gulped it down noisily and closed his eyes.

The rocket was moving eastward. The moon was just over our heads now. It was 12.45 a.m. Crole and Saunders had gone quiet. I could understand their feelings. After all they had witnessed the destruction of St Peter's Basilica. Sheng was muttering, 'We have preserved the Imperial

Palace at Beijing so carefully. It houses countless and priceless documents and artefacts. If this too—'

We all remained silent for another hour or so. We had been rendered utterly helpless. Such dreadful destruction was going on before us and we were mute witnesses.

The rocket started to descend.

Soon enough, I could figure out the mountains and rivers of India in the moonlight. Even knowing the devastation I was to witness, I couldn't take my eyes off from the window. Maybe I would see the Taj Mahal for the last time.

I could hear Carboni humming a tune in the next room. The man was quite insane!

The humming stopped and he started speaking.

'You know, Shonku, I have never seen the Taj Mahal. I only know the latitude and the longitude of Agra. That's enough. The computer will take care of the rest. The spacecraft will automatically reach the exact spot. Just imagine the greatness of science.'

Again he burst into a song.

Now the rocket was descending at a high speed. The view of the ground was becoming clearer with each moment. Crole, Saunders and Sheng had all gathered near the window. I could feel a lump in my throat. I knew I would not be able to control my tears if I had to witness the destruction of the Taj Mahal. Perhaps death would be a better choice.

Yes, I could see the lights of Agra. But they weren't as bright as those in the cities of Italy.

Then came the Yamuna, looking like an unsheathed shining sword in the moonlight.

And there was the Taj Mahal. The spacecraft was moving towards it very fast. Sheng was standing behind me. Twice he whispered, 'Beautiful!' He had only seen of it photographs and read about it in books. But he was looking at the real thing for the first time.

But what's this?

The humming in the next room had stopped. I shuddered.

Where was the Taj Mahal? We had been looking at it a moment ago but now it had vanished! Was this some sort of magic?

And where had all the lights of the city gone?

Only the Yamuna was still there. The moonlight too was present but every other thing had changed. The Taj Mahal had been replaced by thousands of shimmering torchlights.

The rocket was rapidly descending towards the Taj. The scene was very clear. In the moonlight and torchlight, thousands of ant-like humans were moving about. White stones were strewn all over the area.

Suddenly the oval door opened and there emerged Rudolfo Carboni looking completely baffled. 'What happened? Where has the Taj Mahal gone? I saw it so clearly in the moonlight!'

I glanced at Nakurchandra. His eyes were closed and he was meditating. Then I looked in the direction of Carboni and said, 'Your amazing spacecraft has taken us back to a pervious era, Carboni. How can you locate the Taj Mahal? The construction of the Taj Mahal has just started. Can't you see that thousands of artisans are working by torchlight cutting and arranging the pieces of marbles? How can you destroy an object which is not there, Carboni?'

'Nonsense!' shouted Carboni. 'Nonsense! There must be some problem in the mechanisms or with the computer!'

He rushed back to the computer. But this time the door did not close behind him.

We all moved towards the door and entered the room. Carboni could not be trusted. God alone knew what his next course of action would be.

In a frenzy Carboni began to press all the buttons present on the panels. The rocket now swung dangerously.

I signalled to Crole and Saunders. They immediately pounced on Carboni and forcefully pushed him away from the control panel.

I examined the panel thoroughly. It was not at all difficult to understand the meaning of all the geometric symbols and the graphic motifs. We were used to following such clues. I noticed the sign of an upright arrow beside a button, indicating that to gain height one had to just press it. In one jerk, the spacecraft rapidly rose higher as soon as I pressed it.

In the meantime, Carboni had managed to free himself from the grips of Crole and Saunders with one desperate blow. So what if Carboni looked pale and thin! In his state of frenzy he had become a bundle of energy. But he lost his balance and fell once again on the instrument panel, his right hand touching a prominent yellow switch.

Crole and Saunders were again moving in the direction of Carboni but I gestured them not to do so. I had noticed the robot had been switched on as soon as Carboni's hand had hit the yellow switch. The robot was now moving towards the demented scientist, the yellow eyes on his chest glowing brightly.

The robot clasped Carboni by the neck with his two hands and started squeezing. It was like a python coiling round a goat.

We saw Carboni's eyes bulging out and his face turning red all over. It was all over in half a minute. The robot removed his hands and the lifeless body fell on the floor. I could guess that among other things the robot had been programmed with instructions to destroy anyone who endangered the safety of the spacecraft.

The robot now moved towards the control panel and his transparent fingers touched some buttons. The terrible vibration and the swinging stopped. I now left the control room and looked through the window. The rocket was moving north across the Himalayas.

The three of us collected our weapons and returned to the oval room. Nakur Babu now looking happy and pleased and was sitting on a stool. I asked him, 'From where did you get the descriptions of the Taj under construction? Was it from the travelogue by Tavernier?

'Exactly so, sir. Mr Ghoshal's library had this travelogue in two volumes written by this French gentleman.'

It took us two hours to reach Xingyuan.

We landed at the same spot in Taklamakan. It was 5 a.m. The robot joined us in the oval room after piloting the spacecraft perfectly from the control room. By that time the front door had opened up and so had the stepladder. The robot stood behind the door and extended his right hand as if to say, 'Now you may leave.'

Stepping out we were now exposed to the morning cold—quite a change from the pleasant air-conditioned room.

We began moving towards our camp and then turned to look back at the spacecraft. The door had closed and the ladder had vanished. The eastern sky was already turning red. I could not understand why a throbbing noise was coming from the rocket. Suddenly the noise increased manifold.

'Move away, move away, the rocket is about to take off.' Hearing Nakur Babu's warning we all rushed behind the boulders. Immediately we saw the rocket lift off at a tremendous speed. It vanished from our sight within five seconds. All that was left behind was a lot of dust and a huge crater.

All of us rushed towards the crater created by the rocket. Dr Sheng burst into a cry of joy.

Peering into the crater hole caused by the rocket, we could see beautifully carved ancient stonework.

Undoubtedly this was the long lost eighth-century Buddhist monastery described in the scroll. Dr Sheng must be a very happy man now.

EA

7 August

Today was a remarkable day.

This morning when Prahlad returned from shopping, I noticed he was carrying two bags instead of one. I asked him the reason. He replied, 'Just wait, sir, let me first keep the shopping bag aside. I've got something for you. You'll be amazed to see it.'

I was quite amused to think that my elderly man Friday, who has worked with me for thirty-three years, could produce something to surprise me. What had he brought in that bag?

I soon had my the answer and the intense surprise I felt was quite beyond Prahlad's comprehension.

What Prahlad took out of the bag was an animal. It was the size of a kitten. It isn't possible even for a scientist like me to easily describe it in one word. According to zoologists, there are almost two lakh species of animals in the world. I've personally come across quite a few of them, seen pictures of some and of the rest I've come to know of by reading about their breed and descriptions only. But I've never come across any description of the animal which Prahlad presented me with. The face suggests it to be of the simian family. The nose is sharper and the temple is broader than a monkey's, the head is bigger and the lower part, narrower. The ears are large and compressed with the tops pointed like that of a jackal or a dog. The eyes are somewhat larger compared to his face— but not as big as a loris. Instead of a paw you can see five toe fingers, which remind you of a monkey. There's also the hint of a tail. There are no whiskers, but the body is covered with a short layer of fur, copper in colour. This is a rough picture. The head may look large as he is in his infancy–though I used this word as a conjecture. It could be that he is a full-grown animal and his breed itself is small in stature.

In one word, it's a very odd animal. Prahlad said it had been gifted to him by Jagannath. Jagannath lives in the village of Jhalsi across the river Usri. He collects herbs and roots and comes twice a week to sell them in the market. I too have bought a few of these roots from Jagannath to use in my medicines. Jagannath apparently found the animal in a jungle. He knew that Prahlad's master was in the habit of collecting peculiar stuff, so he gave the odd creature to Prahlad with me in mind.

'Has Jagannath said anything about what he eats?'

'Yes.'

'What has he said?'

'He said he eats everything—vegetables, fruits, rice, lentils—almost anything.'

'Good. Then there's no need to worry.'

How easily I stated that there was nothing to worry about but how could I escape from worry regarding this extraordinary arrival? A completely new breed, of whom I know nothing—whose name, nature, description or any kind of reference I have never come across in any book on animals. Such a being has now landed up in my hands—how could I not worry about it? What kind of an animal is he? Passive or mischievous? Where will I keep him? Inside a cage? Within a box? In a confined state or in the open? How will my cat, Newton, react when he meets him? What will others say when they see such an animal? The questions are endless.

Before deciding on how to deal with him, I observed the creature for a long time. I lifted him up from my lap and put him on a table. Happily he settled himself there, his eyes constantly focused on me. His looks were so amazing. I doubt if I have ever seen such an expression in any other animal. His expressions are completely devoid of any signs of fear or inhibition; there are no hints of violence or wildness in them either. His attitude clearly indicates that he fully trusts me; he seems to understand that I will in no way harm him. In addition to this, what his expression suggests is pure wisdom. Even if one still hasn't seen much to believe if the animal is intelligent in reality, the glow in the pupils of his eyes clearly indicates that his mind is constantly alert. Having observed this, I feel the animal is not young. Perhaps we'll never be able to find out his age. If I notice that he is growing by the day then of course I'll realize that he is not too old.

The animal came to me at seven in the morning, and now it is 10.45 p.m. In the meantime, I've gone through all the bird and animal books and the encyclopaedias which I have in my collection. None of the available animal descriptions match him wholly.

Newton met him this morning. Newton comes to nibble biscuits with me, while I have my coffee in the mornings. Today was no different. The animal was still sitting on the table. The instant Newton spotted him he stood near the door, startled. I observed his hair standing, a sign of a cat's fear or anger. But there were no signs of excitement in the animal. The only change was that his focus shifted from me to the cat. But there was a difference in that look. For a brief moment he seemed cautious. Immediately Newton's hair returned to its normal position. He now shifted his gaze from our new inmate and, jumping into my lap, began to eat biscuits as usual.

I've measured the animal. From the tip of the nose till the tail end it extends to nine-and-a-half inches. I've also photographed him with my camera from different angles. These are in colour; so that if he eventually changes his complexion I will have evidence of this change. As for food, he eats whatever I eat and consumes everything with relish. This evening I took him with me to my garden for a stroll. I'd thought of putting a collar around his neck but in the end I picked him up and having carried him out left him loose on the grass. He walked alongside me. It seems he has already grown tame. I've noticed it always takes me very little time to strike up a friendship with animals. This case was no exception either.

Now I'm writing my diary sitting in my bedroom. I've arranged bedding for him inside a packing case. It's been five minutes since he has settled down inside that box.

The unexpected arrival of this new companion has cheered me up considerably.

23 August

I've received a few important letters. Before I go into details, let me inform that in the last sixteen days the animal has crossed Newton in height. He is now sixteen inches tall. A few interesting changes have occurred in his personality as well. I will discuss this in detail later.

A couple of days after acquiring this animal, along with his photographs, I'd written to three of the most renowned zoologists of the world. These three individuals are—John Davenport of the University of California, Sir Richard Maxwell of England and Dr Friedrich Eckhart of Germany. I'd written about how I'd acquired this animal and whatever else I'd discovered about his nature. I received all three replies together. Davenport wrote: 'It's clear that this whole thing is a hoax.' He added that in the future I shouldn't trouble him with any further correspondence. According to Maxwell, there no doubt that this animal is a hybrid creature. Hybrid is a result of two different animals which breed together and produce a new breed. For instance a mix of a horse and a donkey produces a mule. He finished his letter saying, 'There's almost no chance of discovering a new animal in this world any more. We may not know all about the living beings inhabiting the seas, but we are well informed about all beings living on land. One needs to study your animal for a long period of time. If you notice something unusual in his behaviour you must let me know.'

Amongst all three, Dr Eckhart is the most distinguished. As his letter is somewhat different I'm producing it here in its entirety:

Dear Prof. Shonku
I couldn't sleep the whole night after receiving your letter.
If this was written by anyone other than you, I'd have

treated it as a hoax. But such a question can never arise in your case. I realize what an extraordinary animal has come under your care. This knowledge has come to me after doing research on animals for the last fifty-five years. Your photographs suggest this animal's unique qualities. I'm now getting on in years. I cannot possibly visit your country to inspect him personally. But please reply to me soon about your view on an alternative arrangement. If you agree to come here I'm ready to sponsor you. You'll be my guest. I'll also ensure suitable arrangements for your animal as well. Right now I'm indisposed; the doctor has advised me to rest for two months. It'll suit me fine if you can visit me in November. I'll contact you in due course—of course, only if I get to know if your trip is a possibility.

Please accept my sincere greetings.

Yours
Friedrich Eckhart

I'll let him know that I'm keen on this trip—only if my animal remains fit and fine.

Now let me talk about my animal.

For a few days now I have noticed that he no longer sits quietly in front of me. Of course, he hasn't renounced me totally but he has certainly acquired an independent spirit. When I read or write he silently moves around the room. It seems as if he is interested in all the stuff present in the room. The books inside the almirah, the flowers in the vase, paper, pens, inkpot, the telephone—he is curious about everything. Till now he was content examining all the things in my room, but today I saw him leave the chair, climb on to my table, pick up the pen in his hand and begin to study it. I also noticed something special about the way he was handling it. His thumb worked just like a monkey's. The simians had acquired this thumb in order to grip the branches while climbing trees in search of food. I realized that he too had had the experience of climbing trees in a jungle.

Other than this I found another thing—he was looking at the pen while standing on his two feet. In the family of monkeys, one has seen orangutans and occasionally chimpanzees standing upright and walking for a brief spell. A gorilla stands up to beat his chest—but it's limited only to this. Yet my animal stood upright for quite some time.

While standing he picked up a piece of paper with his hand and began to scribble on it with the pen. It was my favourite Waterman pen. I got up quickly in case the nib was spoilt by his handling, and the animal, having guessed my reasons for getting up, handed over the pen to me.

From this incident I could infer three new things about him:

1. His thumb works just like a monkey and a human being's.

2. He can stand up on two feet longer than a monkey.
3. His intelligence is far superior to any member of the simian family.

I wonder how much more I will get to learn by studying this strange animal.

2 September

In these past few days the animal has gained another three inches in height. Now his size is more or less that of a medium-sized dog. Or like a four-year-old child. I mentioned this because this animal often walks on his two feet, uses one of his hands to put food in his mouth and uses both hands to hold his glass to drink milk. Not just that, he no longer needs to be taken to the fields. He uses my bathroom. Last week, I purchased a few colourful pantaloons for him. He didn't object in wearing them. Today I saw him trying to wear them on his own.

I've noticed another thing. If there's any conversation taking place in the room he listens to it intently. His eyebrows knit while listening—a clear sign of concentration. I know for a fact that such a quality has never been observed in any other animal. I noted this in particular when I was talking to Avinash Babu last evening.

Avinash Babu is my neighbour and is very sociable. Among all the people I know, only this gentleman has never given me any importance. Neither has he shown any curiosity about my work. After spotting the animal, he raised his eyebrows and inquired, 'What's this creature?'

I said, 'He is a totally new breed of an animal. His name is EA.'

Avinash Babu looked at me patiently. Then he said, 'You can't remember his name?'

'But I just told you—EA.'

'Oh yeah?'

'Yeah. EA. This can be treated as an English name. EA stands for Extraordinary Animal.'

I had decided on this name yesterday. I called him by the name 'EA' a couple of times as well. The instant turning of his head suggested that he responded to it.

'Well, that's an interesting name,' said Avinash Babu, 'but will he be troublesome?'

The animal proceeded towards Avinash Babu and took his left hand to look at his wristwatch. I said, 'If you don't provoke him, he will not do anything to you.'

'Hmm . . . so will you keep him here or donate him to the zoo?'

'For the time being he'll stay with me. And I've a request for you.'

'What's it?'

'Please don't tell anyone about him.'

'Why?' He looked curious then and asked me, 'Suppose I say you've acquired an EA, where's the harm? I need not mention what an EA is. That's all.'

'Then that's fine.'

Prahlad brought coffee. EA was reclining on the sofa, holding the handle of the mug just like us, using the thumb of his right hand and thereby bringing the mug close to his mouth and sipping from it.

Even after watching this amazing scene all Avinash Babu had to say was, 'Just imagine!'

It's amazing to see someone so completely devoid of any sense of wonder.

4 September

An extraordinary incident that happened today has dismissed all the understanding I'd hitherto had of EA.

In the afternoon, while sitting in my study I was leafing through the pages of *Nature*, which had just been delivered by the post. EA was sitting on the sofa beside me, playing with a glass paperweight in his hands. I didn't notice when he had slipped out of the room. All of a sudden I heard the sound of a box falling down in my laboratory, and when I rushed there I was momentarily transfixed. It was a horrifying scene.

During the monsoon snakes sometimes appear in my garden. One of them must have slid into the laboratory through the verandah. It was no ordinary snake; it was a cobra and it was now in EA's grasp. EA had dug into the snake's neck with a deathly bite while his forelegs were preventing the swishing of the reptile's tail.

The struggle was over in not more than a minute. There was no question: the snake couldn't have survived such an attack. EA dropped the smashed body of the snake and stepped aside.

He was breathing rapidly. I could hear him from the opposite side of the room.

But what was puzzling was that I'd examined EA's teeth previously; it's almost impossible for him to perform this kind of savage act with his set of teeth. EA does not possess the sharp canine teeth of a carnivorous animal. Moreover, the snake's body had been severely wounded. Claws are needed to create such damage. EA has no claws either.

After calling Prahlad and asking him to throw away the snake, I went to EA.

'EA will you please open your mouth for me?'

Like an obedient child this wonder creature obeyed me.

He had never ever had such a pair of teeth before. When did this happen? I also noted that all twenty fingers of his four paws were now tipped with sharp nails, which too had been absent before.

Moreover, stranger occurences were to follow.

Within ten minutes, his teeth and nails returned to their normal shape.

Can any animal study solve this mystery? I doubt it.

1 November

I'm leaving for Germany tomorrow. I will be visiting the city of Koblenz, which is approximately seventy kilometres north-west of Frankfurt. I'd written to Eckhart describing the events of the last two months. He once again extended his invitation, his excitement now brimming twice over. All the arrangements for the trip have been finalized. I'll be staying as Eckhart's guest for a week.

In the last one-and-a-half months, EA hasn't increased in height though he is gaining in leaps and bounds in intelligence. Nowadays quite often he looks at books. One hesitates to call him four legged. Most of the time he walks on two legs.

From my observations I've learnt a few more facts, which I'm jotting down now:

1. He possesses an amazing capacity to quickly adapt himself to meet the demands of the current climate. Even if he has come from the jungles, now that he is living with humans his nature is becoming more human-like.

2. After the cobra episode, it has been proved that nature has bestowed a unique quality on him to defeat an enemy. The mongoose has the natural ability to capture a snake. To do this a mongoose is aided by his teeth and claws. The frog possesses no such capacity and hence often turns into the snake's prey. But suppose one day the frog develops sharp teeth and claws and can attack a snake? That would indeed be a bizarre event. My animal's sudden growing of nails and teeth also amounts to a similar matrix. I now know, if he ever has to confront a snake ever again he'll once more produce a new set of nails and teeth.

3. This animal breed is perhaps mute, because over the last few months not once has he produced any kind of sound.

4 November

EA has once again taken me by surprise.

I'd got a box made for EA which, after making special arrangements with the airways authorities, I had arranged to be kept at the tail end of the plane's cabin. Ten minutes before reaching Frankfurt I went to EA to help him wear a warm coat and immediately noticed a marked change in him. He had grown a layer of fur three inches in length. Once again this is evidence of his ability to acclimatize himself to suit the present condition.

After landing in Frankfurt, I saw that the eighty-year-old Dr Eckhart himself had come to receive me. I decided not to take EA out of the box at the airport as his unusual appearance would have created a stir amongst the passengers. But Eckhart had wisely organized police presence. Besides, he had not informed the press or photographers about our arrival.

After meeting Eckhart I couldn't help but tell him there was no way one can make out that he is eighty. To be frank, he doesn't look beyond the age of fifty or fifty-five. He smiled and answered that the credit went to Germany's weather.

On our way I gave him the news of EA growing extra hair. Eckhart remarked, 'The more I hear of him, the more amazed I am. I've deliberately withheld the news of your arrival here to other scientists and zoologists because I know that to many of them India is still a land of rope tricks and snake charmers.'

Within an hour we reached Koblenz. Eckhart lives in a pleasant locality, a little away from the city. I knew that the Eckharts are one of Germany's most noted noble families. On the main gate the plate 'Schloss Eckhart', i.e., Eckhart Castle bears that evidence. Surrounding the castle grounds is a huge garden full of various kinds of trees and bushes. There is a profusion of roses all over the place. Before we entered the house, Eckhart mentioned that he had lost his wife about four years ago and that apart from himself and some family retainers, the only other person living here was his secretary, Madam Erika Weiss. I met her soon. She has a charming personality but I could sense an element of listlessness in her.

After entering the house the first thing I did was to open the box. Instantly, EA jumped out and walked towards Eckhart with his right hand extended in the gesture of shaking hands. This act was so unpredictable that Eckhart didn't reciprocate immediately. Then EA proceeded towards the secretary. I'll never forget the look of wonder and surprise in her eyes. Her expression spoke of a natural love and affection for animals.

Eckhart said, 'I've kept my dogs locked up at present. It's difficult to say how they'll react when they meet this animal.'

I said, 'I feel if your dogs are well behaved then there's nothing to fear because my cat accepted him very easily.'

When I entered the main drawing room, the setting stunned me.

Was this a zoologist's house or a hunter's? Why was there such a large number of stuffed animal heads on display?

Guessing my thoughts, Eckhart said, 'My father was a well-known hunter. This room is his creation. I've had many altercations with him on this.'

EA was rambling around, looking at all the stuffed animals. When tea was served he too took a cup in his hand and sipped from it. I was aware that Eckhart's attention was totally focused on EA; he couldn't take his eyes off him! I hope he is now convinced that EA is no hoax or magic.

Looking at him, I was again awestruck by my host's youthful looks. I am determined to get down to the bottom of this mystery. Maybe after I am slightly more familiar with him.

When we finished tea, Eckhart got up from the sofa and said, 'You should take it easy for the rest of the day. Erika will show you your room. Tomorrow morning at breakfast you'll meet one of my friends. He is an animal-lover. I know you'll like him.'

One of Eckhart's lackeys had already taken my two suitcases to my room. And now I went to the first floor along with Erika, up the regal carpeted staircase. The arrangements were indeed excellent. I was allotted two adjacent rooms—one for me and one to be used by EA. When asked what EA's diet was, I told Erika that he would eat whatever we ate. 'There's no need worry over him.'

Erika appeared very relieved to hear this but within minutes her looks turned into despair. It seemed as if she was trying to tell me something but was hesitating in doing so.

'Would you like to ask me something more?' I said reassuringly. She bit her lip. 'Hmm . . . I was wondering . . . are you carrying any weapon with you?'

'Why? Do you have any trouble with thieves or swindlers in this area?'

'No. Not that, but I just thought . . . your animal might need some protection. It's such an amazing animal . . .'

'Not to worry. I'm carrying a pistol.'

'Pistol?'

Erika wasn't reassured. Perhaps she would have felt more secure if I'd mentioned a rifle or a Sten gun.

But I did not disclose the truth about my Annihilin gun to her. All I said was, 'Not to fear. The pistol is good enough.'

The lady whispered a faint goodbye and left. Her behaviour, however, left me a bit rattled, even though I am confident of my weapon.

Meanwhile, EA had gone to his room on his own. I saw him looking out of the window. I hope he is not worried. I cannot always follow the thinking of mute animals. If any harm is done to him I'll be in deep misery. Within the past few months I've developed a deep affection for him.

6 November

A few significant events have troubled me considerably. And coupled with these are a few startling incidents that are related to EA.

Eckhart's friend was called Kasper Maximilian Heilbroner. But I'll refer to him as Kasper, since Eckhart too calls him by that name. He is lean and lanky and his jutting-out cheekbones and chin give his face a hard look. He has bushy eyebrows and a crew cut. Such an appearance evokes fear rather than respect. You are never sure what action he is capable of.

After introducing Kasper to me, Eckhart said, 'Kasper is a longtime friend of mine. He is very enthusiastic about animals as well as an expert on them.'

All along EA was with me. Looking at EA for quite some time he came up with just one comment: 'What exquisite fur!'

Everyone will admit that EA's fur is rather smooth and attractive. I don't think I've ever seen any animal fur like this—a mix of yellow with a pink glow.

But I immediately distrusted Kasper. He seemed to cast lustful looks on EA's fur. There's no estimate of how many harmless animals have been violently killed for their fur. Particularly in the West. There's an animal called the chinchilla, which belongs to the rodent family, and some royal ladies are so passionately fond of its fur that for the coat of one such animal they are ready to shell out Rs 20,000 to 30,000. I thought to myself—Oh lord, let no one from the fur industry notice EA.

We continued to talk while having breakfast. Watching EA have his meal with us at the table, Kasper remarked,

'You've trained him very well, I see. He beats a chimpanzee hollow.'

I was forced to comment that EA's grooming was not my doing. He has a tremendous capacity to observe and emulate.

'You were talking about his ability to transform himself to match his surroundings. Can't you show us such examples?'

With a wry smile I said, 'I haven't brought him here for demonstrations. You can see these changes only if they happen on their own. In fact, nature has created all animals with an ability to protect themselves. The stripes and dots on the tiger's body helps it to merge easily amidst trees and leaves in jungles. Also, nature has made sure that one animal can save itself from another. A porcupine can also put a ferocious animal into a tight corner thanks to the quills on its back. Sometimes the pungent smell on an animal's body can save its from its enemies. Those who are comparatively meek—like a deer or rabbit—have been endowed with the ability to run fast. But there are also exceptions to such rules. Not all animals are equally safe from their enemies.'

'You mean to say this animal knows how to protect itself?' asked Kasper.

I said, 'I have found evidence of this twice. He not only saved himself when he was attacked by a cobra but also killed it. Moreover, you can see for yourself how he has protected himself from the cold. You obviously know that many creatures have evolved over time because of environmental changes and needs. In the beginning, life was entirely based in the water; then as water receded and land appeared, amphibians emerged. Later animals that evolved were fully based on land. The lizards grew wings and took to the skies but again this was due to environmental changes and needs. But all these changes took millions of years. Evolution does not happen in a flash.'

'But that's exactly what has happened in the case of your animal?' commented Kasper.

'That's what I have observed with my own eyes.'

I don't think Kasper was convinced. I thought Eckhart would support me. So I was surprised when I noticed a frown on his face.

After breakfast, Eckhart suggested that I take a look at his extensive garden. The garden was carpeted in snow. I had seen it this morning through the window in my room.

I didn't reject his offer.

I'd no idea about the expanse of this garden. Bu it would be wrong to describe the entire area as a garden. The undergrowth of bushes and flowers were now replaced by long and large trees, the majority of which were pines. It'll be more apt to call this as "woods".

I was about to ask a zoology-related question to Eckhart but was interrupted by a sudden animal sound.

It was the barking of a hound. An Alsatian.

'I see Hansel and Gretel too have come out for a walk,' said Eckhart.

Initially, I had been walking holding EA's hand. But at some point we had started walking on our own. Now when I looked at him I saw him frowning.

About a hundred yards away I spotted the two dogs. They both had collars on; Eckhart's' servant was holding on to their leather leashes.

We were now getting close to the dogs. When the distance between us was less than thirty yards, I noticed that the eyes of the Alsatians were transfixed on EA. We stopped walking. I went closer to EA and held his hand. I realized Kasper and Eckhart were both waiting to see the turn of events.

The dogs were now fiercely straining at their leashes and growling. And suddenly, with a forceful pull they threw Eckhart's servant on the snow. Both Hansel and Gretel now came charging towards us. And at that precise moment I felt EA let go of my hand and I turned to see him run like lightning behind a snow-covered busch.

I realized he was scared. Nature hadn't given him the ability to protect himself from this pair of enemies.

I too ran after EA, with Eckhart and Kasper behind me.

I'd already noticed the aggressive looks in the dogs' eyes; now I saw them run helter-skelter, hunting for their prey. They were desperately looking for my animal.

I was alarmed. I was forced to shout and tell them, 'For god's sake, Dr Eckhart, please stop your dogs.'

'Impossible,' Eckhart spoke in a choked voice, 'even God can't stop them in this state.'

The dogs went in the same direction EA had gone but there was no sign of my devoted pet animal.

After five minutes of uncontrollable romping both Hansel and Gretel gave up the hunt. They were panting with their tongues sticking out. Their trainer came forward and took up the leashes in his hands.

'Take them back to the house,' Eckhart ordered.

'But where did your animal disappear?' Kasper asked.

My thoughts also ran along the same lines. But I couldn't spot any hole on the ground or a crevice on a tree where he could have hidden himself. It was only when the dogs were about to reach the house that my amazing animal resurfaced.

But what had he done to himself? Had he been rolling in the snow?

No, not really. The colour of his body from head to toe had now turned white. He looked like a snowball. It would be impossible to locate him now in a snow-covered garden.

'Gott in Himmel!' Kasper screamed. Yes, it's normal to pronounce God's name under such scenarios. I'm sure the two Germans had never witnessed such an astonishing incident.

We returned to Eckhart Castle. After settling down on the sofa, it was Kasper who spoke first.

'Have you decided on the future of this invaluable property?'

The answer was simple. I said, 'Till I'm alive he'll stay with me. He is my companion. Over the last few months I've nurtured him.'

'But as a scientist don't you have any responsibility towards the zoologists of the world? You want to conceal this animal from them?'

'If I wanted to hide him why would I bring him here? In future if anyone wants to see him they're most welcome to visit my home in my country. My door will remain open to all. The animal will stay safe in my custody. You saw what happened to him after bringing him here. There's no guarantee that such a thing won't happen again.'

'Do you have any objection to keeping him in a zoo?'

'If I decide to do that I'll keep him in a zoo in my own country. The reputation of the Calcutta Zoo is not that bad.'

'Hmm . . .'

Kasper got up.

'Well. I had a proposal, which I don't know if you will accept or not. Both Eckhart and I are ready to pay you 20,000 marks together for this animal. If you give it to us the whole world will get to know about his existence. Along with it, your name will become immortal. We will not conceal the fact that we got the animal from you.'

'You guessed right. I cannot accept this offer.'

Along with Kasper, Eckhart too left the room, perhaps to see him off in the car. As soon as they stepped out a third personality appeared.

Madam Erika Weiss! She looked very disturbed.

'Since you're alone,' said Mrs Weiss, 'I must tell you one thing. The zoologist Eckhart died a month ago. It was he who wrote you the first letter. This man is his son. His name too is Friedrich. He is a hunter. He has no compassion for animals. If possible you must leave tomorrow. I'll arrange for your tickets. It's not safe for you to stay here.'

'Then whose secretary are you?'

'Not his. I was his father's secretary. I'll leave within a week after winding up a few jobs.'

'And who's this Kasper fellow?'

'He is the owner of the Odeon Circus. Along with the circus he also has a zoo which keeps all sorts of weird animals . . .'

Then we heard the sound of footsteps. Erika immediately left the room through the side door.

'I won't disturb you today,' Eckhart stated after entering my room. 'Do think of our proposal carefully. We'll discuss this again tomorrow morning.'

Eckhart left. I hadn't looked at EA all this time. When I looked at him now, I realized he had gone back to his normal self.

It's about 11 p.m. now. EA is sleeping in his room. Was today's confrontation a horrible experience for him or does he enjoy such episodes? Any living being generally goes through life with two missions in mind—one is self-defence and the other is to consume food in order to provide nutrition for the body. The latter is of no concern for EA—certainly as long as he is with me. And as for the former, he can handle it with competence which has been proved already. But the question is—what kind of danger has Erika warned me about? Against other animals EA is capable of self-defence but we don't know how skilled he is at protecting himself against human conspiracy.

I will ponder over this tomorrow.

Let's see how events unfold eventually.

7 November

I shall never be able to forget the spine-chilling event of last night and its bizarre conclusion.

Even after hitting the bed at 11 p.m. I couldn't fall sleep. Eckhart's deceitful act was weighing heavily on my mind. It's clear that taking advantage of his father's death he had called me over only to grab my animal. He had promised to pay for my travel, which he still hasn't. Perhaps he thought the 20,000 marks for the animal would compensate for my expenses. Could he imagine that I would not accept this money?

Almost magically I fell asleep. The grandfather clock on the landing of the staircase was just chiming midnight. I heard the beginning of the chime but didn't hear the end. That is, I had already gone to sleep by then.

I woke up soon after. Initially I thought an earthquake had woken me up. Then I realized my body was being handled by someone and I was soon rendered immobile, confined. I have been tied up. My Annihilin gun was under my pillow but there was no way I could reach it. When I looked up by chance, the wall clock said 3.30 a.m. The light of the full moon lit up the room almost as if it were dawn.

I could see the forms of at least four or five people inside the room. One was holding a torch focused at me. I could hear the sound of footsteps from the next door too. Did that mean EA was also captured?

'Professor Shonku, can't your animal transform itself according to the demands of the environment? And can't he adopt peculiar strategies of self defence in the wink of an eye? Now let's see how far his capacity works.'

It was Eckhart's voice. He was standing in front of the door.

'Schienner, Schultz—make him stand in front of that door.'

Two fellows dragged me out of the bed and forced me to stand in front of EA's room.

The moon's light was reflected in this room too. Here, at least six or seven people were present, shining their torches in different directions of the room. Three of them were carrying ropes, a sack and a net—that is, paraphernalia needed to trap an animal. Seeing the reflection of metals in the hands of the other two men I realized that they were all armed.

But it's obvious that the bed was empty.

Two men were bending down to throw light under the bed when a commotion broke out.

The whiff of a sharp pungent smell entered my nostrils, bringing tears to my eyes. As I'm used to experimenting with various chemicals in my laboratory no smell can upset me; but I could make out that this revolting stench would have the capacity to disable a man.

Those present in the room could not bear the disgusting odour and, covering their noses with handkerchiefs, dashed out of the room. Needless to say, Eckhart belonged to this group.

This was soon followed by Eckhart's shout to the group of men waiting in the garden, 'Stay ready with your weapons—the animal may try to escape from the window!'

Even for the fraction of a second my eyes hadn't moved from the room.

From below the bed appeared my beloved amazing animal. In one leap he jumped to the window facing the garden and then with another leap he sprang out of it. Was he about to become the prey of those armed men outside?

No. Not quite. In that prime moment of acute crisis, the animal had devised the only possible mode of escape. Breaking the infallible rule of evolution, in a nano second this four-legged land animal acquired a pair of wings.

When he jumped out of the window, instead of falling down he spread out his wide wings and flew swiftly upwards. I managed to run towards the window and saw in the moonlit sky a swiftly moving birdlike object soon turning into a tiny dot. I heard two rounds of shots from the garden but it was impossible for anyone to aim correctly in situations like these.

17 November
Courtesy Mrs Erika, my release and the arrests of Eckhart along with his friends by the police took place simultaneously.

Seven days after returning to Giridih I read in the newspaper that in a deep forest in Nicaragua a group of animal collectors has discovered a completely new animal. Apparently this animal was standing at a distance, and touching the right side of his head again and again, as if saluting the men. But when they tried to capture him with a net he flew to the top of a hundred-foot tall tree and disappeared into the foliage. The group extended the stay of their expedition in the hope of capturing this new species.

From the descriptions it was not difficult to identify the animal as my own EA. While staying within the human habitat he had adapted himself to our way of life but now he has become accustomed to forest life. It's very easy to predict that after a few days of searching for him the group will finally have to give up on him.

But does that mean EA will never come back to me?

In a way perhaps it's all for the good. Let him survive and enjoy life to the brim along with all his amazing qualities. One part of me—the scientist—regrets not being able to study him fully; so much could not be understood. And the other half tells me there should be a limit to a human's greed to know everything. Some things should remain to arouse curiosity and sustain wonder in the human mind.

1915. In 1916, it was taken over by his eldest son and in 1961, revived by his grandson, all Ray work and published only adventure...

Translator's Note

In my ten-year-old mind, the word 'science' had always formed a daunting image but the thrilling exploits of Prof. Shonku opened up a completely new world of the imagination. I began to discover that science could also be full of fun, rich with anecdotes about travel, fascinating details of geography, enticing glimpses of world history—all rolled into one rollicking adventure. Satyajit Ray conjured up this world with all the chronicles of Prof. Shonku and of course in the process crumbled to dust all my fears of science! Years later, I can still experience the thrill of exploration and discovery as I revisit the tales of Professor Shonku. And when Puffin asked me to translate this collection of stories for them, it was like being reunited with an old friend.

The Shonku stories first appeared in 1961 in *Sandesh*, a magazine for children that had been started by Satyajit Ray's grandfather, Upendrakishore Ray Chowdhury, in

1913. In 1916, it was taken over by his father, Sukumar, and in 1961, revived by Ray himself. In all, Ray wrote and published forty adventures—the last two appearing only as incomplete drafts. Out of these, eighteen were written for the annual editions of, *Anandamela,* another popular children's magazine. Ray continued to write and captivate us with the Shonku escapades for the next thirty-odd years. I still remember waiting with bated breath for the latest issue of *Sandesh* to appear at our doorstep, especially as the adventure was often serialized. And much of the excitement of the Durga Puja festival lay in devouring a fresh new Shonku story in the annual *Aanadamela* with colour illustrations adding to the appeal of every story.

How did Ray's interest in science begin? In the author's own words: 'In my own case, it happened at the age of ten when my grand-uncle Kuladaranjan Ray's splendid translation of Jules Verne's *Mysterious Island* came out in two yellow volumes. I was enthralled then as I'm now by Verne's power to grip and persuade by abundance of convincing details... An interest in science was always there. After all, my father (Sukumar) and grandfather Upendrakishore were both men of science, in addition to being writers and artists.'

In an interesting article written in 1966, Ray cogently defines two schools of science fiction writing—one of

Jules Verne and the other H.G. Wells. Ray believed, 'Wells's approach to science fiction was poetic and romantic. Wells chose in his science fiction to skirt technology and concentrate on fiction...' While Jules Verne uses 'the available scientific data as the springboard, but never lets the imagination soar beyond the limits of probability.' It's clearly evident that Ray's Shonku adventures belong more to Wells's school of writing, culminating in what we today call sci-fi fantasy.

Prof. Shonku lives in Giridih, a cozy town in Jharkhand, but each and every one of his adventures takes him all over the world. Thus the globetrotting Shonku takes us to Austria and Switzerland to unravel the mystery of Dr Schering's loss of memory; to an ancient castle in Norway to free himself from the clutches of the terrifying personality of Alexander Craig; and to Innsbruck to confront a daring doppelgänger. Prof. Shonku also lands up in Montefrio in Granada to undertake an incredible experiment to create pure gold and travels to an unknown island in the Atlantic Ocean to look for an amazing fruit following a clue left behind in a diary! What is the message in the mysterious papyrus found in Cairo and why did scientists go missing in the deep jungle of Congo? Is there any truth in the reported sightings of the UFO and what happens when he takes along an extraordinary animal to Koblenz in Germany?

His neighbour, companion and dispassionate friend, Avinash Babu, once appears in this collection of stories and Prof. Shonku is often accompanied on his sojourns by old friends we have met before—his colleagues Saunders, Crole and Summerville, Nakur Chandra Biswas—the man with the uncanny power of predicting the future, his trusted servant Prahlad and his feline friend, Newton.

These stories offer a reader not just the suspense, thrill and excitement of the mysteries; they present a wonderful travelogue across the world and the opportunity to study the scheming and devious minds of people in the garb of scientists, businessmen and ordinary people. They take the reader to faraway yet imaginary lands while reiterating the eternal human values and emphasizing right from wrong.

It's interesting to note that Ray manages to give such accurate and graphic description of these countries and their cities and as well as their life and culture at a time when Google, Wikipedia or Google Maps was essentially the material for science fiction! How did he do it?

Ray's work is indeed a culmination of both hard work and research. He took the trouble to write to all the friends who lived in these distant cities he was planning to make Prof. Shonku visit and talked to the local consulates and embassy officials for authentic information. He also procured maps, postcards and brochures of all these cities.

And the net result was not only an authentic description of these places but those striking illustrations done by him, often adopting a new style to describe each adventure. The end result is just magic.

Another charming highlight of these stories is that they all seem to be wrapped up in a distinct time warp. Generally, for communications across the world, the professor only depends on handwritten letters and for urgency it was always the telegram. Public telephones are frequently used and even in a hotel in a city like Innsbruck guests had to share a common telephone kept out in a corridor. For checking on facts and gathering information Shonku faithfully delves into the ever dependable *Encyclopaedia Britannica*. A few modern contraptions cited are a tape recorder and photocopy machine! Yet Shonku's own ingenious discoveries mentioned in these adventures will continue to marvel each reader. Inventions like the Remembrain, Annihilin, Miracurol pills, Nervigour, Omniscope remain a mystery and a matter of envy to the scientific fraternity, even today.

Ray, throughout these stories, instills great value and faith in the world of science and objectivity. However, children will be fascinated to observe that Ray's interest in the field of fortune tellers, planchettes, oracles, clairvoyance, telepathy, past regression, hypnotism, and revocation of angry souls also find a place of pride in the plots of these adventures. In his tales Ray also imparts the notion of patriotism—all told very gently, not once sounding didactic. References of Tagore's *Geetanjali* and the Taj Mahal are bound to touch a chord indeed. Another facet to these stories is mention of various personalities such as Oral Stein, Tavernier and Jābir ibn Hayyān who are sure to intrigue the young reader to discover more.

Will today's children be able to appreciate these old-time scientific impressions? Will this prolific professor become as credible as the precocious Potter? Let the young readers decide. All the same I'm sure each episode of the Shonku escapades will enchant all readers of this volume. And perhaps inspire some children to pick up a pen and start writing a diary!

Puffin has agreed to use some of Ray's original drawings in this collection. I am grateful to Sandip Ray not just for granting the permission to use his father's illustrations but also for sending me the scanned images of these drawings. My thanks also go to Souradeep, Satyajit Ray's grandson. I'm grateful to my brother, Jyotirmoy Majumdar, for looking into my initial drafts and correcting and fine-tuning all the technical and scientific language used in the stories. And my thanks of course go to my editors Renu Rao and Mimi Basu for polishing up my translation considerably.

This will be the third collection of Shonku adventures

produced by Puffin. The last two volumes were translated by my sister Gopa Majumdar, whose flair for translation will always remain an inspiration to me.

Indrani Majumdar *lives in Delhi but has her roots firmly based in Bengali culture. Her bilingualism has helped her career as she has translated Bengali texts into English and vice versa. A keen researcher, her vocation in life has been to explore the various facets of Satyajit Ray's work. At present she works with the Programme Office, India International Centre, Delhi.*

PUFFIN CLASSICS

The Mystery Of Munroe Island
and Other Stories

With Puffin Classics, the story isn't over
when you reach the final page.
Want to discover more about the author
and his world?
Read on . . .

CONTENTS

AUTHOR FILE

NAME: Satyajit Ray

BORN: 2 May 1921 in a progressive Brahmo family of Kolkata

FATHER: Sukumar Ray

Famous writer, poet and printing technologist

MOTHER: Suprabha Ray

QUALIFICATIONS: B.A. in Economics (Hons) from Presidency College, Kolkata. Trained in Oriental Arts for three years at Vishwa Bharati University.

PROFESSIONAL LIFE: Worked in the advertising agency DJ Keymer for almost twelve years. Started as a Junior Visualizer and went on to become the Art Director.

MARRIED TO: Bijoya Ray

CHILDREN: One son, Sandip Ray, also a film-maker.

FAMOUS FOR: Internationally acclaimed films. One of the earliest Indian directors to have won prizes at major film festivals around the world like Cannes, Venice, Berlin, London and San Francisco. An extremely versatile person, he wrote the script, composed the music, designed the sets and costumes, prepared posters in addition to directing the films.

Ray was also a writer of repute, and his short stories, novellas, poems and articles, written in Bengali, are still immensely popular. Many of his books became bestsellers. He also illustrated them.

MAJOR AWARDS: Bharat Ratna, highest civilian award of India; Legion D'Honneur, highest civilian award of France; and the Oscar for Lifetime Achievement

SHONKU FACT FILE

★ FULL NAME: Trilokeshwar Shonku
  In Bengali, Shonku means a cone. Trilokeshwar means the 'lord of heaven, earth and hell'. It is also a play on the name Trishanku, a mythical figure who tried to reach the heavens but was punished by the gods to forever remain stranded somewhere between heaven and earth.
★ BIRTHDAY: 16 June. Birth year estimated to be 1912
★ QUALIFICATIONS: B.Sc. in Physics and Chemistry. A child prodigy, he graduated from college when he was sixteen. Honorary doctorate from the Swedish Academy of Sciences
★ HOMETOWN: Giridih
★ PET: Cat called Newton
★ MANSERVANT: Prahlad
★ NEIGHBOUR: Avinash Babu
★ FRIENDS: William Crole Jeremy Saunders

How did Professor Shonku come to be?

The first book in which Prof. Shonku appeared was simply called *Professor Shonku*. Published in 1965, it was Ray's first book, though the stories had been written between 1961 and 1965. Professor Shonku was dedicated to Ray's son, Sandip, who was eleven years old then. The inscription in the original book read 'To Sandip Babu'. (Sandip's pet name is Babu.) This was the only time Ray dedicated any of his books. One of the earliest examples of science-fiction writing in any Indian language, this book won the Government of India's prize for Best Book for the Young.

THINGS TO THINK ABOUT

Travel Trails

Professor Shonku is an avid traveller. His adventures become more exciting on account of their exotic locations. Here are some fun facts about the places Shonku has travelled to.

Read on. Maybe they will excite the traveller in you.

Switzerland

There are more banks than dentists in Switzerland.

Norway

There is a town called Hell and it freezes almost every winter.

England

In Medieval England animals were brought into court, and tried and sentenced by the judge for any mischief or damage they did!

Egypt

Ancient Egyptians shaved off their eyebrows to mourn the death of their cats.

Congo

The maximum population of these rainforests consists of pygmies.

China

Chinese police use geese instead of dogs because of their aggressiveness and superior vision.

Austria

The first postcard was used in Austria.

Germany

German don't sing their whole national anthem.

Atlantic Ocean

Due to the shift in the tectonic plates, the Atlantic will replace the Pacific as the largest ocean in the next few hundreds of years.

Innovational Idiosyncrasies

Professor Shonku's inventions have set extremely high standards for scientists all across the world. Here is a complete list of his inventions that will leave you awestruck and convinced of our beloved professor's incomparable genius:

Innovation	Description
Bidhushekhar	A rather comic robot, capable of inexplicably brilliant stuff
Mangorange	A hybrid fruit of mango and orange—tastes a bit of both
Invisibility Potion	A liquid version of Harry Potter's Invisibility Cloak!
Microsonograph	Device to record every tiny sound made in the world
Air-conditioning pill	A pill to keep in your pocket, which keeps you comfortable irrespective of the temperature
Electric pistol	Pistol to deliver an electric shock of 400 volts
Somnolin	Super-effective sleeping pill
Neospectroscope	Device to summon ghosts of the departed
Miracurol	Pill to miraculously cure all diseases
Room freshener	Natural fragrances of thirty-six flowers
Onmiscope	Telescope + Microscope+ X-ray in a device that looks like a pair of normal spectacles
Ornithon	Device to impart knowledge to birds
Annihilin gun	A gun to make anything disappear
Remembrain	A helmet that helps you remember old or forgotten memories
Cerebrilliant	Nerve-soothing pill that helps recover quickly from head injuries
Shankalan	Extremely strong yet light plastic